Also by Ray Hobbs and Pul

An Act of Kindness	2014
Following On	2016
A Year From Now	2017
A Rural Diversion	2019
A Chance Sighting	2020
Roses and Red Herrings	2020
Happy Even After	2020
The Right Direction	2020
An Ideal World	2020
Mischief and Masquerade	2021
Big Ideas	2021
First Appearances	2021
New Directions	2021
A Deserving Case	2021
Unknown Warrior	2021
Daffs in December	2022
A Worthy Scoundrel	2022
Fatal Shock	2022
Last Wicket Pair	2022
Knights Errant	2022

Published Elsewhere

Second Wind (Spiderwize)	2011
Lovingly Restored (New Generation Publishing)	2018

A Baker's Round

Ray Hobbs

Wingspan Press

Copyright © 2023 by Ray Hobbs
All rights reserved.

This book is a work of fiction. Names, characters, settings and incidents are either the product of the author's imagination or used fictitiously. Any resemblance to actual events, settings or persons, living or dead, is entirely coincidental.

No part of this book may be reproduced or transmitted in any form or by any means, electronic or mechanical, including photocopying, recording or by any information storage and retrieval system, without written permission from the author, except for the inclusion of brief quotations in reviews.

Published in the United States and the United Kingdom
by WingSpan Press, Livermore, CA

The WingSpan name, logo and colophon are the trademarks
of WingSpan Publishing.

ISBN 978-1-63683-046-9 (pbk.)
ISBN 978-1-63683-964-6 (ebook)

Printed in the United States of America

www.wingspanpress.com

This book is dedicated to the memory of my late mother,
a truly excellent baker.

As always, I wish to acknowledge the assistance of my brother Chris in the preparation of this book, and particularly his input into the technicalities of baking.

    RH

A Baker's Round

London, April 1990

1

The End of It

It was the most contentious conversation with the band's agent that Jeff could remember, and he was determined it was going to be the last. Unfortunately, Ollie Murchison wasn't inclined to give way without a struggle.

'You just have to be joking, Jeff.'

'No, Ollie, I'm quite serious. *Finito.* It's the end of the road.' He transferred the phone to his left hand as he'd been holding it in his right for some time, and it was tired.

'So, the band's split up. That's bad enough, but to say you want out of the business altogether is too much.'

'It's quite straightforward, Ollie. Our contract ends on the twenty-ninth, and it will not be renewed.'

'But you haven't given me one good reason why you're doing this. Your name's highly regarded in the business, for goodness' sake. The studio and the session musicians respect you, and that's a rarity in itself. It would be the easiest thing for you to start up another band.'

'It wouldn't be difficult,' agreed Jeff, 'but I don't intend to, and that's final.'

There was a deep sigh at the other end. Eventually, Ollie asked, 'What am I going to tell the media?'

'Just tell them the truth, that Tantum Somnium has split up, citing irreconcilable differences, and that I'll be publishing an open letter of thanks and farewell through the music channels to those who've followed the band. Otherwise, I'm not available for comment. If they ask you what I'm going to do next, tell them you've no idea, and that's also true, because, at this very moment, neither have I.'

A Baker's Round

On an almost pleading note, Ollie said, 'Don't disappear altogether, Jeff. You've so much to offer as a songwriter, it would be criminal if you dropped out for good.'

'Mine is a modest talent, Ollie. All I have to offer, that sets me apart from the rest, is the ability to read and write dots. That's why I'm popular with the session men. That, and I treat them with respect, a courtesy they find somewhat novel in this business, to say the least.'

'But to say you're dropping out for good....'

' "For good" is a reckless way to describe it, Ollie. I can't rule anything in or out at this stage.'

'You're making a big mistake.' Ollie was now sounding sorrowful, rather than critical. 'Keep in touch. That's all I ask, Jeff. Don't disappear altogether.'

'I'll be in touch all right. You owe me money.' Looking down at the street, he saw a familiar white Toyota coupé park outside the flat. 'Listen, Ollie, I've just seen Michelle's car, and she doesn't know a thing about this, so I have to go.' Impatient to end the call, he put the phone down and went to the kitchen to fill the kettle while he braced himself for the next confrontation.

The water was boiled by the time Michelle came into the flat, a fact that earned her instant, if fleeting, appreciation as he handed her a mug of tea.

'Cheers, Jeff.' She leaned forward, inviting him to kiss her. 'What's new?'

'Come and sit down.'

'That sounds ominous.' Nevertheless, she took her tea into the sitting room and sank into the Farnham leather sofa. 'Okay, tell all.'

'For one thing, the band's split up. I've just been on the phone with Ollie about it.'

'You said things were looking dicey. What happened?'

'Joby's joined a new band called "Running Sore", and now Kevin looks like going the same way. Just when I thought Heavy Metal had died a well-deserved death, it's flourishing again.' He grimaced. 'And if that's the case, those two are welcome to it.'

'What about Merv?'

'He was so far gone on whatever he fixes himself with nowadays, he'd no idea what was happening on our planet.'

'So, who have you approached?'

'About what?' The conversation was beginning to follow the same lines as the one he'd just had with Ollie.

'About forming a new band, of course.'

He had to tell her now. There was nothing to be gained by delay or prevarication. 'I'm not going to form another band,' he told her.

'What?' Her reaction had always been predictable. 'What are you saying?'

'There won't be another band.'

Surprise had given way to impatience. 'So, what are you going to do?'

'I don't know.'

'What do you mean, you don't know?'

'Just that.'

Tight-lipped and business-like, she stood up. 'This tea's far too strong.'

'I'm sorry.'

'Your mind must have been on other things,' she said, taking her mug to the kitchen.

Through the open door, he heard the kettle element struggling in its limescale straitjacket, just as he would struggle to explain himself to Michelle while she was in that fiery-redhead mood that was so alien to his own nature. In that moment, he wondered a little about the connection between pigmentation and temperament. Was it her red hair that made her so quick-tempered, and were his fair colouring and blue eyes the reason he was usually so placid? Maybe it was all an old wives' tale. At all events, and whatever the cause, he and Michelle were direct opposites in more than one respect.

She returned, tight-lipped as before, and took off her shoes to make herself comfortable on the sofa. 'So, what prompted this brainstorm?'

'It's been coming for some time. I'm sick of the music industry. I've been wanting to get out, and the band splitting up when it did helped me make the decision.'

'You want to get out of the business that made you famous and enabled you to buy a flat in Hatch End and run a Porsche?' She shook her head vigorously. 'I don't believe I'm fucking hearing this.'

A Baker's Round

'That's what the music industry means to you, isn't it? Fame and fortune.'

'It makes more sense than poverty.'

'What do you know about poverty, Michelle?'

'You'll know all about it when you try to run this flat on zero income. Have you given any thought at all to what you're going to do for money?' She sounded like a despairing parent trying to reason with a teenager, and her Antrim accent was now prominent, as it always was when she was angry.

'There's more than enough in the bank and investments.'

'But how long is it going to last? You've got to be realistic!'

'I got realistic today, when I told Ollie I was getting out.'

'Oh, somebody tell me I'm dreaming this whole thing. Jeff, you're talking about getting out of a lucrative industry, and all because you're bored with it! Do the words "grow up" mean anything to you? You're thirty. Try to remember that.'

'Twenty-nine, actually.'

'That's no excuse.'

'Can't you just accept that I'm finished with all of it?'

'But why?' She'd gone from impatient and angry to furious. 'You haven't explained why!'

'Okay. Calm down and I will.'

' "Calm down," he says, just like that.'

'Give it a try, Michelle. It's not difficult.'

'You're so calm, you're fucking infuriating!'

She was probably right, but he decided to make a start, anyway. 'Think of some of the things the media and the fans call us. "Geniuses", "legends" and "icons" are names that spring to mind, but what are we in reality? I can count on the fingers of one hand the bands that have any real ability, and I wouldn't call them any of those things.'

'Tell me, then, why the kids can't get enough of your music.'

'They don't know any better. They're excited by the gimmicks, by distortion, pinch harmonics, mindless use of the whammy bar.... They really think those things are clever, and if they only knew it, they're nothing more than cheap tricks.'

In a theatrically patient tone, she asked, 'What, exactly, are pinch harmonics?'

'They're called "squealies" in the trade.' He got up to switch on an amplifier and plug a guitar into it. 'On an electric guitar,' he demonstrated, 'you pluck a string with the pick and then immediately touch it with your thumb and let go. That way, you get the fundamental note followed immediately by the octave harmonic.' He played a few for her. 'There's nothing clever about it.'

'Maybe I'm missing something here, but if the kids like it so much, what's wrong with it?'

'Don't you see? It's taking their money by false pretences. They think they're hearing talent, and all they're getting is technical hocus-pocus.'

Exasperated, she insisted, 'But they don't know that.'

'That's what I'm saying, but it's no excuse for pulling the wool over their eyes.'

'I give up,' she said, adopting her familiar and exaggerated weary tone. 'I suppose I'd better do something about dinner.'

'If you promise to calm down, I'll take you somewhere to eat. Where do you fancy?'

'As you've taken leave of your senses, I think we should go somewhere that's not very expensive, just to get you into practice for when you're broke.'

Michelle finished undressing and joined him in bed, wrapping herself tightly round him. 'Tell me today was a bad dream,' she pleaded. 'Tell me I'll wake up tomorrow and everything will be as it was.'

'I'm sorry, I can't.'

'And you can't decide what you're going to do next. What can you—?' She broke off when she became aware of movement beneath the duvet. 'I'm glad someone's feeling decisive,' she said, reaching downward to lend encouragement.

They kissed for some time, as if no disagreement had ever taken place, and she welcomed him in the same spirit.

Later, as they lay side by side, she said wistfully, 'Trust you to make it special, tonight of all nights.'

It was an odd thing for her to say, and he was about to ask her what

A Baker's Round

she meant by it, but the pressures of the day had left him drained, and sleep claimed him even before he could frame the question.

———•———

He turned over and, finding an empty space, imagined he'd slept longer than usual, and that Michelle had left for the auction house. He turned the other way to read the time on the radio alarm. It was only seven thirty-seven, but he could hear no movement in the flat. It was uncanny, and he meant to investigate, but the need to relieve himself was more urgent, so he slipped out of bed and went to the bathroom.

His eyes gradually cleared and, as he washed his hands, he saw something unusual reflected in the shaving mirror. He turned to dry his hands and saw that a sheet of paper had been pinned to his bathrobe where it hung behind the door. With his eyesight now fully restored and aided by Michelle's characteristically generous handwriting, he read the message.

Jeff, you really are some kind of fucking loser. All the same, good luck. I hope things work out for you. I took one of your suitcases, but I've no doubt you can spare it. Love, Michelle. XXX

Returning to the bedroom, he opened the wardrobe and drawers to find all her clothes gone, and that final discovery cleared his lingering doubts and confirmed that she was, in fact, gone from his life.

Later, fully dressed, he went to the door of the flat and found her key on the mat. In the past twenty-four hours, he'd lost a band and a girlfriend. Now, he really had to decide how he was going to spend the rest of his life.

2

An Echo of Innocence

*S*lam was playing on the worktop a few days later as Jeff put the eggs on to fry. It was the Ben Nicholson Hour, and the presenter was being his customary irritating self.

'We have news, just in, that will surprise us all and disappoint some, that Tantum Somnium have split up and gone their separate ways. It's true! No *fictum* about it. Jeff Mort has sent an open letter to the media for the band's followers – I should say, *ex*-followers – and I can read it to you, as I'm now holding it in my hand. Jeff writes, "I am sorry to announce that, because of irreconcilable differences, Tantum Somnium is no more. The band split up amicably yesterday, and its members have moved on to the next stage in their respective careers. I wish to thank all of you who followed us for your loyalty, which has meant a great deal to us." Well, Jeff always did use words that most people can't begin to understand, but let's not worry about that this morning. Let's listen instead to one of the band's singles, "Night Drift".'

Jeff switched off the radio and pushed down the levers on the toaster. Maybe he should have sent pictures with speech balloons. What did the plonker expect?

The phone rang four times, and the answering system cut in. At such a time, it was almost as good as a guard dog. Not surprisingly, the caller was a reporter wanting an interview. That was his bad luck.

While he waited for the toast to pop up, he considered his jobs for the day, and began making a list, using Michelle's pink-edged shopping pad, possibly the one item she'd not taken with her.

A Baker's Round

Speak to the Porsche dealers.
Speak to an estate agent, probably the one who sold me the flat in the first place.
Chuck out torn jeans, T-shirts with mindless slogans, and other trappings of band life. It's time for a complete change.
Buy some decent clothes and shoes.
Have a haircut.

He considered the last item before crossing it out. He might need to make an appointment for that. On second thoughts, he might well find a hairdressing salon where appointments weren't always necessary, so he reinstated the item.

As he put down Michelle's pink shopping-list pen, the toast popped up, so he buttered it and then scooped the eggs out of the frying pan, hoping as he placed them on the toast, that Ben Nicholson was starving, and with another hour to go before lunch. It was no worse than he deserved.

He sat down at the table with the eggs and toast, reflecting that the disadvantage in letting Michelle do the shopping was that he had no control over what she bought. He'd spoken to her more than once about the tasteless, mass-produced, sliced bread she brought from the supermarket, but her response was always to tell him that if he didn't effing like what she bought, he should do the effing shopping himself. He reflected that, not only had she no taste where bread was concerned, she also relied on a vocabulary so limited, she had to pad it out with expletives so as to sound even semi-articulate, and that couldn't possibly do her any favours at the auction house. He wondered for a moment if she effed and blinded at the telephone bidders during an auction. That thought, and others of a similar kind, helped him cope with her dramatic departure from his life.

'A Nine-Four-Four Turbo? Let's take a look.' The salesman followed him outside. 'Nineteen eighty-seven, "D" plate, I see. Of course, we could only offer you trade price, I'm afraid, although it looks like a fine motor. That would be twenty-four, seven-fifty.'

'Couldn't you sell it for me on commission?'

'No, that's not a service we offer.' He peered inside and said, 'It's nicely kept. What's the mileage?' Another look inside answered his question. 'It's had a bit of use,' he observed.

'I didn't buy it so that I could leave it in the garage,' Jeff told him. He was beginning to lose patience with the man and his slick dismissiveness.

'Just a minute,' said the salesman, 'aren't you Jeff Mort?'

'Yes.' He prepared himself for the burning question, but it never came. A Porsche dealership must deal almost daily with well-known personalities.

'A celebrity connection always helps sell a car. I'll tell you what,' he said, taking the price guide again from his pocket. 'I can offer you a bit more than basic trade.' He thumbed through the guide.

'Don't bother,' said Jeff. 'I'll sell it privately.' The dealers would have no difficulty in selling it, but he stood to lose too much that way.

'It's your best bet.'

It was, too. He took his leave of the salesman, resolved to put an advertisement in the *Evening Standard*.

He'd arranged for someone to come from the estate agency the following morning, so his next job was probably to get a haircut, so that he didn't look too much of a plonker when he went clothes shopping. Accordingly, he set out to find a place that could accommodate him.

It was quite an ordeal, but his fourth try was successful.

'Yeah, we can fit you in,' said a young man. He had a mullet cut and facial adornments that appeared to be breeding. 'Donna can do it for you. She's recently qualified as a stylist, so she hasn't got a lot of clients yet.' Raising his voice above the chill wave rubbish that was coming through the speakers, he called, 'Donna!'

The girl who answered his call looked out of place among the heavily-pierced and elaborately-coiffed staff that Jeff had noticed so far; in fact, her modest collection of piercings and medium-brown, no-nonsense bob were a welcome sight.

'Donna, this gentleman wants a cut and blow-dry.'

The girl had been staring at Jeff, but with a visible effort, she regained her concentration and said, 'Would you like to come this way?'

Jeff followed her to a row of wash basins and, finding a vacant one,

A Baker's Round

she invited him to take a seat. In arranging a towel and waterproof cover round his shoulders, she bent her head to whisper, 'I hope you don't mind me asking, but aren't you Jeff Mort?'

'Yes,' he whispered, 'but don't tell anyone.'

She shook her head and said, 'No, you can trust me.'

He thought he probably could.

'Would you like a conditioner?'

'Yes, please, it needs all the help it can get.'

'It's nice hair, really,' she said, plying the shower head. 'Have you thought about how you'd like it cut?'

'I'd like it a lot shorter, but not silly.' He hoped that made some kind of sense.

'I'll give you some pictures to look at, just to give you some ideas.'

'You've dealt with idiots like me before, Donna. I can tell.'

'No, I just try to be helpful.' She rubbed shampoo into his wet hair, and he closed his eyes in sheer ecstasy at the scalp massage he was receiving.

'Are you purring? That's what they say, isn't it?'

'Yes, I'm purring, Donna.'

She worked in the conditioner and then rinsed everything out. Finally, wrapping his hair in a towel, she led him to a chair. 'I'll get you those pictures,' she said.

For the moment, Jeff was happy to sit peacefully, knowing that no one was going to recognise him with damp hair.

'There you go, Mr Mort. These are the pictures of short hairstyles. Can I get you any coffee or tea or anything while you're looking?'

'No, thank you. I'll just flick through these.'

'Take your time.'

He looked to either side and confirmed to himself that they were less than in the earshot of other staff and clients. 'Donna,' he said, 'as it's fairly private here, can you call me "Jeff"? "Mr Mort" makes me feel like someone from that American horror-comedy thing they used to show.'

'*The Addams Family*? Of course I can.' She began combing out his damp hair while he thumbed through the pages of photographs.

'I've found it.'

'There's no hurry, Jeff.'

'No, this is the one,' he said, pointing to the photograph. It was neat, but not severe, on the business-like end of stylish, and not at all trendy, but it appealed to him nonetheless.

'If that's what you want, that's what I'll give you,' she told him confidently.

'I used to part it on the right,' he said, 'if that helps.' Now that he could see her in the mirror, she looked rather pretty.

'Well, your crown's on the right, so it makes sense, and you know what they say about a right parting.'

'No, I don't think I do.'

'It gives the impression of care and sympathy.' She made the parting with her comb and picked up her scissors.

'That's a new one on me,' he admitted.

'You strike me as a sympathetic kind of bloke,' she said as she began cutting.

'It's just possible I am. I've never really thought about it.'

She went on cutting, and asked, 'Why did the band split up, Jeff?'

'Two of them wanted to join a new Heavy Metal band, and the other wasn't in a fit state to know anything.'

'Are you going to start a new band?'

'No, and that's why I want you to make me look like the Jeffrey Mortimer I was before my agent took the scissors to my name. I'm getting out of the music business, and I'm not overjoyed at the idea of people recognising me all the time.'

Sweet girl that she was, she didn't ask the obvious question, but turned her attention to his new lifestyle. She asked, 'Are you going to buy new clothes?'

'Yes, I am. It's time I changed into something civilised.'

'So, are you going to have a grand shopping spree?'

'I suppose so.'

She gave him a wistful look and said, 'I wish I could come with you. I love helping people to shop.'

'Do you really?'

'Yes, it's fun, and I just like clothes. You have to remember that it's possible to go shopping without actually buying anything.'

'Incredible. Do you do a lot of shopping for yourself?'

He suspected it was a silly question, and her expression confirmed

A Baker's Round

it. 'Not your kind of shopping. I've been on an apprentice's wages these last few years.'

'I'm sorry, Donna. That was clumsy of me.'

'There,' she said, as if she'd just won a bet. 'I said you were sympathetic, didn't I?'

'You did,' he agreed. 'When's your day off?'

'Tomorrow. Why?'

'Would you like to come shopping with me?'

Her reaction would not have been out of place had he asked her to marry him. 'Do you mean it?'

'Of course. Tell me where you live, and I'll pick you up at, oh… eleven.'

'I'll write it down for you before you go.'

The man from the estate agency remembered the flat from the time of Jeff's purchase, and the valuation took very little time, so that Jeff had no difficulty in driving to Stockwell for eleven, as arranged.

Donna answered the door, dressed and ready to go. A little surprised, she accepted a kiss on her cheek and walked out to Jeff's car. 'I don't believe it,' she said. 'Is it really yours?'

'Yes, but not for long.' He opened the passenger door for her. 'I'm hoping to sell it.'

When he was in his seat, she asked, 'What will you get instead of this?'

'I don't know yet. Something sensible, I suppose.'

She appeared to consider that decision, because she said, 'Sensible hair, sensible car…. Are we going to buy sensible clothes today?'

'I hope so.'

'Well, it's your money you're spending. Where are we going, anyway?'

'We're going to leave the car in the multi-storey carpark and take a taxi across the river. When did you last eat?'

'About three or four hours ago.'

'Right, we've time to make one or two calls, and then we'll have lunch.' He saw her hesitate. 'It's on me,' he assured her.

Relieved, she said, 'You know, I could get used to this.'

He smiled and said, 'Make the most of it, Donna. I'll be out of your life after today, much as I value your skill with the comb and scissors, not to mention the very real pleasure of your company.'

Leaving the Porsche in the carpark, they took the lift to the ground floor. Jeff looked at his watch and asked, 'Shall we do lunch and then start shopping?'

'You're the boss.'

'Okay.' He hailed a taxi, which dew up beside them. 'Harvey Nichols, Knightsbridge, please.'

Donna gave him a stunned look.

'We'll have lunch there,' he explained, 'and do the shopping somewhere more sensible.'

Laughing, she climbed into the taxi. 'I'm glad I put my best five-oh-ones on,' she said. 'Now, that was sensible.' Still laughing, she said, 'I still can't believe you're going in for the sensible life.'

'Being a rock star isn't all it's cracked up to be.'

'But you're not at all what I expected.'

'I'm flesh and blood, just like you,' he said, carrying out a discreet survey, 'but with a few differences. You're a pretty girl, Donna.'

'Thanks, Jeff.'

At that moment, the driver broke his silence to say, 'D' you know what, guv'nor? If your hair was a bit longer, you'd be a dead ringer for that Jeff Mort. D' you know who I mean?'

Donna giggled, but Jeff told him seriously, 'You're not the first person to say that.'

'You're a lot tidier than him, though. He's a scruffy git on stage, an' I can't stand his band.... What's it called?'

'Tantum Somnium. They've split up, by the way.'

'An' not before time, if you ask me.' Now fully wound up, he asked, 'Goin' to do a bit of shopping, are you?'

'That's the idea.'

'I thought so when you said Harvey Nic's.' He pulled confidently into a stream of traffic, ignoring a horn blast from one irate motorist.

A Baker's Round

'Mind you, you'll pay through the bloody nose at that place, if you ask me.'

'I'm not asking you, but I will ask you to curb your language. There's a young lady here who's not used to it.' He squeezed Donna's hand to discourage her from laughing.

'Sorry, guv. Sorry, miss. No offence.'

They continued to Knightsbridge in silence. The driver pulled up outside their destination and reported, 'Harvey Nichols, guv'nor.'

Having paid off the taxi, Jeff offered Donna his arm somewhat incongruously in his denim jacket, and they walked into the store. 'This way,' said Jeff, heading for the restaurant.

A waitress came to them and said, 'Good morning. If you're looking for a table for lunch, I'm afraid we're rather busy....' Her mouth remained open, and she stared at him.

'Yes,' he confirmed, 'I'm Jeff Mort. I had a rather superior haircut yesterday, which makes me harder to identify.'

'Oh well, I'm sure we'll find you a table, Mr Mort. For two, is it?'

'That's right.'

'Would you like to follow me?' She led them to a table in a far corner of the restaurant and left them with the menu.

' Feel free to have whatever you fancy,' he told Donna, 'but I usually just have a main course at lunchtime, a salad or something with pasta.' Reading confusion in her features, he pointed to the quiche salads and said, 'These are always good.'

'Oh, yeah, I like quiche Lorraine. I'd like that, please.'

'Consider it yours. What would you like to drink?'

Confusion returned, so he said, 'A dry white wine would go well with the quiche.'

'If you say so. I won't have very much, because I'm not used to wine.'

'Don't worry.' He caught the eye of the waitress.

'Are you ready to order, sir?'

'Yes, we'd both like the Quiche Lorraine salad, please.'

'And to drink, sir?'

'Two glasses of the house Chablis, I think.'

'Very good, sir.'

Donna was still in Wonderland. 'You're not real,' she said. 'You're too smooth for a rock star. From what I've heard, they're always effing and blinding and insulting people.'

'It's just as well I'm getting out of it, then.' Smiling at her bewilderment, he said, 'I don't think I'm at all suave. I went to a posh school, but they threw me out when I was sixteen.'

'Was it one of those schools where you go to live?'

'I was a boarder, yes.'

She was quiet for a spell, possibly unable to imagine life in such a place, and then she said, 'Now you've got a sensible haircut, and when you get your sensible clothes and car, what are you going to do?'

'The short answer to that is that I haven't decided yet, but I intend to go on my travels and see what ideas occur to me.'

Suddenly excited, she said, 'You're going to seek your fortune, just like….'

'The Three Little Pigs?'

'No,' she laughed, 'you know what I mean.' Then, returning to an earlier topic, she asked, 'Why did they send you home from school?'

'It was overreaction, really. Some of us got up to harmless mischief with the local girls, and steps had to be taken. The headmaster waived the usual two terms' notice and asked my father to take me away. I have to say, my father was very decent about the whole thing. He thought I'd been unjustly punished.'

'Good for your dad.'

'Yes, he was a fair-minded man.'

'Was?'

'Both my parents were killed in a motorway accident almost six years ago.'

'Jeff, you poor thing.' She reached across the table for his hand. 'That's awful.'

'It was, I have to agree. It was probably the shock of it that made me chuck in my job and go into the music business.' He considered that for a moment and confirmed it. 'Yes, I wasn't in a fit state to make a sensible decision.' He grinned in spite of it. 'It turned out to be a lucrative decision, in the end.'

Their conversation came to a close when the waitress arrived with two quiche salads and two glasses of Chablis.

A Baker's Round

When circumstances were normal, Jeff wasn't a devotee of clothes shopping, but Donna's lively participation turned it into non-stop entertainment. She encouraged him to try on more clothes than he would ever have considered, and each time he emerged from the changing room, she gave him her candid opinion, usually with an emphatic shake of her head, a look that told him she was unconvinced, or a beaming smile of complete approval.

Eventually, he declared the innings closed, asking her, 'Where do you buy your clothes, Donna?'

'Miss Selfridge when I can afford it, but that's not very often.' Having answered his question, she asked, 'Where are we going next?'

'Oxford Street.'

As accommodating as ever, she accompanied him to the famous street of clothing stores, until they stood outside Miss Selfridge, where she asked, What have we come here for?'

'To look at what they've got.'

'But I can't afford anything here.'

'You told me that shopping doesn't necessarily involve buying.'

'All right. I can manage that.'

They walked through the store, with Donna's practised eye taking everything in until her progress was arrested, not by a dress or a trouser suit, but by a stone-coloured trench coat.

Jeff asked, 'Do you like it?'

'Like it? I'd kill for it,' She looked at the price and said, 'That's the only way I'd ever get my hands on it.'

'Try it on.'

'What for? I can't afford it.'

'I want to see you in it.'

She hesitated and said, 'All right, if that's what you want.' She looked at the sizes and picked out two, saying, 'I may as well get the size right and let you see it properly.'

Jeff waited while she tried them on.

'I'm still size ten,' she reported, tying the belt loosely around her waist.

'And you look the perfect picture in it. Let's put the other one back.' He took it from her, inserting the hanger and returning it to the rail. Having done that, he took the coat she'd worn for him and guided her to the checkout.

'What are you doing, Jeff?'

He made no reply, but handed the coat to the nearest assistant and asked, 'Will you wrap this for me, please?'

'Certainly, sir. How are you paying?'

'Card.' He took out his credit card while Donna stared in astonishment. Conscious of her state of mind, he said, 'I usually regard clothes shopping as an almighty nuisance, Donna, but you've made it a pleasure. You've been great company and full of advice, so I'd say you've earned this coat.'

'Jeff, that's....'

Hearing his name, the assistant looked again at the name on the credit card machine. 'You're... but your hair's different,' she said.

'This delightful young lady cut it for me yesterday, and you're right. I am guilty of being Jeff Mort.' He took his card and receipt, leaving Donna to claim the carrier and its contents.

'Jeff,' she said as they left the store, 'you're the loveliest fella ever. Thank you.'

'No, you're confusing me with someone else.' He hailed a taxi, and when it drew up beside them, said, 'Stockwell Park Carpark, please.'

'Right you are, guv.'

The journey was relatively brief. Before long, they put their shopping into the Porsche and climbed in.

'No one's ever going to believe me about today, Jeff.'

'Well, it obviously means a lot to you, so I'd better do something about that.' He took out a pen and the bill from Harvey Nichols, and used the car handbook as a firm surface to write:

Donna,
Thank you for your delightful and helpful company, and for making today's outing the most enjoyable shopping trip ever.
Lots of love,
Jeff (Mort) XXX

A Baker's Round

'There,' he said, returning his pen to the pocket of his denim jacket, 'you've got it in black and white.'

'Thank you, Jeff. I'll never forget today. It's been brilliant for all kinds of reasons.'

'Neither will I.'

'Can I ask you for one favour before we go?'

'You can always ask.'

Shyly, she said, 'I feel a right wally, asking you this, but will you kiss me properly, just once?'

'It'll be a pleasure.' He took her in his arms and kissed her deeply and at length.

Eventually, she emerged, flushed and fulfilled. 'Jeff, that was... brilliant.'

'I'm glad.'

'Have you got a girlfriend?'

'I had, but she walked out the day the band split up. I think it meant more to her than it did to me.'

She seemed to be nerving herself to say something. Suddenly, in a now-or-never burst of confidence, she asked, 'You see, if you need company, you can call on me.'

'Nothing would give me greater pleasure, Donna, but I can't offer any degree of stability. I could be away by next week, and I don't yet know where.' He kissed her again and started the engine.

3

Final Preparations

Jeff took several phone calls about the Porsche and experienced no difficulty in selling it for twenty-seven thousand. Once the banker's draft was in place, and he'd handed the car over to its delighted new owner, he could turn his attention to other matters, the first of which was a replacement for the Porsche.

After a great deal of thought, he sacrificed speed and glamour for practicality and visited the Volvo dealership.

The salesman asked him, 'Are we looking at a new vehicle?'

'I doubt it. I need something fairly quickly.'

'Saloon or wagon, sir?'

'Or what?' Suddenly, he had a mental image of something hauled by a team of oxen.

'Station wagon. Most marques offer an estate car, sir. Volvo prefer to call it a "wagon".'

Thinking quickly, he decided that an estate car must be the ultimate combination of comfort and practicality. He asked, 'What estate… wagons have you available?'

'As it happens, sir, we have a lovely Two-Forty that's four months old. It's an ex-demonstrator, which means it's been maintained by us from new, so we know all about it.'

'I should hope you do. May I see it?'

'By all means, sir.' The salesman appeared to be examining him covertly.

'Is something the matter?'

'Not really, sir. It's just that, with longer hair and in more casual

A Baker's Round

clothing, you'd bear a strong resemblance to Jeff Mort of Tantum Somnium.'

'It's not the first time I've been told that.' In fact, it was happening too often for his peace of mind, despite the haircut and smart, casual appearance. He intended to do something about that later. For the time being, he followed the salesman to the rear of the showroom, where a number of vehicles lined the compound. The salesman led him to an estate model in dark red.

'Have you your driving licence with you, sir?'

'Yes.' Jeff fumbled in his pocket for the folded paper document. 'Here it is.'

The salesman stared at the name on the licence and said, 'You *are* Jeff Mort.'

'Yes, I am, but don't tell anyone.'

'Are you forming a new band, Mr Mort…imer?'

'No, I'm trying to buy a car. Can I take this one out to try it?'

'By all means.' The salesman handed him his licence and the key. 'There's plenty petrol in it,' he said. 'Just let me move a couple of cars so that you can get out.

When that was done, Jeff said, 'Right, I'll see you in about fifteen minutes.' He got into the driving seat, which seemed comfortable enough, and started the engine, smiling to himself. It was going to be a new experience after the Porsche. Reminding himself he could get used to anything if he gave it a fair chance, he drove it into the main road.

Once in the stream of traffic, performance meant nothing, but he felt comfortingly safe, much safer than he had in the Porsche, and this car was going to do everything he wanted it to do. When he was able, he made his way back to the dealership, where the salesman was waiting.

'Thank you,' said Jeff, handing back the key. 'Let's go inside and talk.'

In the office, the salesman asked, 'Have you anything to trade in?' His look said that he doubted it.

'No, I'll pay in ready cash.'

'All right. For cash, I can do it for ten thousand, five hundred.'

'I was thinking in terms of nine thousand, seven-fifty.'

The salesman looked doubtful. 'I don't think we can do that.'

'Call it a straight ten thousand and you've got a deal.'

'Will you excuse me for a minute?'

'By all means.'

The salesman went through an internal door, presumably to gain approval from above. Meanwhile, Jeff was happy to wait. The dealer was asking a fair price, but it was a point of honour not to agree too readily.

After a few minutes, the door opened, and a relieved-looking salesman returned to say, 'We can do it for ten thousand.'

'There you are. You never know what you can do 'til you try. All right, I'll give you a deposit, if you like, and I can pay the balance on delivery. How much do you need for a deposit?'

'Is a hundred acceptable, Mr Mortimer?'

'Fine.' Jeff handed him his credit card.

The salesman finalised the paperwork and asked, 'What have you been running until now, Mr Mortimer?'

'A Porsche Nine-Four-Four Turbo, but don't ask me why I'm changing, because you wouldn't believe me if I told you.'

The salesman could only wonder.

On leaving the Volvo agency, he walked to the optician's he'd noticed that morning. Somewhat unimaginatively, it was called Belle Vue Optics, and, unusually for him, he had no difficulty in finding it again.

A stern matron confronted him. She asked, 'What can we do for you, sir?'

'I'd like a pair of glasses with clear lenses, please.'

'*Clear* lenses?'

'Devoid of optical artifice,' he confirmed, 'except that they must obviously fit the frames.' He couldn't wear sun glasses all the time, and neutral lenses seemed to be the only option.

The woman remained nonplussed. 'Have you never needed glasses?'

'Not to my knowledge.'

'When did you last have your eyes tested?'

'Oh, you've got me there. Let me see. I was still at school, so it was before October 'seventy-seven.'

'Twelve years or more,' she said in a reproachful kind of way. 'Don't you think you should have them tested again? Our optometrist is on the premises and she's free now.'

'Oh, I don't think so. I haven't been aware of any problem.'

'Well, if you're happy with that.'

'Quite happy, thank you.' The sound of a door being opened and closed distracted him for the moment, but not as much as the sight that passed before his eyes. 'Belle Vue indeed,' he murmured.

'This is Miss Hopkins, our optometrist. Miss Hopkins, this gentleman hasn't had an eye test since nineteen seventy-seven.'

'Oh, tut, tut,' chided the vision good-naturedly.

'On second thoughts,' said Jeff, 'maybe I should have a test.'

'I can do it now,' she offered.

'Lead the way.' He followed her into the examination room, where she invited him to take a seat, and having done that, peered at him more closely.

'It's uncanny,' she said.

'What is?'

'With longer hair, you could be Jeff Mort of Tantum Somnium.' She shook her head to dismiss the thought, and said, 'We have to complete this form. First of all, your full name.'

'Jeffrey Andrew Mortimer, initials J-A-M, known throughout school life as "Chivers", a reference to the jam manufactured by them. Parents never think, do they?'

Miss Hopkins wasn't interested in nicknames. She stared at him again and said, 'You *are* Jeff Mort.'

'So people keep telling me.'

'Are you going to start up another band?'

'People keep asking me that, as well, but no, I'm not.'

Adopting a professional air once more, she continued with the questionnaire, noting his general health and medical history, which was reassuringly blank. 'So, you've never needed glasses?'

'Not as far as I know.' He certainly had no need of them at that moment. Miss Hopkins had crossed her legs, causing her delightfully short skirt to take an upward journey.

'All right. Let's find out what you can see.'

He gave a start, and then realised guiltily that she was talking about the test card reflected in the mirror.

'First, I'll cover your left eye.'

He responded to each instruction and question, forcing himself not to look too obviously at her delectable limbs, and finally, she said, 'You need a little help with your distance vision. You're a bit short-sighted, but it's nothing awful.' Then, as if suddenly reminded of something, she asked, 'If you thought you had no need of glasses, what brought you here today?'

'Can you keep a secret?'

'Of course.'

'I'm tired of being Jeff Mort and being recognised as him. I want to go back to being boring old Jeffrey Mortimer, and I thought a pair of glasses would help with the *incognito*.'

'Good thinking. My boyfriend had to start wearing glasses recently, and quite a few people commented on how different they made him look.'

He was down to earth with a bump. The boyfriend was bad news, but he had to say something neutral. 'Is he trying to avoid recognition?'

She laughed. 'No, but listen. What will you do?'

'I don't know yet, but "'Tis not too late to seek a newer world".'

'If you say so.' She had a boyfriend and she was a stranger to Tennyson. He was almost relieved when she said, 'Let's go and find you some frames.'

The receptionist at Bligh's Removals wasn't particularly good-looking, and her legs were mercifully well-covered, but she was efficient, and that virtue compensated for a great deal.

'So, you don't want a removal.'

'No, I just want my furniture and bits and pieces taken into store. When I find somewhere to live, I'll let you know and then you can reunite me with my worldly goods.'

'Do you want us to pack for you?'

'Absolutely. I'm hopeless at that kind of thing.' The great advantage of dealing with middle-aged women, he decided, was the cosy probability that they'd never heard of either Jeff Mort or Tantum Somnium.

'When would you like them to come round and pack for you? Next Tuesday morning is free, if that's any good.'

A Baker's Round

'It's perfect, thank you.'

'Right, I'll just make a note of the address where you want the packing done, and a phone number where we can reach you, and if you'll sign here, you can leave the rest to us.'

He was aware that he was preparing for a journey, and an important one, too, but with no real idea of his route or destination. As Donna had put it, he was going to seek his fortune – or spend it. The latter was the likeliest outcome.

He spent the afternoon browsing his dilapidated AA Road Atlas of Great Britain, concentrating on the area north of London, as it seemed to provide greater scope for discovery, a hypothesis based on the fact that it covered a greater area than the south.

He studied the double page that led enticingly northwards, until a hint of some childhood fancy stirred his memory, and he looked around for place names that meant something to him.

Presently, his eye fell on Banbury in Oxfordshire, and the nursery rhyme he'd known from infancy came to him.

Ride a cock horse to Banbury Cross,
To see a fine lady upon a white horse;
Rings on her fingers and bells on her toes,
She shall have music wherever she goes.

Banbury would be his first stop. His late grandfather would have approved of that. As Rural Dean of Binningford and surrounding parishes, he often delighted in surprising his congregations by referring to the stories behind popular nursery rhymes. He spoke with some authority, as well, having written a book on the subject.

Now enthused, Jeff hunted his bookshelves until he found *Ding, Dong Bell* by A. C. Mortimer. It was a timely find, and he would keep it within reach for his journey while the rest of his books were in store.

He found the Contents page and ran his eye down it, finally locating 'Ride a Cock Horse'. He turned to the relevant chapter and read:

The most obvious 'fine lady' has to be Lady Godiva, who pleaded with her husband Leofric, Earl of Mercia, to ease the tax burden on the poor. His response, in the year 1040, that he would lower the taxes only when she rode naked through the streets of Coventry, must be the earliest recorded challenge of its kind. The rings on her fingers that indicated her marital and noble status, and the bells on her toes that reminded the populace to look the other way are referred to in the rhyme, and were possibly the only adornments she was allowed on the journey.

There are, of course, other possible origins.

Jeff scanned the rest of the chapter, but was unimpressed. The Lady Godiva story was the one he wanted to believe, and that was how it would remain. When his belongings were packed and taken into store, and when he'd collected his new glasses and taken delivery of the Volvo, he would set out on the first stage of his quest, to Banbury.

4

To Banbury Cross

It was a shame that Jeff had to make the first part of his odyssey through a conurbation of Greater London and its commuter belt. He felt that a succession of unspoilt villages would have been a more fitting approach to the ancient town of Banbury, but the thought was born of his romantic nature. He remembered his old geography master calling him a fanciful idiot when he was twelve years old, because he regarded new spring growth as a source of excitement and wonder, rather than the product of chlorophyll and photosynthesis. With that memory in mind, he continued along the M40, concluding that his decision not to make geography one of his 'O' levels had been a sound one. There was a limit to the boredom a teenage lad could be expected to endure.

One benefit the M40 had to offer was that after less than an hour and a half he was on the outskirts of Banbury. Very soon, he found his way to the town centre and was looking around for signs to carparks, which seemed plentiful, so he opted for the nearest. It would be pleasant to explore Banbury on foot, but first of all, he had to find somewhere to stay. He had a list of possibilities, which he consulted, noting that the third on his list was located in Castle Street, which was not far from where he stood, at least, according to the map, which he had no reason to doubt.

Jeff had never been at home with maps, which was another good reason for dropping geography at the end of the third year. Yet another was his appalling sense of direction and his naïve surprise when the map and the local signs and street names turned out to be in agreement.

Even so, he located the house in Castle Street with no more than the usual difficulty, and was rewarded by a sign outside it advertising bed and breakfast vacancies. So soon after Easter, it was welcome news, so he rang the bell confidently.

He didn't know why he imagined landladies to be middle-aged, but he was surprised when the woman who answered the door seemed quite young, maybe about his age or even younger. Maybe she was the landlady's daughter, or even a hired help. 'I'm looking for accommodation,' he told her, 'and I see you have vacancies.'

'Yes, for how long?'

'I can't really say at this stage, but maybe a week. Would that be difficult?'

She smiled. 'Not at all. I really don't know why I asked you that. Would you like to come in? Is it just for you, or will you be requiring a double room?'

'Thank you. No, a single room will be fine.' He followed her into the passage, and he noticed her wedding and engagement rings for the first time.

'I'm Mrs O' Connell, by the way.'

'Jeffrey Mortimer.' In shaking her hand, he was able to see her more closely. He didn't find her startlingly attractive in the conventional way, but she had an other-worldly, almost maidenly, appeal. Clearly, she was no maiden; the wedding ring was witness to that, but the effect was still there. With her dark, flowing waves, held for the moment by some kind of clasp, and her gentle lines and brown, contemplative eyes, she might have stepped out of a renaissance painting.

'I'll show you the room and the bathroom first, if that's all right.'

'Absolutely,' he said, gathering himself again. 'Lead on.'

She took him upstairs and pointed out the bath and shower room, and then, straight across the landing, a single room with the figure 2 screwed to door. It seemed more than adequate.

'Excellent.'

'I'm glad you like it. I'll show you to the breakfast room now.' She led him downstairs to a room at the front of the house and opened the door. 'I serve breakfast between seven and nine-thirty.'

'Very convenient.'

'You'll find copies of the breakfast menu here, on the sideboard.'

A Baker's Round

Almost apologetically, she said, 'My husband usually functions as breakfast cook, but he's currently working away from home.'

'I've no doubt he's left the job in perfectly capable hands, Mrs O' Connell.'

'Thank you.' She smiled again, Jeff thought, a little uneasily, although he admitted to himself that he might have imagined it. Then, she said, 'I haven't told you about my charges, yet, have I?'

'No, but I'm sure you're about to.'

'For a single room and breakfast, it's just ten pounds per night.'

'That's absolutely fine.'

Seemingly pleased that the matter was out of the way, she asked, 'What brings you to Banbury, Mr Mortimer?'

'Curiosity. As a matter of fact, you could call it idle curiosity, but from the little I've seen of it, Banbury's a lovely town, so I'm quite keen to explore it.'

'Have you no work or family ties?' Immediately, she recollected herself. 'I'm sorry,' she said. 'I'd no right to ask you that.'

'Not at all. I'm happy to answer your question, but I don't think you'll find it at all entertaining.'

'If you come through to the kitchen, I'll give you a cup of tea. Is tea all right, or would you prefer coffee?'

'Tea will be very welcome, thank you, Mrs O' Connell.'

He followed her to a large, square kitchen, where she offered him a seat before filling the kettle.

'My only remaining family is my brother, who lives in America. He's a vicar there, in what Americans call the Episcopalian Church.'

'I've heard of it. I suppose the Church of England is episcopalian in character. We just don't call it that.'

'It's too much like hard work, and speaking of work, I made myself redundant a short time ago, I'm trying to decide what to do next, and while I'm coming to that decision, I'm going to visit places with names that mean something to me. I chose Banbury for obvious reasons.'

She laughed. 'Banbury cakes?'

'No, although they have their appeal. It was actually the fine lady upon a white horse that beckoned to me. I remembered her from childhood, and I read about the connection in a book my grandfather wrote.'

'Who was your grandfather?'

'A. C. Mortimer.'

'*Ding, Dong Bell?*'

'That was the book, yes. You know it, obviously.'

'I have a copy.' The thought seemed to please her. 'So he was your grandfather, and your brother's a vicar. I gather you're not.'

'No, I departed from the family tradition. Can you imagine me with longer hair and untidy, casual clothes? Until a couple of weeks ago, I was lead guitarist and songwriter with a band called Tantum Somnium.' It felt strange, offering the information, but Mrs O' Connell somehow inspired confidences.

For the first time, she seemed puzzled. 'I don't know much about the current pop music scene,' she said, 'but that seems an odd name, Unless I'm mistaken, it means "only dreaming".'

'Yes, but used in a scornful sense, "*somnium*" means "illusion", as in "dream on". It was as close as I could get to "Only Make-Believe".'

'That was the name of a song, wasn't it?'

'An excellent song,' he agreed, 'written by a proper songwriter.'

'Who was that?'

'Jerome Kern. I saw *Showboat* in London when I was at school. It was a half-term treat.'

'I've heard of it.' Still intrigued, she asked, 'What made you give it that name?'

'Cynicism. It was why I left the music business.'

'Don't keep me in suspense,' she said, getting up to make the tea.

'I was tired and ashamed of being a party to the pretentiousness that's so much a part of the music industry.'

'I know nothing about the music industry, but I think that was noble of you, Mr Mortimer.'

'Thank you. My girlfriend left me because of it. She said I was a loser.'

'That's awful.'

'Not really. We hadn't been together long, and we had little in common.'

She nodded to register her understanding, and then, remembering something, she said, 'As you're a visitor to Banbury, maybe you'd like a Banbury cake.'

'Yes, please. It's been quite a while since I tried one.'

She got up and took a cellophane packet from a cake tin. 'They're mass-produced and not brilliant,' she said, putting two of them on plates, 'but the symbolism's there.'

'Thank you.' He tried the cake and considered the taste and texture.

'Don't tell me,' she said. 'They're not very good.'

'They're actually pretty good, and I appreciate the symbolism, Mrs O' Connell. Thank you for an unusual welcome.'

'Go on,' she said. 'You were going to say something else.'

'No, really. Only that, as Eccles cakes, they deserve at least six out of ten.'

'But they're supposed to be Banbury cakes.'

Confidently, he nodded in agreement while he ate another mouthful. Finally, he said, 'In all fairness, that was pretty good.'

'All right, Mr Mortimer. What makes them Eccles cakes rather than Banbury cakes?'

'Mainly, the absence of honey, cinnamon and rum. There are other, less-important ingredients as well.'

She was shaking her head in bewilderment. 'That was quite an appraisal. Are you keen on baking?'

'Yes, I am.'

'I'm not, largely because I'm not particularly good at it.'

'Who taught you to bake, Mrs O' Connell?'

She had to think about her answer. Finally, she said, 'My mother was very impatient with me, and that's an excellent way to turn someone against the thing they're supposed to be learning.'

'I agree. What about school?'

'Oh, I did some at school, but the circumstances weren't ideal.' After a little thought, she said, 'Neither was the teacher. Like my mother, she was demanding and very impatient.'

Maybe he was already influenced to some extent by what he saw as her vulnerability, but her talk of insensitive treatment at home and at school found Jeff's soft centre, and he felt sorry for her. 'I'll tell you what,' he said. 'Even though I'm a visitor to the town, I can bake Banbury cakes. It's not difficult, and I'll teach you how to do it, too. Have you got a mixing bowl, a sieve, a rolling pin, a baking tray and a fine grater?'

She thought. 'Oddly enough, yes. They were my mother's.'

'Then I think we're in business. There's just one thing I have to ask.'

'Yes?'

'Is there off-the-road parking here? I left my car in a carpark, and it's probably earned a ticket by now.'

When Jeff went down for breakfast at eight o' clock, he found the dining room deserted, and concluded that the other guests must have left early. A copy of the day's *Independent* lay on the sideboard, so he took it to the table to acquaint himself with the news from the outside world.

He was reassured to find that May had begun with very little happening in Britain. Even rioting on prison roofs seemed to have lost its appeal, and he was about to return the newspaper to the sideboard, when Mrs O' Connell came into the room.

'Good morning, Mr Mortimer. Did you sleep well?'

'Good morning, Mrs O' Connell. Very well, thank you.'

'What would you like for breakfast?'

He glanced quickly at the menu and said, 'I'd like two poached eggs on toast, please, and coffee.'

'Would you like juice? I have orange, grapefruit or tomato.'

'Oh, orange juice, please.'

A little nervously, she asked, 'As you're currently the only guest in the house, do you mind if I join you for breakfast?'

'Not in the least. I 'd welcome your company.'

She smiled much more confidently and said, 'You know, I can't imagine anyone less like a rock star than you.'

'You're not the first person who's told me that, Mrs O' Connell.' The agreeable memory of Donna came freshly to mind. 'Do you find me too urbane?'

'You're unusually urbane for that role, yes. You're a charming man, and I welcome that.' Remembering the reason for her visit, she said, 'I must put your eggs on to poach.'

A Baker's Round

Left alone again with his thoughts, Jeff began to plan his day, and was still putting it into some kind of order when Mrs O' Connell came in with a tray.

'I usually eat in the kitchen,' she said, 'but it seemed a nonsense with only one guest in the house.'

'Some things are better shared,' he agreed.

'What are you going to do today?'

'I was just thinking about that when you came in. I have to do some shopping, and I'm certainly going to look at the sights. Banbury Cross is a must, and I caught a quick glimpse of the fine lady on her white horse when I arrived, but I'd like a closer look.'

'You'll find her fully clothed,' she warned.

'Good, I'd hate to be embarrassed.' Thinking once more about his plans for the day, he asked, 'Is there a leisure centre hereabouts?'

'There's more than one.' She took a brochure from the sideboard and gave it to him. 'If you like open-air swimming, you've come to the right place.

'Thank you. It's the gym I need as much as anything, now that I'm spoiling myself with Banbury cakes and cooked breakfasts.'

'There is a gym,' she assured him. 'I've noticed it on my way to the pool. I go there quite often.' Lifting the coffee pot, she asked, 'Would you like your coffee now?'

5

Baking Therapy

Jeff managed to find everything he needed at Sainsbury's for the baking session, after which he phoned the estate agent in London to learn that some interest had already been shown in the flat. It was an encouraging sign, and he arranged for the agents to pick up any mail from the flat and send it to Mrs O' Connell's address until further notice. It wasn't a service they offered, as a rule, but he reminded them, and they agreed, that they wouldn't be doing it for nothing.

With those jobs out of the way, he walked the streets of Banbury, enjoying the architecture and the statue of the 'fine lady', robed though she was. As a passing local confirmed, they couldn't show her in her original state. It simply wouldn't have been right with so many children about. The same man explained that the original town had been destroyed by Puritans in the early seventeenth century. His story strengthened Jeff's resolve to avoid becoming fervent about anything. Unquestioning zealots, he decided, could be an awful nuisance.

He did well to find the leisure centre after only three wrong turnings and, after a spell in the gym, he made his way to the outdoor pool, or 'Lido', as it was delightfully known. It was certainly popular, but he was sure there was room for him as well.

He began with two lengths, after which he hauled himself up on to the side to look around him. As he did so, a voice said, 'Hello, Mr Mortimer. I see you found the place in spite of your doubts.'

A Baker's Round

He looked in the direction the voice was coming from. It had to be Mrs O' Connell's voice, but it was only when she spoke again that he recognised her.

'It's the swimming cap, isn't it? It makes everyone look the same.'

'I wouldn't say that, exactly.' Not everyone looked like Mrs O' Connell in a swimsuit. He tried not to make it obvious, but he knew that women could always see where a man was looking. 'Hello, Mrs O' Connell. Yes, I only got lost three times.'

'Are you having a rest?'

'Yes, I've already done an hour in the gym.'

'You're keen, evidently.' Sitting beside him on the edge of the pool, she said, 'When you're ready, I'll race you to the shallow end.'

'Okay. As we're playing out together, do you think you could call me "Jeff"?'

'All right. In that case, my name's Lynn.'

Jeff nodded. 'I'm ready for that challenge, now. In fact, we could make it two lengths, if you like.'

She gave him a wary look. 'I have a feeling I'm about to be humbled,' she said.

'I wouldn't do that to you.'

'No,' she said, standing up, 'I don't think you would.'

They stood side by side, waiting for an elderly man to complete an unhurried breadth.

'Right,' said Jeff, 'on your marks, get set, go!'

They dived in, he a little ahead of her, but he took his time in surfacing. When he did, he found that she was actually swimming quite strongly, but he maintained his short lead to the shallow end, where he made a leisurely turn, and they set off on the return lap almost together. He reached the deep end a few strokes before her.

As she hauled herself up beside him, she said, 'You weren't even trying.'

'I said I wouldn't show you up, and you're quite a strong swimmer, anyway, Lynn.'

'You are. You obviously do a lot of swimming.'

He could see that she was eyeing his muscles discreetly. He enjoyed it when women did that, discreetly or otherwise. 'London isn't the healthiest place to live, and I had to keep fit somehow.'

'Will you go back to London?'

'I don't know.' He hadn't even thought about the possibility. 'It all depends on how I decide to spend the rest of my life.'

'Oh well,' she said, standing up again, 'let's start the rest of your life with another swim. It's what we came here for, after all.'

He ate at the Olde Reindeer Inn, where he'd had lunch earlier, and arrived at Lynn's house a little after seven-thirty, as arranged.

She was wearing her hair down and, whilst it was certainly appealing, he had to say, 'You have lovely hair, Lynn, but I'm afraid I have to ask you to tie it up.'

'I'm sorry,' she said. 'I never thought. It's my off-duty look.'

'And very nice too, but we don't want hair in the baking. Have you got one of those munchie-things handy?'

'*Scrunchie*,' she corrected him. She found one and caught her hair back with it. Then, looking at the bag of ingredients, she said, 'You must tell me what I owe you for those things.'

'No, I shan't. It was my idea, and I'm doing it partly for the pleasure it gives me.'

'And what else?'

'I'll tell you later. Now, did you leave that pack of pastry I gave you to stand?'

'Yes,' she said confidently, as if she were relieved that she'd got something right.

'Good. The first job is to preheat the oven.' He glanced at the oven control and saw that it was in Celsius.

'Okay, preheat it to a hundred and eighty, and, having done that, let's line a baking tray. I see you've got one ready.' He passed her a roll of greaseproof paper.

'It's not very obliging.'

'It'll lie down all right when it gets nine or ten cakes on it.' He picked up the large mixing bowl she'd got ready, and placed it in front of her.

'Are you doing all this from memory?'

A Baker's Round

'No, I've got my secret recipe book with me.' Taking a pack of butter from his carrier, he said, 'First, we put fifty grams of butter in the bowl.' He opened the pack and was about to cut a piece off, but he stopped and said, 'As you're learning to do this, would you like to weigh fifty grams? It's about a quarter of a pack,' he prompted. While she was doing that, he took out a jar of honey, a nutmeg, a box of allspice, one of cinnamon, a bag of raisins, one of currants, another of candied peel and a miniature bottle of rum. Then, seeing what looked like fifty grams of butter in the bowl, he said, 'I want you to follow the method and do exactly what it says.' He placed the notebook in front of her. 'A good way to do this is to measure everything beforehand into individual containers, but we didn't have time for that.'

'So, I have to cream the butter along with the honey?'

'Take a tablespoonful of honey and dribble it over the butter, and then cream them together.' He watched her do it and then put a hand on her shoulder. 'Good girl, well done.' Then, seeing her smile, he apologised quickly. 'I'm sorry. That was so patronising.' He removed his hand, saying, 'So was that.'

'Don't apologise.' She smiled as she said it. 'No one's said anything like that to me in a long time. It was rather nice.'

'You surprise me. Now, here's the nutmeg and here's the grater. Give it a dozen strokes. Don't be too gentle.'

She showered the mixture with nutmeg and asked, 'What's next?'

'The spices. You've already put the nutmeg in.'

'Half a teaspoon of allspice.'

He gave her the box of allspice.

'Half a teaspoon of cinnamon.' She took the box from him and repeated the procedure.

'Now weigh out fifty grams of currants and the same weight of raisins.' He watched her as she did it. 'Now, fifty grams of candied peel.'

She completed that and said, 'Now the rum. Honestly, Jeff, these things must have cost you a fortune.'

'It's going to be worth every penny.' He broke the seal on the cap of the rum and said, 'Pour a tablespoonful into the mixture and stir it all together until it's an even mixture.'

When it was stirred to his satisfaction, he pushed the bowl aside. 'What does it say next?'

'Roll out three hundred grams of pastry.' She was sounding more confident as she went on, and Jeff took her through the rest of the process without a hitch. When the cakes were in the oven, she set the timer for twenty-five minutes, as the recipe told her.

'Now it's time to wash everything up,' he told her.

'You can leave that to me.'

'No, we're doing this according to my rules. Most of these things won't fit into the dishwasher, so you wash, and I'll dry, and when we've done that, if you like, we can have a drink.' He took a bottle of Burgundy from his carrier. 'Have you a corkscrew?' She handed him one, and he opened the bottle in readiness.

When they were done, they took it with two glasses to the small sitting room.

As he handed her a glass of wine, she said, 'You can have no idea what this evening's done for me.'

'I've a rough idea.'

'Was it what you meant when you said you were doing it only partly for your pleasure?'

He smiled. 'It was all for my satisfaction, really. I just hate the idea that you think less of yourself than you deserve, and when those Banbury cakes come out of the oven, you'll have the pleasure of seeing, smelling and tasting your own achievement.'

'It was very kind of you to do that.'

'Honestly, it was my pleasure, too.' As another thought occurred to him, he said, 'Also, think of the reaction when you welcome your husband home with home-made Banbury cakes.'

She looked down guiltily. 'When I told you my husband was working away, it was basically true.' She faltered.

Seeing that the subject was causing her some embarrassment, he said, 'It's your private life. You don't have to tell me anything.'

'No, I want to tell you, if only because you're the first person I've been able to talk to about it.'

'In that case, take your time.'

She sipped her wine, and it seemed to brace her. 'He left me for someone else,' she said. 'It was almost four months ago.' Looking up again, she said, 'He really is working away, but he's also playing away, except, this time, I think he means it.'

'So it's not the first time he's done it?'

'No, it's not. As they say in all the worst crime dramas, "he has previous for it".'

He topped up her glass and said, 'I can't think of anything original to say except that he doesn't deserve you any more than you deserve to be treated in that way. The other thing is that you mustn't see it as a reflection on you. It never is with the wives of serial hunters.'

'Hunters?'

'Yes, that's what it's about, the thrill of the chase. They pursue their quarry with wild enthusiasm, and then, when they've succeeded, they lose interest.' He wondered quite how to complete the analogy, and another occurred to him. 'It's rather like buying a car.'

'Are you serious?'

'Yes, it's the only bit of real shopping we blokes ever do. We look at the range of options, narrow it down, drive the best bargain we can, and then we experience the ultimate thrill.'

'Not paying for it, surely?'

'No, I'm talking about getting inside it for the first time.' As the words left his lips, he winced and said, 'I'm sorry. That was clumsy of me.'

'It was,' she laughed, 'but it was amusing, all the same. One way and another, Jeff, you've cheered me up this evening.'

'It's the cruellest thing to make a person feel unworthy for any reason, so I'm only too glad to be able to redress the balance.'

'You've certainly done that.'

The oven timer shrilled, interrupting their conversation, but signalling the next excitement.

Lynn took out the baking tray. 'I think they're done,' she said. 'They smell delicious.'

'Done to a turn,' he confirmed. 'It's time to turn them out on to a cooling tray.'

Suddenly alarmed, she said, 'I haven't got one. At least, I don't think I have.'

'Is there a rack in your grill pan?' He opened the top compartment of the cooker. 'Here it is,' he said, taking out the stainless steel rack and putting it on the deal table. 'Now you can leave them on that to cool.'

They returned to the sitting room, and he said, 'Your achievement is just there, on the kitchen table, and you'll come downstairs in the morning and see it afresh. It'll be a second-stage boost for your morale.' Then, as an afterthought, he said, 'I'll give you some more recipes before I leave, and you'll soon realise how easy it can be.'

'Don't talk about leaving, Jeff. I'm just getting used to the luxury of having you here.'

'Well,' he said, pouring the wine again, 'I can't stay forever, but I must say I've enjoyed it so far.'

'I certainly have.'

'I wonder,' he said thoughtfully.

'What do you wonder?'

'As you're effectively a single person, would you consider joining me for dinner?'

'When?'

'An evening of your choice. Tomorrow or whenever.'

'Tomorrow is fine.'

'Perfect. I'll do some scouting around and find the perfect place.'

She shook her head in disbelief. 'Rock stars just don't behave like this,' she said.

'I was a misfit all along. It's just as well I got out when I did.'

6

Pillow Talk

The meal and the wine were good; they both thought so, and that was what really mattered.

Jeff asked, 'Would you like coffee?'

'Shall we have it at home? I have a bottle of cognac, if that helps.'

'You've just found my Achilles' heel,' he told her. 'I'm now helpless and ready to be taken to wherever you will.' In addition to that, she was looking rather fetching in a turquoise dress that looked perfect on her.

He paid the bill, asking the waiter to phone for a minicab. While they waited, Lynn asked, 'Would you describe yourself as a gourmet?'

'Nothing so pretentious.'

'And, of course, you're leaving the world of pretentiousness behind. I remember.'

'I like to eat.'

'And bake.' The thought seemed to lead to another, because she said, 'There was something surprisingly professional about last evening's baking lesson.'

'I should hope so. Baking was my trade before I succumbed to the lure of the music industry.'

'Really?'

'Time-served and qualified,' he confirmed.

A taxi pulled up outside, and the waiter opened the door for them.

'Thank you.' Jeff stepped back to allow Lynn to go ahead of him. She gave her address to the driver, and they got into the taxi.

'But you enjoy baking. What made you give it up?'

'Circumstances. I'd recently lost my mother and father in a motorway collision.'

'I'm sorry.' She put her hand on his, and he held it.

'It was a difficult time made worse by a family disagreement. Lots of disturbing things were happening, so it's fair to say that it was hardly the time for making important decisions.' He smiled suddenly, realising that the mood of the evening had taken a downward turn. 'But, now I've come to my senses and left the music business behind me, so things can only improve.'

'I hope so, Jeff.'

The taxi pulled in outside the guest house, and Jeff got out to offer his hand to Lynn and to pay the driver. 'That's just right,' he said, allowing for a tip.

'Much obliged. Goodnight to you both.'

'Goodnight.'

Lynn unlocked the door. 'I'll put the coffee on,' she said. 'Come through to the kitchen and I'll give you the cognac.'

Jeff took the bottle of Remy Martin and two glasses to the sitting room, where he waited in the pleasant abatement that follows a good meal in the right company. He poured two measures and left them to find room temperature while he took a seat at the end of the sofa.

When Lynn came in with the coffee things, he took the tray from her and placed it on the low table.

'You must understand,' she said, 'that this is not something I do regularly with my guests.'

'Are you talking about drinking coffee?'

'No, the whole thing,' she explained, pouring the coffee. 'I mean going out to dinner and carousing until all hours.'

Looking at his watch, he said, 'It's not ten-thirty, yet.'

'But I'm not used to keeping late hours.' Something made her say, 'I don't suppose you are, either. They say bakers are early to bed and early to rise.'

'I fell into bad habits some years ago,' he admitted, 'but yes, when I was at the bakery, I kept to the rules. I must confess, it was a girlfriend's nightmare.'

Initially surprised because she'd obviously never considered it, she said, 'Yes, I suppose it was.'

A Baker's Round

'It was a measure of a girl's keenness.'

'Did many fall by the wayside?'

'All of them,' he told her gloomily, 'but it was the price I had to pay for my chosen trade.'

'I don't believe you,' she said, accepting a glass of cognac.

'I'm still single,' he said, as if that proved his point. Then, because the conversation had been all about him, he asked, 'What did you do before you went into the hospitality business?'

'Just that. I was a trainee in hotel management, on placement from university, when I met my husband.' She stopped to say, 'You don't really want to hear all this, do you?'

'I'm happy, but it's your life, so it's entirely up to you.'

'Really?'

'I'm awkwardly conscious that we've talked a great deal about me, and I'm genuinely interested in your background. That's if you want to talk about it.'

'All right.' She inhaled the heady vapour of the cognac and took a sip. 'Like you, I made a hasty decision, I became pregnant, and I left university and married my husband, whose name, by the way, is Tony. Then, I had a catastrophic miscarriage that caused all manner of problems.'

'I'm sorry,' he said, taking her free hand. 'No wonder you weren't in a hurry to talk about it. I shouldn't have asked in the first place.'

'It's all right. Just to finish the story, when I was well again, we bought this place, and the rest of it you know.'

'You've had rotten luck.' In the absence of anything more useful to say, he squeezed her hand gently.

'Well, now you can understand why last evening meant so much to me. It was comfort, and you radiate comfort.'

'Do I?' He genuinely had no idea.

'Oh, yes. They say that men who part their hair on the right exude sympathy and sensitivity.'

'I've heard that,' he said, as memories of Donna returned. He had to stop feeling guilty about her. A relationship with her would have been impossible, as he'd explained at the time.

'What's on your mind?'

'I'd just remembered someone else saying that to me, quite recently.'

'A woman?'

'A very young woman. She was cutting my hair at the time.'

'She was taking a professional interest in your parting, I suppose.'

'Yes, it had been missing for several years, and she had to remodel it.' He was trying not to look too obviously into her eyes, but the initial impression he'd formed on meeting her had returned, and he was captivated by them.

'Is something the matter, Jeff?'

'No, nothing at all. I was just wondering….'

'About what?' She seemed to have a pretty good idea.

'I was wondering if it would spoil things at all, if I were to kiss you.'

With her expression unchanged, she said, 'No, I don't think it would spoil anything. I'd even go as far as to call it a good idea.'

Taking her cognac glass from her and placing it on the table, he leaned towards her to brush her lips with his. She responded by opening them in invitation, and he joined her in a lingering kiss of a kind that no Renaissance maiden could ever have imagined.

After a while, she said, 'Those girls didn't know what they were missing.'

'Which girls?' His concentration had been elsewhere.

'The girlfriends who fell by the wayside.'

'Oh, them,' he said dismissively.

They kissed again until, once again, Lynn broke the silence by asking, 'Do you think it would spoil things if I invited you to spend the night with me?'

'Now, why didn't I think of that?'

'You've been thinking of nothing else, the whole evening.'

'Guilty as charged,' he admitted. 'I really must be more enigmatic, or at least, discreet.'

'I'm sure no one else noticed,' she said, standing up and taking his hand.

He followed her upstairs and into her bedroom, where he took her in his arms and kissed her again. 'Aphrodite,' he said.

'What?'

'When you opened the door to me, I saw a slender version of one of those Renaissance paintings. You know, the deities.' He kissed her. 'I see you now as Aphrodite.'

A Baker's Round

'That old nympho, eh?'

'In the nicest possible way,' he assured her, unhooking her dress and running the zip down.

'That was clever,' she said. 'You couldn't even see what you were doing.'

'I felt inspired.' He let her step out of her dress and hang it up.

'I'm glad I decided to wear hold-ups,' she said. 'Tights are too prosaic for words.'

'I'm glad you did, too.' He performed another act of dexterity and removed her bra, celebrating the event by greeting each full breast with a courteous kiss.

That seemed to amuse her. 'You like them?'

'I'm an avowed fan.' He lowered his trousers while she sat on the bed to peel off her stockings. Presently, they faced each other with only their nether garments in place, until, as if at an unspoken cue, they uncovered themselves in a single movement that brought them once more in face-to-face contact. Kissing her repeatedly, he ran his hands over her back and hips, delighting in their smoothness and the new intimacy. Eventually, she turned back the duvet, and they subsided into bed together, still entwined.

They kissed at length, with Jeff breaking off occasionally to share his favours with her neck, shoulders and breasts. As he did so, she carried out her own quest, as eager as he was to give and receive enjoyment. Her excitement seemed to have no limit, but then, she hooked one leg round him and whispered urgently, 'Turn over.'

Ever-ready to oblige, he moved on to his back while she knelt above him.

'Ohhhh.' It was the merest breath, but it conveyed a wealth of feeling as she subsided into a world of ecstasy. Now fully engaged, she rocked insistently while he stroked her thighs and breasts. How long it went on, he had no idea; time was of no consequence, but then, almost without warning, she erupted into an expression of bliss. As it subsided, she held up one hand, as if directing traffic, and said, 'Don't move yet.'

'You're the one who's doing the moving,' he pointed out.

'Yes, all right.' She nodded, and that small movement caused her to cry out again. 'Aah-ah!'

'I never even twitched,' he protested.

'Yes, don't twitch, whatever you do.'

'I'll try not to, but now you've put the idea into my head....'

'Don't you dare.' She bent slowly and kissed him to show that it was all in fun. Then, having kissed him, she asked, 'Could we swap places?'

'Mothers and fathers?'

'I think so. I never saw mine do it, thank goodness.'

'Neither did I.'

'Do you think we can rearrange ourselves without coming apart?'

'Oh, Lynn, you do ask a lot.' He waited for her to straighten her legs behind her, and then took her in his arms and rolled over.

'What are you doing?'

He removed his hand and said, 'Making sure everything's still where it should be.'

'Aah. Wear one for protection, by all means, but I'm bullet-proof as far as the other is concerned.'

He didn't ask, feeling that it wasn't the right time. Instead, he tested the *status quo* with an exploratory twitch.

'Oh!'

'Was that too much?'

'No, it was lovely.'

He kissed her softly and then began to move.

Later, as they lay together, Jeff asked, 'What was that you said about contraceptives?'

'Only that this is the most adventurous I've been since before I met Tony, but you're probably right to use one of those things, because it's anybody's guess who he's been with.'

'You also said you were bullet-proof.'

'Yes, after the miscarriage. The emergency operation left me unable to conceive.'

'Hell, I'm sorry.'

'There's no need to be sorry, Jeff. I decided some time ago that I wouldn't have wanted to have a baby with Tony, anyway.'

A Baker's Round

He thought for a while, and asked, 'Do you still feel anything for him?'

'Yes, I do. It's been impossible to get him out of my system in the time he's been gone, and he does have some good points.'

'I suppose everyone does.' He waited for her to offer a few examples, but none seemed to be forthcoming.

'Although, sex with him was very ordinary, and not just in the light of tonight's experience, which was… extraordinary.' She gave the appearance of enjoying it again, in retrospect, which did seem to mark it out as special.

'It takes two, Lynn,' he said generously.

She appeared to miss the immediate message, because she went on to say, 'The trouble is, each time he's gone on his travels, he's returned full of apology and repentance, but he's always known I'll be here for him to come back to.'

'Maybe that's the problem.'

'Just knowing that?'

'Yes, it's worth thinking about if he does show up again.'

7

June

A Timely Arrival

It was an easy and enjoyable relationship that continued for several weeks, but they both knew it couldn't go on indefinitely. Jeff was still looking for the life that eluded him, and Lynn also realised that, although it was unfortunate that it should have ended the way it did.

Jeff returned from a minor shopping trip to find that Lynn had company. The man in question looked quite at home, an observation that set Jeff thinking, and his suspicion was proved right when Lynn introduced him.

'Jeff,' she said uneasily, 'this is my husband Tony.'

'Pleased to meet you, Tony.' Jeff countered the weak handshake with a fierce grip, enjoying the resulting wince. Tony had the appearance of a lightweight in every sense, but now was no time for resentment. The guest house was his home, and Lynn was his wife, even though he didn't deserve her. Jeff took a can of shaving gel and some razor blades from his bag and said, 'I'll leave your stuff here, Lynn.'

'Thank you, Jeff.' She was clearly unsettled, which was no surprise. As Jeff left the room, he heard Tony ask, 'Since when have you been on first-name terms with paying guests?' He was pleased to hear Lynn say, 'That's how I treat long-term guests. In any case, wouldn't you say that any objection to familiarity is downright impertinent, coming from a serial adulterer?'

Jeff retired to his room to pack his bags, hoping for Lynn's sake that she could maintain her resolve.

He managed to speak to her alone when he took the recipes he'd promised her to the kitchen.

'Bless you, Jeff,' she said. 'I'll never forget this or anything else about you. You've changed my life.'

'Oh, surely that's an exaggeration.' It was certainly a surprise.

'No, it's not. You changed the way I see myself, and that's going to make a huge difference. I've already told Tony that if he goes on his travels again, he's not going to find me waiting for him on his return.' She smiled thinly and said, 'It's a pity you couldn't have been here to see him. "Shock" wasn't the word.'

'Where is he now?'

'He's gone into town, probably to buy me a present. That's what he usually does, not that it'll make any difference to me.'

He had to tell her. 'I'll be leaving in the morning, Lynn.'

'I thought you might.' Suddenly, her eyes were wet.

He opened his arms to her.

'I'm going to miss you, Jeff.'

'And I'm going to miss you.'

They kissed for the last time.

Jeff had spent some time studying his atlas, and he knew exactly where he was heading when he started the car. The journey would not be a long one – he reckoned about an hour and a half – but it would take him to Shrewsbury, the county town of Shropshire and home of the famous Shrewsbury Biscuits or Shrewsbury Cake, as it was once called.

From time to time, his thoughts returned to his stay in Banbury, but then he told himself to draw a line beneath it. Lynn was no longer available, and there was nothing he could do about that. He made himself concentrate on his next stop.

It was both remarkable and wonderful, how a tiny island such as Great Britain could produce and then maintain through the centuries so many regional recipes. It was possibly true of France, Germany, Belgium and a host of other countries, but none of them was as tiny as Britain. He felt himself glow at the thought, and another thought that buoyed him up in spite of his sudden departure from Banbury was the news that someone was buying his London flat. The buyer had made an offer, and Jeff had accepted it. He now had to give his new address to the estate agent, the solicitor and the bank, once he knew it.

He continued along the M40, still feeling that he should be threading his way through the kind of picturesque villages that would have had Constable setting up his easel. Of course, that was a nonsense; Constable was a son of Suffolk, and chances were he'd never even heard of Shrewsbury, and why should he? He was part of that regional sense of pride and belonging that made Jeff wish he'd been born anywhere but in London.

In a little over an hour and a half, he drove into Shrewsbury and found a carpark. He was surprised to see architecture of a similar kind in the town centre to that which he'd found in Banbury, and he spent some time admiring it before remembering with a start that he had to find somewhere to live. He had a list of guest houses, procured by a phone call to the tourist office in Shrewsbury, and he set out, with the help of various locals to find the first on the list.

When he reached the address, it was to find that there were no vacancies. Summer was "icumen in", and that was something he would have to remember. He turned to the second on the list, which was thankfully not far away.

The notice read: *Vacancies*. That, also, was a stroke of luck. He rang the doorbell before anyone else got the idea and jumped in ahead of him.

The door opened, and it was immediately apparent that this would not be an experience of the Banbury kind. The woman who stood before him was possibly in her forties, but she was plain and drab. He wondered where she'd dug up the flowered pinafore that was reminiscent of a theatrical period costume. Maybe she'd inherited it along with the guest house.

'Yes?'

'I see you have vacancies. I need a single room.'

'How many nights?'

A Baker's Round

'I don't know.' That seemed to unsettle her, so he said, 'A week, to begin with, then I'll have a better idea.'

'Come in, then.' She looked around his feet and said, 'You'll have luggage, I imagine?'

'It's in my car. Is there any parking here?'

'Through the passage and into the back,' she told him, opening a register.

Behind her was the bed and breakfast tariff. It was inexpensive, but the whole place was as uninviting as its owner.

'I charge nine pounds fifty for a single room, and I lock the doors at eleven o' clock. If you intend to come in later than that, you'll need to take a key and come in quietly. I'll have no ladies in gentlemen's rooms and vice versa.'

'I don't know any.'

'Any what?'

'Ladies. I only came to Shrewsbury an hour ago, and so far I've yet to meet one.'

'Good.'

That it had sailed straight over her head failed to surprise him. He asked, 'When do you serve breakfast?'

'Seven o' clock to eight-thirty.' She pointed to a dining room that was no more inviting than the parts he'd already seen. 'Come down after eight-thirty and you won't be served.'

Taking all that into account, he asked, 'Would you rather I went elsewhere?'

'Of course not. What makes you think that?'

'Simply by standing here, I feel like a nuisance.'

'I don't know why you should think that. You don't look like a nuisance.'

He wondered how she would have felt had she seen him two months earlier. 'It's just an impression,' he told her.

'Well, I suppose you'll want to see the room.'

'If it's not too much of an inconvenience.'

'No, it's quite normal for guests to see their rooms.' She seemed untouched by irony, but led him up a dingy staircase and pointed out a small bedroom and the bathroom, both of which were in need of modernisation. There was still time for him to back out, but there was no guarantee he would find anywhere else, so he decided to make the best of it, at least for one night. He could look for somewhere else the next day. Accordingly, he signed the register and paid for one night's accommodation in advance. He would give the agent and solicitor his address when he was more certain of it.

After an uncomfortable night and an unremarkable breakfast, he set out to explore Shrewsbury. So far, he found the architecture engaging and compelling. Breakfast was lying heavy on his stomach – he suspected an abundance of oil – so he gave lunch a miss and settled for a lunchtime drink at an ancient pub that seemed friendly enough, but the clientele were either visiting or passing through. Such high street pubs were seldom favoured by locals.

In all, he enjoyed a very pleasant day, but the highlight occurred a little after four in the afternoon, when he was exploring one of the side turnings off the High Street. A young woman had just parked her car in one of the numerous back yards, and she emerged with two little girls, presumably just out of school. As he stepped aside, and they passed him, the woman smiled and thanked him. That alone would have been enough to make him take notice, such courtesy being rare in London, but the smile was so open and natural that it seemed to light up her already attractive features.

They walked as far as a teashop, about thirty metres or so from the High Street, the woman reached out to open the door, and that was when things began to happen, because one of the girls shouted, 'Look at that dog!'

At a first glance, the dog appeared to be loose, but as the girls ran towards it, and Jeff set off after them, he realised it was on an extending lead. Even so, it was off the causeway and in some danger, a fact that seemed to have passed its owner's notice.

Behind him, the young woman was shouting to the two girls to stay where they were. Whether or not they heard her, they continued to the kerb edge, where, quite unexpectedly and in its excitement, the dog turned and slipped its collar. In that moment, with the person

A Baker's Round

who was presumably the dog's owner calling it, the animal stood still, seemingly mesmerised by the traffic around it, and the two girls were about to leap into the road, when Jeff reached them. Taking one in each arm, he plucked them from in front of a minicab and deposited them, startled, on the pavement. Somewhat unnecessarily, the driver of the minicab sounded his horn and pulled into the side of the road to vent his feelings. Lowering the passenger window, he shouted, 'You want to take better care of your kids!'

'I'll pass the message on.'

'I'm just telling you.'

'All right, you've told me. Now bugger off.'

The driver eyed him warily and decided to take his advice. Jeff turned to find the two girls in the care of their mother, and the dog now restored to its embarrassed owner, who was refastening its collar. He returned his attention to the girls, who were both crying, and the mother, who was both relieved and upset.

He asked her, 'Are they all right? I'm afraid I hadn't time to be gentle.'

'They're fine,' she assured him. 'Thank you ever so much for what you did. I'm very grateful.'

'It was no trouble.' He looked at the girls, who were now more collected, and said, 'Do you think these two are in line for a treat? I expect you could use one, too.'

She gave something between a laugh and a sob. 'You're probably right. Look, it's my teashop. Will you join us?'

'You know, I think I will.' He'd noticed her wedding ring, although that meant nothing. Her hair was the colour of Fine Cut Oxford marmalade, and now that she was dry-eyed again, the rest of her was quite appealing.

'I'm Wendy Ashurst and these are Rebecca and Rachel, the Terrible Twins.'

'We didn't mean to be naughty,' said the one called Rebecca.

'No, we didn't,' said Rachel. 'The dog was going to be run over.'

'He's all right now,' Jeff assured them.

'And I know you didn't mean to be naughty,' said Mrs Ashurst.

'I'm Jeff Mortimer.' He offered his hand.

'I'm glad to meet you.' She led him to the teashop in the side street and welcomed him inside, where a middle-aged woman viewed the twins with alarm.

'A dog ran into the road, Maureen,' said Wendy. 'The twins ran after it, and this lovely man grabbed them before they could be hit by a car.'

'Well, I never.'

'Mr Mortimer….'

'Jeff.'

'Jeff,' said Wendy, 'Will you excuse us while we clean ourselves up? Maureen will get you whatever you like to drink, and we'll be with you as soon as we're presentable.'

It seemed that Tuesday afternoon was a quiet time, or maybe it was an isolated occasion, but his table was one of only two that were occupied. He took his seat and said, 'I think a pot of the English Breakfast is called for.'

'Certainly, sir.' Maureen retired to the kitchen to prepare it.

He was stirring the tea and wondering idly what Wendy's other half did while she was running the teashop, when she and the twins came to join him. He stood until they were seated.

'Now, Jeff, please order whatever you'd like, and I'll find something for these two adventurers that won't spoil dinner and make me unpopular with their mum.'

'Oh, I beg your pardon. I thought you were their mum.'

'I'm their auntie, although they do spend a lot of time with me, don't you, twins?'

'Mm.' It was a single, unison response. The twins weren't identical, but they did seem to do things in tandem, and their current shared interest was the tea menu.

'When I was about your age,' said Jeff, who could only guess at their age, 'and I'd had a difficult time, I used to find unbelievable comfort in a soft-boiled egg and toast apostles.'

Wendy looked at him enquiringly. 'Apostles?'

'My father was a vicar,' he explained.

'I see.' She smiled at the thought.

'Yes, please,' said the duo.

'And orange juice?'

'Yes, please.'

A Baker's Round

'What would you like, Jeff?'

He looked again at the menu and said, 'I'll stay with the English Breakfast, if I may, and just a piece of the Victoria sponge would be excellent.'

'Great minds really do think alike.' She caught Maureen's eye and gave her order. 'Will you cut the toast into soldiers for the twins, please.'

'Apostles,' they said, correcting her.

'I'm sure they'll taste much the same. I'll tell you what. When Maureen brings them and they're on the table, you can call them whatever you like.' With that settled, she asked, 'What brings you to Shrewsbury, Jeff?'

'A new way of life, not necessarily here in Shrewsbury, but that's the nature of the odyssey.' He explained his recent decision and the need to find a different direction.

'I'm afraid yours wasn't my kind of music, Jeff, so you'll have to forgive me for not recognising you.'

'I've gone to some trouble to disguise myself, so please don't apologise.'

Rachel asked, 'Were you really a rock star?'

'I'm afraid so.'

Rebecca asked, 'What was your band called?'

'Tantum Somnium. It no longer exists.'

Rebecca wasn't impressed, anyway. 'Our teacher says that people give bands silly names, thinking they sound clever,' she said.

'Rebecca, that was very rude,' said Wendy.

'But true, nevertheless,' said Jeff. Then, changing the subject for her sake, he asked, 'Can you tell me if there's a pool and a gym hereabouts, Wendy?'

'There certainly is. Is fitness part of your odyssey?'

'It's part of my life, really. When I feel fit, I feel good, and it helps me to face down angry minicab drivers and send them on their way.'

'Was he terribly angry?' Her question alerted the attention of the children, who waited to hear his answer.

'I'd give him seven out of ten for it. In fairness, though, it's a natural reaction after a near miss.'

'Yes, I suppose it is.' After a little thought, she asked, 'Where are you staying in Shrewsbury?'

The question made him smile. 'The Wenlock Guest House, home of the landlady from hell, the original shrew in Shrewsbury.'

Rachel asked, 'Is she a witch?'

'There's no such thing,' Rebecca told her.

'She sounds bad enough,' said Wendy, 'and the place looks pretty grim from the outside. Jeff, you can't stay there. Move your stuff out and stay here.'

'Do you do B and B?'

'Not as a rule, but I can.'

'Well, if you're sure it's no trouble, I'll give Mrs Broomstick the bad news.'

'It's no trouble at all. I don't know what the going rate is for B and B. What's Mrs Broomstick charging?'

'Nine pounds fifty.'

'We'll call it that, then.'

'Fine.'

8

Pâtisserie

As well as bed and breakfast, Jeff was invited to dinner, which made proper conversation possible, the children having gone home to their parents.

'I don't know why my successful sister had children,' said Wendy. 'They spend more time with me than they do with her.'

'Aunties are special people. I imagine they enjoy being with you.'

'What makes you think that?'

'I could see it when you were together.'

'You're an unusual man. More wine?' She picked up the bottle and topped up his glass. 'What did you do before you went into pop music?'

'I was a baker.'

'No, really?'

'Cross my heart with flour and yeast.'

'I've had to work hard at baking,' she admitted. 'It's important in a teashop.'

'The Victoria sponge was very good.'

'Ah, but that's basic.'

'Everyone has to start somewhere. Have you a "significant other" working in the business?' It was a convenient time to find out before he became too interested.

'Not in the business. My husband works in London and usually joins me at weekends. Why do you ask?'

'I only wondered if he provided the missing skill, but evidently not.'

'No, everything you saw on the menu was made with my own hands.'

He nodded. 'I can only speak for the Victoria sponge, which was very good, as I said, even though I'll have to work it off tomorrow.'

'Something I'd really like to learn,' she said, sounding genuinely like someone with a long-term goal, 'is how to make those amazing cakes and tarts you get in France.'

'I can see how they'd go down well here. I mean to say, Shrewsbury biscuits are very nice, but there's a sort of sameness about them that must wear thin after a while.' Then, after very little thought, he said, 'I can teach you *pâtisserie*. It can be quite time-consuming, depending on the item, but it should draw people in.'

Her eyes widened suddenly. 'Could you really do that?'

'No problem. I spent some time with a *maître pâtissier* in Normandy, learning the ropes. We could make a start tomorrow evening.'

'Saturday evening's a good time. My husband will be home, but that's no problem.'

'Okay. I'll have a work-out and a swim in the morning, and then we'll get floury.'

He spent a more comfortable night than the previous one, and breakfast was infinitely better, so he was in good spirits when he set out for the shops.

Because of their brief shelf life, the items he had in mind called for a limited range of ingredients, including some exotic fruits, but within reason, and he was able to take everything that was needed back to the teashop, where a surprised Maureen relieved him of them.

He found the leisure centre with only moderate difficulty, and spent the next hour in the gym. A shower and then a spell in the pool were sheer luxury, as always, and he arrived back at the teashop charged, refreshed and ready for most things. He took a seat at a free table and requested coffee.

Before long, Wendy joined him and introduced her husband, a seemingly pleasant, if ordinary, young man. 'This is Paul,' she said. 'Paul, meet Jeff, my *patisserie* guru, if you'll forgive the mixed-race description.'

A Baker's Round

Jeff took Paul's hand. 'Glad to meet you, Paul.

'How do you do, Jeff.'

Wendy picked up the menu. 'You can't go through the day on coffee,' she said, 'so have a look at the lunch menu. It's eating-up time.'

'Let me see. Temptation lurks within, but I think the turkey salad will do the trick.'

'Good.' She caught Maureen's eye and gave her order.

'Was I wrong to suggest an evening session? With Paul at home, you surely don't want to work all hours.'

'I'm sure it won't take all night, and I have Sunday to recover.'

'If you're both happy, I am.'

'I'm happy enough,' said Paul, 'as long as you let me taste the end product when it's made.'

'There's no problem there,' Jeff assured him.

With that dealt with, Wendy asked, 'What are you going to do this afternoon?'

'Don't laugh.'

'We shan't.'

'I'm going to the public library to learn about Shrewsbury and its past.'

Wendy smiled. 'What's funny about that?'

'I don't know, but the other boys at school would have called me a big swot.'

'Oh dear. How long did that go on?'

'For less than half a minute, and then I flattened them.'

'You had me fooled for a minute.'

'I fooled them as well, but only for half a minute.'

During the afternoon, Jeff learned about Shrewsbury's history, going back to Medieval times, about its importance as a trading post with Wales. It was a troubled time, apparently, because of the ongoing animosity between England and Wales, but the city survived the centuries, so that to the present day, it was the county town of Shropshire, and in Jeff's opinion, deservedly so.

He arrived at the teashop a little before closing time and found Wendy in the kitchen.

'Hello,' she said. 'Did you have a useful afternoon?'

'Very. In view of your kindness, I was thinking of asking you and Paul out to dinner, but I think we should do that another time.'

'Yes, it's a lovely idea, but it wouldn't leave us much time. In any case, I've laid something on for us tonight.'

'You're too kind.'

'Let's just say we're level. When were you thinking of dining out?'

'How about tomorrow evening?'

'Paul will be back in London by then.'

'Okay, let's make it next weekend.'

Being in the food preparation business, Wendy didn't need Jeff to remind her about fastening up her hair; in fact, she provided him with protective clothing in the form of an apron.

'Okay,' he said, 'this is all about things happening at the same time, so it's a good idea to prepare a chart, and then you know what has to be done and when.'

'It makes sense,' she agreed.

He introduced her to the preparation of short pastry, frangipane, gelatine, *crème anglaise* and fruit, leaving other items for a later date, when he would still be around to guide her. Thereafter, they concentrated on a batch of tarts with blueberries and Cape gooseberries set in gelatine.

'The problem is that these things have a short life,' he said. 'Just for now, we'll make enough for you, me, Paul, Maureen if she's around, and....'

'I shan't see Rebecca and Rachel until Monday, although I could take some round to them.'

'If you don't, I really will have something to work off.'

Eventually, they put the batch of tarts into the fridge and dusted their hands in satisfaction.

He asked, 'Are you happy with that?'

A Baker's Round

'Very happy,' she said, 'and in need of a shower.'

'It's the flour, isn't it?'

'It is when I use it. It gets everywhere.' Inclining her head upward, she asked, 'Would you like to go first?'

'I wouldn't dream of it. Off you go, and I'll have mine when you're finished.'

'Help yourself to a drink while I'm gone. Paul will have gone up to bed, so don't worry about him.'

Jeff poured himself a glass of wine and sat at the kitchen table. In truth, he'd always enjoyed *pâtisserie*, so he'd been happy to pass on his knowledge. He was looking forward to the next session, when they would try something different, maybe the *milles feuilles*, or 'vanilla slice', as the prosaic Brits called it. The custard would be of superior quality, however, and so would the pastry. He finished his wine and went up to his room to undress, wondering a little about Wendy's relationship with a husband who worked in London, and who made a practice of going early to bed.

He was almost ready when he heard Wendy say, 'The shower's free.' He heard her door close, and made his way to the bathroom.

For the second time that day, he indulged himself in the luxury of a well-earned shower, enjoying every second up to the moment of Spartan self-denial, when he had to turn off the water and dry himself.

He was back in his room when he heard Wendy's voice through the wall. 'Damn and blast!' It was tame stuff. His father might have objected to it, had he been around, but he would have been in a minority. Opening his door, he asked, 'Are you all right?'

'Yes, but my hairdryer's conked out. It'll be the fuse or something.'

'I'll get you a towel.' He knew where the airing cupboard was, because he remembered Wendy taking his bedding from it. Tightening the sash of his bathrobe, he looked in the cupboard for a hand towel and, having found one, took it to Wendy's room, where he knocked on the door.

'Come in,' she said, 'I'm decent.'

He opened the door and found her alone in the double room. Presumably, her husband was spending the night elsewhere.

'Thank you, Jeff,' she said. 'You're too good. This is such a nuisance.'

'I'm glad I could help.'

Patting the place beside her in invitation, she said, 'You must be wondering, so I'll explain.'

'Your personal life is no business of mine, Wendy.'

'I really don't mind. The fact is, Paul and I lead an unusual life. Some years ago, he was involved in a traffic accident that damaged one shoulder in such a way that he spends much of his life in great pain, and there are times when he has to be alone to cope with it. Those times are when he takes himself off to bed.'

'Poor man. I imagine he takes something for it?'

She sighed. 'He'd tell you himself, that he's probably addicted, by this time, to prescribed pain killers.'

'How awful for both of you.'

'It's worse for him, believe me.'

'I'm sure,' he said, getting up. 'I imagine you'll be all right now?'

'Yes, thank you. Good night.'

'Good night, Wendy.'

9

Straight Talk

Wendy soon became adept at *pâtisserie* in its various manifestations, and Jeff had the satisfaction of watching his pupil develop new skills that could only enhance the business. Running the teashop, however, was a routine that often had to accommodate collecting the twins from school and safeguarding their wellbeing until they were able to return to their official home. At such times, Wendy's sister Sandra regarded Jeff as a convenient minder, popular with the children and clearly trustworthy. He also had the considerable virtue of lending his services free of charge, but then, Sandra was high-up in tourism, which made her important enough, at least in her own estimation, to regard such assistance as hers by right.

A few weeks after his arrival, Jeff collected the children from school, and was driving them to the teashop, when Rebecca asked, 'What are we going to do today, Jeff?'

'I don't know yet. Give me thirteen minutes to think about it.'

'You've had all day to think about it,' said Rachel, whose grasp of tact owed much to her mother, 'so why do you need thirteen minutes?'

'Yes,' asked Rebecca, 'why thirteen, and not ten or fifteen?'

'It's an old tradition,' he explained, parking the car in the yard behind the teashop. 'It's known as the "bakers' dozen". We do everything in thirteens.'

He took them into the teashop to let Wendy know they were back, and continued into the kitchen and the table that was set well away from where food was being prepared for customers.

'I've finished with the oven,' Maureen told him. 'It's all yours, if you want it.'

'Thank you, Maureen. We'll keep out of your way.' He pretended to study the oven, looking purposefully at his watch if either of the twins tried to speak to him. It was usually the closest either of them came to disciplined behaviour, unless they were actually baking.

Eventually, he turned to face them. 'Today,' he said, 'we're going to make rock cakes and raspberry volcanoes.'

'I've never heard of rock cakes,' said Rachel.

'And I've never heard of raspberry volcanoes,' said Rebecca.

'You both have,' he told them, 'just now, but you were too busy talking to notice it. A rock cake,' he explained, 'looks like a rock with currants in it, and maybe raisins or sultanas if I'm feeling generous, but it tastes wonderful. A raspberry volcano is similar, except that, when you squeeze it, raspberry jam comes squirting out of the top, like lava out of a volcano.'

Rachel was inclined to be sceptical. She asked, 'Whoever heard of raspberry jam coming out of a volcano?'

'It happens all the time. You can't move on Mount Etna for raspberry jam. Mind you, it means that you don't have to buy it, which is good.' He clapped his hands and asked, 'What do we do first?'

'Measure the ingredients,' said Rachel.

'No, we don't.'

With heavy patience, Rebecca said, 'Tie our hair up and wash our hands.'

'Right in two. Hair up, both of you, and then you can wash your hands.' He waited until they were ready, and said, 'Right, roll up your sleeves.' He threw each of them an apron and made allowance for height by tucking some in round the waist. 'Now, we're ready. We need four hundred and fifty grams of self-raising flour, into the scale pan, here.' He let Rebecca weigh it out. 'Now, Rachel, a hundred grams of butter cut up into small pieces, and Rebecca, seventy-five grams of currants and raisins and twenty-five of mixed peel. You can weigh them together.' When those things were weighed into separate containers, he asked Rebecca to weigh a hundred grams of caster sugar, and Rachel to get two eggs. He switched the oven on at two hundred and set the twins on lining two baking trays with greaseproof liners.

A Baker's Round

Dropping two pinches of salt into the flour, he got them to start mixing. 'Now,' he said, 'you both know how to make a rubbing mixture, so I want you to rub the butter into the flour. Keep your hands high and let it fall to keep the air in. Well done.'

'It's yucky,' said Rachel.

'It won't be when it comes out, trust me.' When he was satisfied with the rubbed mixture, he said, 'This is where we separate the mixture into halves.' With that done, he added the fruit and peel to one bowl, and the sugar to both. 'Right, ladies, get stirring.'

'We're not ladies yet,' said Rachel.

'If you don't start stirring, you will be by the time these things are made.' He watched them stir the ingredients together, and whisked up the eggs and milk.

Rebecca asked, 'Why has she got currants and raisins and there are none in mine?'

'Because you're making the volcanoes. For you, the fun comes later.' He added the eggs and milk and let them mix everything into a stiff dough. 'Rachel, I want you to plonk handfuls of mixture on to a baking tray. Use your hands and don't try to make it look pretty. They have to look like rocks.' Turning to Rebecca, who felt clearly left out, he said, 'You do the same, Rebecca, and then we'll add the special ingredient. You can make yours a bit tidier than Rachel's, if you like.'

Rachel asked, 'Why do mine have to be untidy?'

'I told you, so that they look like rocks.'

'But everyone will say Rebecca's look better than mine.'

'No, they won't. They'll say that yours look like rocks, and Rebecca's look like Mount Etna, or Vesuvius, or somewhere else where you can't move for raspberry jam.'

Having dealt with Rachel's latest objection, he took out a jar of raspberry jam. 'Put one teaspoonful of jam on to each, and then, when you've done that, we'll fold them up so that the jam's lurking on the inside, just waiting to make it on to the six o' clock news.'

'Why will it be on the six o' clock news?'

'Because that's when they report the disasters, Rachel.'

'Is our baking going to be a disaster?'

'No.' Rachel was a very literal child, who struggled with metaphor and exaggeration. 'When a real volcano erupts, that's a disaster. I was just being silly.' He helped Rebecca enclose the jam inside the mixture and placed both trays in the oven. 'We'll have a look after ten minutes,' he said.

'Is that all?'

'How long would you like to wait, Rachel? We could put some Christmas cakes in, if you like, and then you could wait four hours.' He kept them occupied by letting them do the washing-up.

When Sandra called for the twins, they naturally wanted to show her what they'd made.

'What on *earth* are these things?' She peered into the bag containing rock cakes as if she expected something to leap out and bite her.

'They're rock cakes,' said Rachel, immediately deflated. Wendy simply looked embarrassed.

'These things look more civilised,' said Sandra, squinting at the volcanoes. Warily, she took one out and bit into it. 'It's very pleasant,' she said, 'but not exactly healthy. I hope you two haven't been gorging on these things so that you won't want dinner.'

'You're supposed to squeeze it to make the jam jump out,' Rebecca told her.

'Don't be silly, Rebecca.'

To answer her criticism, Jeff said, 'When I was a child, a treat was something rare and fleeting. That's all they are, a treat. That, and a way of entertaining two children while their auntie concentrates on the demanding task of running a business, spared as she is, during the week, the responsibility of a disabled husband.'

'Yes,' said Sandra, missing the point entirely, 'don't go anywhere in a hurry, Jeff. You're far too useful here.'

'Even though I encourage the children to make things you don't recognise and that must surely result in clinical obesity and coronary thrombosis?'

Sandra looked at him sharply and asked, 'Are you trying to say something?' In the same breath, she turned to the children and said, 'Go and get your school things ready to take home.'

A Baker's Round

'I think I just said it quite eloquently. Wendy has been able to take the children off your hands because I've been looking after them. When I turned up, she was run ragged, trying to work and marshall the children at the same time. I shan't always be here, so I hope for her sake you're going to find a sensible way forward.' He could see that Wendy was unhappy, but it had to be said.

'How dare you?' She made the challenge without raising her voice, possibly because of the children in the next room, but her anger was no less real. 'How dare you criticise the way I bring up my children and treat my sister? I've never heard anything like it.'

'How dare I? I'll tell you how I dare. For one thing, I object to my efforts being taken for granted and even criticised, and I dare to voice my objection because I'm a straight-talking chap who speaks his mind. I'm going now, so you'll need to look elsewhere for someone to entertain your children, and I hope you'll think about what I've said.'

He'd finished packing by the time Wendy came upstairs, anxious and tearful.

'Do you really have to go, Jeff?'

'Yes, it's time I went. I'm not going to let her treat me as an unpaid family retainer, if there is such a thing. She's your sister, I know, and I'm sorry, but that's the way it is.'

Wendy looked down at his bags. 'It would be a shame for you to go now,' she said.

'If you're happy for me to stay one more night, I'll leave in the morning.'

'I'm not happy with anything, just now. I've just told her that, much as I love those children, I won't be treated as a convenient child-minder any longer.'

'I'm glad you have, Wendy.' He meant it. 'But I still have to go.'

'She's been ordering my life for as long as I can remember,' she said, 'and she's turned every situation to her advantage.'

He could only show that he was listening and sympathetic. He kissed her cheek, and his lips came away wet with her tears. Still, he knew that if he stayed, he would only damage relations between her and Sandra further. Their quarrel was for them to settle, and he'd probably said too much already.

10

No Cause for Shame

It had to stop. Jeff kept telling himself that as he drove along the A5 towards Oswestry. He had to stop interfering in people's lives and leaving in his wake a succession of… well, if not broken hearts, it was certainly true to say that both Lynn and Wendy had been saddened by his leaving. As he thought about it, he remembered Donna as well. She'd virtually offered herself to him. There were those, he told himself, would be proud to be so popular, but he could only feel remorse. As for interfering in people's lives, who was he to give advice? He who didn't even know where his life was going.

With that thought, he drove into the outskirts of Oswestry and parked as soon as he could, to consult his road atlas. For some reason he could neither identify nor dismiss, Wales suddenly appealed quite strongly, so he set about searching the road signs for the B4580, as that road sounded like the kind of pastoral route he'd had in mind since leaving London.

Almost an hour and several horn blasts later, he succeeded in finding the road and, in a state of renewed optimism, left Oswestry behind.

For once, he was not disappointed. The route became increasingly rural, if not exotic, as he passed several places with unpronounceable names. He struggled with Rhydycroesau, Lledrod and Llansilin, and then gave up, content to drive past them and leave others to pronounce their names. He pressed on until a mid-morning coffee break felt like a good idea, and with that in mind, he took the side turning into a village called Llandaron, which looked promising.

A Baker's Round

Driving into the village, he passed a grocery, a bakery and a café, where he pulled in and parked.

The café was completely empty, but the sound of the door opening and closing attracted the attention of a smiling woman of forty or so, wearing a blue tabard.

'*Bore da.*'

'Good morning,' he said, 'I'm sorry. I'm afraid I don't speak Welsh.'

'Oh, it's English you are, is it? Well, you're welcome all the same. What would you like?'

'I'd like coffee, please.'

'Of course. You English are great ones for coffee, isn't it? You take a seat and I'll bring it to you.'

'Thank you.' He took a seat at the nearest table, reflecting on the way Welshness in attitude and language imposed itself within miles of the boundary. That was what pride was about, he fancied.

The café owner was with him shortly, bringing coffee, milk and sugar.

'Thank you,' he said, 'I don't take sugar.'

'I suppose you're sweet enough.' She made the observation with a smile.

'Not really. I just like to keep fit.'

'Well, I suppose there's that to it as well.'

She seemed friendly, so he said, 'You're very quiet this morning.'

'Am I?' Clearly, there was an element of misunderstanding.

'The café,' he explained. 'I meant there's no one about.'

'Oh,' she said, realising her mistake, 'there will be, soon enough.'

Having decided that Llandaron was as good a place as any, he said, 'I'm looking for bed and breakfast. Is there somewhere you can recommend?'

'Oh, well now.' The question had evidently given rise to thought, because she gave the appearance of being in deep concentration. Eventually, she said, 'A couple of weeks from now, there'll be signs up all over, offering bed and breakfast, because of the Festival, the Eisteddfod, you know, but most places don't offer it all the year round.' Suddenly, as if inspiration had just flown in through the window, she said, 'You could try the bakery. Mrs Jones the Bread might be able to help you.'

'Mrs...?'

'You see, the baker is called Jones the Bread. That's to tell him apart from Jones the Letters and Jones the Feet. The baker's wife is called Mrs Jones the Bread.'

'I see. I imagine Jones the Letters is the regular postman, but what does Jones the Feet do?'

'He's the local bobby.' Her tone suggested that the connection should have been obvious.

'Of course.' It wasn't at all obvious, but he'd no intention of arguing with her. 'On the subject of names, we're bound to see each other again, so I'd better introduce myself. I'm Jeff Mortimer.'

'And I'm Mrs Powell. I'm glad to meet you, Mr Mortimer.' She shook his hand with a surprisingly strong grip.

'Tell me about this Festival. What is it about?'

'Why, it's a music festival, a local one, not like the big one at Llangollen, but it's well supported, for all that.'

'Is it like Glastonbury, with rock bands coming from all over?' He rather hoped it wouldn't be. There were people he was keen to avoid.

'No, you misunderstand me, Mr Mortimer. When I say music, I mean proper music. We get choirs, instrumentalists, singers.... The baritone who won last year's Eisteddfod had a voice like liquid honey. You should have heard him.'

'I wish I had.' In truth, Jeff was recovering from his gaffe. 'Mrs Powell,' he said, 'thank you for your advice. I'll try the bakery.'

'You'll probably be all right there. Mrs Jones is a friendly soul. Tell her I sent you and you should be all right.'

'Thank you, Mrs Powell. Goodbye.'

'Goodbye and good luck.'

He'd not far to go, as the bakery was only two doors away from the café. As he passed the window, he saw the once-familiar sight of a baker hard at work. From what Jeff could see, he seemed to be making Welsh cakes, an item that couldn't have been more appropriate. He knocked on the door and waited. He was rewarded when the baker came to the door, elderly, portly and serious, and bringing with him the familiar scents of baking.

'*Bore da.*'

'Good morning.' Once more, he had to say, 'I'm afraid I don't speak

A Baker's Round

Welsh. I'm looking for bed and breakfast, and Mrs Powell at the café said that Mrs Jones might be able to help me.'

Without changing his expression, the baker said, 'Is that so?' Then, calling into the next room or beyond, he said, 'Angharad?' He followed the name with a sentence in rapid Welsh. Then, with a nod, he left Jeff on the doorstep and returned to his bakery.

The woman who came to the door was rather younger than her husband, less portly and much less serious. '*Bore da*,' she said with a smile.

Yet again, Jeff confessed to his ignorance of the language and explained that he was English.

'Don't worry,' she assured him, 'you can't help it, I'm sure.'

'That's true, I suppose. Actually, I'm looking for bed and breakfast, and Mrs Powell at the café told me you might be able to help me. It's a single room I'm looking for.'

'Mrs Powell was right. I probably can. How long will you be staying?'

'I'm not sure, but possibly a few weeks, if that's all right.'

Her expression brightened further. 'We can manage that, all right, and you're here in good time for the Eisteddfod, and by that I'm not suggesting you've come for that, although I can recommend it. It's just that all the bed and breakfast accommodation gets taken up by visitors.'

'I gather so.'

'Anyway, come inside and I'll show you your room.' She led him up a flight of stairs to a small, but well-appointed, bedroom. 'My rules are very straightforward. I'll have no strong drink in the house and no women in the bedrooms, unless they're paying guests, of course.'

'Of course. This is a very nice room, Mrs Jones. By the way, my name's Mortimer.'

'Glad to meet you, Mr Mortimer.' Like Mrs Powell, she had a very strong handshake, and he wondered briefly if the local pub fielded a ladies' arm-wrestling team. The thought died at birth, however. In a place such as Llandaron, women would never be seen in a pub, unless they worked there, of course.

'What brings you to Llandaron, Mr Mortimer?'

'Sheer chance. I've turned my back on my previous life, I've sold my flat in London, and I'm looking for a new way of life. Since I left London, I've visited Banbury, Shrewsbury and now Llandaron.'

'My goodness,' she said, shaking her head at the dazzling prospect. 'I've often wondered what it must be like to travel great distances.'

'When you live in such a charming village as Llandaron, Mrs Jones, why would you want to travel?'

'Why indeed? Let me take you downstairs and show you the dining room, where you'll have breakfast. It's usually from seven until nine, but just let me know when you want it, and I'll have it ready for you, as there's only you staying.'

'That's very accommodating of you, Mrs Jones.'

As they left the bedroom, she hesitated and said, 'There used to be an electric alarm clock in there that made tea as well, but it broke down, so I threw it out. That's technology for you, isn't it?'

'It certainly is, Mrs Jones.'

'If you want to be woken up with a cup of tea, Jones will do it for you. He keeps strange hours, being a baker.'

Jeff could only imagine how he would feel if he had to break off making bread to take tea to a pampered guest. 'I wouldn't put him to that trouble, Mrs Jones. I'll just come down to breakfast in the usual way.'

'There's lovely, then.' They reached the bottom of the stairs, and Mrs Jones took him into the dining room, which was quite large and well-lit. I suppose you'll want to know what I charge.'

'Not really. I like the accommodation, and I'm happy to pay whatever you charge.' In any case, the scale of charges was listed on the wall behind her, and ten pounds for a single room was very reasonable.

'If I'm being nosy, you'll tell me, I suppose, but what is your line of work, Mr Mortimer?'

'I'm currently between jobs. Before I left London, though, I was lead guitarist with a rock band.'

'Oh, there's exciting.'

'Not really. I was glad to get out of it.'

'Yes,' she said, changing her expression accordingly, 'you look far too civilised for that sort of thing.' Then, like the busy housewife she was, she asked, 'Is there anything else I can do for you before I get on with my housework?'

A Baker's Round

'Just one thing, Mrs Jones. Do you know of a gym and a swimming pool close by?'

'A gym?'

'A gymnasium.'

'Yes, I know what you mean, but without going to a big town, such as Llangollen, I don't think you'll find either of those things.' As the thought occurred to her, she said, 'If it's swimming you're after, there's always the river. It'll be cold this time of year, mind.'

'Oh, I don't mind cold water. Thank you for telling me that, Mrs Jones. I'll fetch my bags from the car.'

Later that afternoon, Jeff set out for the river and surprised himself by finding it with no trouble at all. Finding a way down from the bank wasn't quite so easy, but he located a natural ledge and, as there was no one about, because he'd no wish to offend anyone, he stripped naked and waded in. As Mrs Jones had warned him, the water was very cold, but that was a luxury in the early summer heat, and he soon became accustomed to it, swimming luxuriously up and down the stretch where he'd left his clothes.

Eventually, he decided he'd been in the water long enough, so he made for the ledge and the pile of clothes beside it.

Looking around him to ensure he was completely alone, he climbed up and on to the bank, where he dried and dressed himself, now resolved to make a swim in the river a regular feature of his stay in Llandaron.

Another feature on his list was the Red Lion, where he found the food very acceptable and the beer different from what he was used to, but palatable for all that.

Having an Englishman in the bar was a novelty for the locals, so he experienced a degree of friendly ribbing.

One of the regulars, an elderly man called Ianto, said to the company around him, 'I wonder if the English have learned to throw darts yet.'

Jeff was always ready to pick up a challenge. 'Where do you think Owen Glendower learned archery? It's the same thing.'

'If you're going to take the great man's name in vain,' said one of them, 'you should learn how to pronounce it. It's "Owain Glyndwr". He pronounced the surname "Glindoor" and challenged Jeff to do the same. After several tries, his final effort was judged 'not bad for an Englishman'. Meanwhile, someone had gone to the bar to get some darts so that everyone would start with the same handicap, as the pub's darts were generally regarded as worthy of that purpose.

'While he's doing that,' said Jeff, 'I'll get the drinks in. Same again, everyone?'

A voice said, 'you can come again, boyo, isn't it, lads?'

There was a chorus of agreement as Jeff went to the bar, motivated only partly by his willingness to stand his round, the other attraction being the barmaid, whose pleasant features and cascade of red hair made her impossible to ignore.

She greeted him with an open smile as he gave her his order. Placing the first two pints on the bar, she asked, 'Did you enjoy your swim this afternoon?'

'Yes, I did. You saw me, obviously.'

'I saw you all right,' she said cheekily.

He decided to brazen it out. 'Well, I'd nothing to be ashamed of.'

'You're right there.' She was grinning now. 'You've certainly no cause for shame.'

'I'm Jeff Mortimer, by the way.' He offered his hand, and she took it.

'I'm Caryl. I only work here three nights a week. I'm in the business of herbal remedies. That's how I saw you this afternoon. I was out collecting plants.'

'Maybe we'll meet there some time, Caryl.'

'I hope so.' She grinned again. 'I'll look forward to it.'

'I'll probably wear something another time.'

'Don't feel that you have to.' She put the last of the pints on the bar and said, 'That lot have accepted you, I see.'

'Why do you say that?'

'They're speaking English, mun. If you'd upset them, you wouldn't have got a word of English out of them. In fact, they wouldn't be speaking to you at all.'

'I'll see you soon, I hope, Caryl.'

'I'll be around,' she promised.

A Baker's Round

The great advantage in having beer glasses with handles was that Jeff could pick up three in each hand, and he delivered the round safely, thus winning the approval of his drinking partners.

'Be careful with that Caryl,' said Ianto, who'd evidently been watching him. 'She's a *gwrach*, you know.'

Jeff was about to ask him to translate, but the process of picking teams had begun, so the moment was lost.

In the end, Jeff established his darts credentials by leading his team to an easy victory, thereby earning the respect of all concerned.

As he walked back to the bakery, he wondered a little about Ianto's warning, but mainly about how soon he would meet Caryl again.

11

Bara Brith and More Besides

It was a magnificent breakfast that Mrs Jones put before him, and he was hungry enough to do it full justice. He was almost finished, when Mr Jones walked in and sat opposite him.

'*Bore da*,' he said.

'*Bore da*, Mr Jones.'

Mrs Jones came in and poured her husband a cup of tea. Turning to Jeff, she asked, 'Breakfast all right, was it?'

'It was excellent, thank you, Mrs Jones. *Da iawn.*' It was a phrase he'd learned from Ianto the previous night, when he'd thrown two double tops.

Smiling at his attempt at Welsh, she said, 'I'm glad you enjoyed it.' She took his empty plate and asked, 'What are you going to do today, Mr Mortimer?'

'I think I'll explore the region. This is a beautiful part of the... world.' He'd been about to say 'country', but thought better of it, nationalist sensitivities being as strong as they were. He'd learned that much at the Red Lion.

'He's quite right, isn't it, Jones?'

The baker simply nodded over his teacup.

When his wife was gone, Mr Jones said, 'I hear you're one of those rock 'n' roll stars.'

'I was. I've given it up.'

'Oh? Why's that, then?'

'I'd rather do something useful.'

The baker nodded sagely and said, 'There's sensible, all right.'

A Baker's Round

After further consideration, he asked, 'Have you ever done a job of useful work?'

'Yes, I have. Before I went into the music business, I was a baker.'

'*Nefi blw!* Is that a fact?'

'Absolutely. By the way, I have to congratulate you on your bread. The toast was excellent.'

'I'm glad you approve of it.' The news about his guest seemed to excite Mr Jones's curiosity, because he asked, 'Do they really have proper bakeries in London? I mean, it's not all that mass-produced rubbish, then?'

'There's a lot of mass-produced rubbish, Mr Jones, but there are independent bakeries, like the one where I served my apprenticeship.'

'I served my apprenticeship with my father, and he with my grandfather before him.'

'It's the best way,' affirmed Jeff. 'To preserve the family's reputation, a father will always make sure his son is properly trained.'

'That's a fact,' agreed Mr Jones solemnly. 'Tell you what. Before you go about your business, come and look around my bakery.'

'I'd like that.' It was the friendliest Mr Jones had been, and Jeff was warming to him. He left the table and followed him into the bakery.

From the start, he was impressed by the standard of cleanliness. Mr Jones would have finished making bread some time since, and the kneading machines were now spotless.

Seeing that Jeff's eyes were on them, he said, 'I use the rotary machine for white bread and the vertical one for wholemeal.'

'Yes, you can't beat it for making wholemeal bread.'

'You recognise it, then?'

'I grew up with one of these.'

That seemed to please Mr Jones, who said, 'Tell you what. I'm going to make some bara brith. Would you like to lend a hand?' He added quickly, 'That's if you've nothing pressing.'

'No, I'd like to do that. I'll just wash my hands.'

'Good.' Mr Jones waited until Jeff had washed and dried his hands, before throwing him a clean apron. 'I've had the fruit and sugar soaking in tea overnight,' he explained. 'I'm making a dozen loaves, so would you like to sift six-and-a-half pounds of self-raising flour and four tablespoons of mixed spice into the bowl of fruit? The spice is on the shelf above your head.' As he spoke, he prepared twelve loaf tins with greaseproof paper. 'Put the eggs in, and then you can mix everything together.'

Jeff looked at the oven, which was set at gas mark 4. Not surprisingly, Mr Jones had thought of everything, and he favoured Jeff with a rare smile when he saw him check the temperature.

'These are for Friday,' he told Jeff. 'I make them two days ahead, and then they're ready to eat.' He looked at the mixture in the bowl and said, 'All right, you can fill the loaf tins now.' He watched Jeff fill each tin with the mixture, ensuring that it filled the corners as well, and smiled. 'You know what you're doing, all right,' he said. 'They don't have anything like bara brith in London, I don't suppose.'

'Not in London. In the north of England, they have tea breads that are similar, but you'll always find regional differences, I imagine.'

'Oh, yes. Well, it's been very interesting, talking to you, Mr Mortimer, but I'll let you get on your way. I expect you have things to do.'

'That's true. Thank you for showing me your bakery, Mr Jones. I'm very impressed.'

'Oh, yes? *Hwyl am y tro.*'

'*Hwyl am y tro.*' As in any other language, 'goodbye' took many forms, and Jeff had just learned one of them.

He returned to his room, where he rolled up his Speedos inside his towel and, uncovering a packet of contraceptives in the drawer, pocketed them to avoid any risk of offending Mrs Jones's moral sensibilities.

It was late morning and another hot day was in prospect as he walked towards the river. Not for the first time, he considered the dramatic way in which his life had changed since the break-up of the band, and part of that change had been his complete loss of interest in the music industry. Even when he'd been driving, he'd either listened to the news on Radio 4 or simply not had the radio on. Life in Llandaron was infinitely more real than the life he'd known, and his brief visit to Mr Jones's bakery had been a blissful reminder of life as it had been. Not that he could return to that life. He would have difficulty in finding references after so long; in any case, no one was going to give him a job after half-a-dozen years out of the industry. No, he would have to press on until some hitherto unconsidered possibility presented itself.

A Baker's Round

His musings took him almost to the riverbank, by which time the sounds of birdsong and flowing water were sufficient to restore his natural optimism. He found the ledge in the bank and, after a cursory look around, undressed beside it.

The water was as cold as ever, but he went in gradually, allowing himself to adjust to the temperature. It took a little time, but before long, he was swimming comfortably. The water was remarkably clear, so that fish, mainly small ones, were plainly visible beneath him. Raising his head above the surface, he saw something else that surprised him. Beside his pile of clothes, another pile had appeared. He wiped his eyes and looked again, but he hadn't been mistaken. Someone had left a pile of clothes next to his, and he had a pretty good idea who that someone was.

'Aren't you a little over-dressed, Englishman?' The voice from behind him was Caryl's, and that confirmed his suspicion.

'I'm not an exhibitionist, Caryl. I only did it yesterday because I thought there was no one about.' Now that he could see her, he could detect no sign of a swimsuit, and when she rolled quite deliberately in the water, she confirmed that suspicion.

'It doesn't do to stay in cold water too long,' she told him.

'Probably not.'

'I'm going to get dried.' She made for the ledge.

'Do you want me to look the other way?' He hoped not.

'Why would I want you to do that? I'm not ashamed of what I've got, thank you very much.'

'And you've nothing to be ashamed of. I'll come and join you.' He struck out for the bank and hauled himself up to find her drying herself with his towel.

'You don't mind, do you? I didn't bring one, as it's warm enough to dry in the sun.'

Hers was a strange kind of logic, as he would be the one relying on nature, having forfeited his towel.

As she rubbed herself dry, he looked at her with new interest, a development that wasn't lost on her. She asked, 'Just what are you looking at?'

'I just noticed that you're a redhead all the way down. It's quite reassuring.'

'What did you expect? A blonde wig?'

'No, that would be awful. I like your shade of red. It was the first thing that caught my attention.'

'You're a strange one, Jeff.' She threw his towel to him, saying, 'It's not completely wet.'

'Thanks. Aren't you going to dry your hair?'

'No, I'll comb it out and it'll dry in the sun.'

He lowered his Speedos, thankful that the shrinking effect of the cold water had worn off, and plied the towel, noticing that Caryl now stood in her briefs.

'I didn't bother with a bra this morning,' she said, pulling her dress over her head and her magnificent breasts.

'Caryl,' he asked as he dried himself as well as the damp towel would allow, 'what is a *gwrach*?' He thought he'd pronounced it correctly.

'A *gwrach*? Why, it's a witch. You don't believe in that kind of thing, do you?'

'Of course not. I heard the word used, that's all.'

'Last night at the pub?' The question was loaded with suspicion.

'Yes.'

'I bet Ianto Price told you I was a witch. Did he?'

From childhood, Jeff had been unable to lie convincingly. It had got him into a lot of trouble both at home and at school. He nodded.

'Ianto believes in pixies and fairies and that sort of thing, the daft old bugger.'

Wishing he'd never asked the question, and feeling he should somehow make amends, he said, 'If it's any consolation to you, I don't believe what he said.'

'It's just as well. Otherwise, I might never have invited you to my cottage.'

'Have you invited me?' He wondered if he'd missed something in all the excitement of mixed bathing and changing.

'I'm inviting you now.'

'Thank you. Where is your cottage?'

'It's not far. Hop on to the back of my broomstick and we'll be there in no time.' She was smiling, so he knew everything was all right. He finished fastening his laces and followed her.

A Baker's Round

After about half a mile, they came to a hamlet that was like an island, quite separate from the rest of Llandaron, and Caryl took him to one of the cottages, where she unlocked the door and invited him inside.

'It's a warm day,' she said. 'Would you like a glass of water or would you prefer a cup of tea?'

'Water would be fine, thank you.' In truth, he wondered quite what to expect after a morning of surprises.

She drew two glasses of water and gave him one of them. 'It's well water,' she said. 'I've been drinking it all my life, so it's safe enough. Make yourself comfortable.' As he did so, she explained, 'All this, the solitary existence, living in my mother's old cottage, carrying on her trade, selling herbal remedies and basically being a free spirit all lend strength to Ianto Price's fixation that I ride on a broomstick and I'm responsible for every disaster that happens for miles around. A sheep has only to cough, and I'm in fear of being burned at the stake.'

'Surely not.'

'No, I'm exaggerating. You are funny, Jeff.' She joined him on the short sofa. 'What did Ianto actually say? I'm not going to make trouble. I'd just like to know.'

'Oh, he just warned me to be careful, and he told me you were a *gwrach*.'

'He probably doesn't know the English word for it.'

'It's possible. I can't believe that we're not all that far inside Wales, and everyone speaks Welsh.'

'Just cross the border and you're already in at the deep end,' she assured him. 'Anyway,' she said impatiently, 'are you going to have sex with me or sit there all day, talking about geography?'

'Geography doesn't stand a chance,' he said, getting up from the sofa.

'Follow me.' She led him upstairs to a small bedroom with a window that looked out on to open countryside. 'It saves closing the curtains,' she told him, pulling her dress once more over her head.

Jeff undressed quickly, but Caryl beat him to it, starting as she did with only two items of clothing. She lay, gloriously naked, on the bed, waiting for him to finish undressing.

'Oh,' she said as he removed his shorts, 'there's lovely. I said as much to myself when I saw you yesterday in the river, and again, today.'

Jeff joined her on the bed, and they kissed unhurriedly, but with great enthusiasm while Caryl acquainted herself with the part of him that had captured her attention on first sighting. 'I'll be back in a little while,' she murmured, journeying downward.

'Take this with you,' he suggested, handing her the vital equipment.

'Oh yes, I suppose so. Better safe than sorry.' She performed the necessary precaution, saying, 'You know, English or Welsh, they all look the same, only this one really is a bit special.'

'I'm glad you think so, Caryl. We're quite attached to each other as well.

'Let's hope you're never parted.' She became quiet for a spell after that, and Jeff could only surmise that things were progressing to her satisfaction.

'*Cariad*,' she said with great feeling, and he deduced that the term of affection wasn't intended for him, but for his popular appendage, which seemed to have attained celebrity status. She then addressed the honoured member in a torrent of Welsh, which sounded passionate enough, but which meant nothing to Jeff. He consoled himself with the knowledge that he was excluded from the conversation, anyway, so the precise meaning didn't matter all that much.

Eventually, Caryl rose to the surface, reverting to English once more. 'You never told me his name,' she said, as if that should have been one of the normal courtesies.

'He just answers to "*Cariad*".'

'He does,' she agreed, kneeling above him and lowering herself into position with a predictable sigh. 'Oh, *Cariad*,' she said, 'your name and mine mean the same.'

'You were made for each other.'

'We most likely were. Oh, Cariad.'

'Are you talking to me or him?'

'Both of you. You're equally special.'

Jeff accepted the compliment, even though he'd done nothing so far.

Caryl continued to help herself, growing increasingly aroused, until she rose up, almost unseating herself, and declaring loudly, '*O fy duw! O fy duw! Oes! Oes! Oes!*'

At length, she became quieter, straightening her knees and subsiding on top of Jeff, who, in the light of recent experience, remained motionless. Even so, Caryl was quick to warn him. 'Don't move yet.'

'I shan't. I can't speak for Cariad. He has a mind of his own.'

'Tell him he mustn't.'

'Okay. Freeze, Cariad. Your life depends on it.'

His warning evidently earned Caryl's approval, because she kissed him with great enthusiasm. It was unfortunate that, in the perverse way of things, that very gesture caused Cariad to respond.

'A-aah!'

'He's sorry. He couldn't help it.'

'Just lie still.'

It occurred to Jeff that he'd done little else since removing his clothes.

At length, Caryl abated, and he manoeuvred her gently on to her back, dividing his kisses between various parts of her anatomy and arousing her again, so that he felt once more in charge of things. And so the roller coaster once more gathered momentum.

———•—•———

As they lay together, Caryl said, 'In Welsh, it's called "*esgynebau*".'

'What is?' He was feeling quite jaded, and a language lesson wasn't high on his list of priorities.

'What we just did. "Climax" is "*esgynebau*".'

'That makes sense,' he observed. 'It sounds more exciting than "climax", and it *is* more exciting when you do it the Welsh way, I've found.'

'Are we going to do it again?'

'What, now?'

'No, at a later date. Tomorrow, maybe.'

'Why not? It must be the best way to keep fit.'

12

A Helping Hand

Jeff continued to see Caryl regularly, and she remained as ready to accommodate him and as appreciative of his company as she had from the outset. There was one interruption to their idyllic routine, and Caryl was quite understanding, as the cause of the hiatus was the Eisteddfod.

Mrs Jones brought up the subject one morning as she served Jeff with breakfast.

'The Eisteddfod is a wonderful thing,' Mr Mortimer.'

'Yes, I'm looking forward to it, Mrs Jones.'

'So is everyone, but it makes an awful lot of hard work for Jones. The business is worth having – don't get me wrong – but it's a lot of work for him in a very short time. As well as all the other things, there's all the bread for the sandwiches, and that's a lot of work in itself.'

By this time, Jeff had deduced that a request was on its way, albeit by a circuitous route, so he saved her further manoeuvring by addressing the problem directly. 'If I can be of any help to him, he has only to ask, Mrs Jones.'

Her relief was immediately evident. 'That's a very kind offer, Mr Mortimer, very kind indeed, but there's a snag, you see.'

'Is there?' The matter seemed quite straightforward to Jeff.

'You see, he's very shy of asking favours. He's a proud man, basically, so he doesn't like to ask, isn't it?'

Jeff refrained from commenting on that disclosure. Instead, he said, 'As soon as I've had breakfast, I'll go and speak to him. How's that?'

A Baker's Round

'Oh, Mr Mortimer, it's too kind you are. He'll really appreciate that. He was only talking about it this morning.'

'Leave it with me.' He was conscious that breakfast was cooling by the minute.

'Oh yes, I'll leave you to your breakfast, and thank you again for your kindness, Mr Mortimer.'

Jeff ate quickly, afraid that Mrs Jones might reappear at any moment with another burst of gratitude, and, as soon as he'd finished, he went to the bakery door and knocked.

'*Dewch i mewn.*'

Jeff pushed the door open. '*Bore da*, Mr Jones.'

'*Bore da,* Mr Mortimer.' If he were surprised to see Jeff, he showed no sign of it.

'I'm sorry to disturb you. I just called to say that if you need any extra help in preparing for the Eisteddfod, I'm happy to provide it. I'm no stranger to hard work, and I'm used to keeping bakers' hours, so it's no trouble.'

Mr Jones stared at him, but with no perceptible change in his expression. Eventually, he said, 'Thank you, Mr Mortimer. It's very kind of you to offer, and I'll take you up on it.'

'Good. I was hoping you would.' There seemed nothing else to say, so Jeff took his leave and went up to his room for his bathing things.

'You're a glutton for swimming, I have to say.' Caryl had a way of creeping up on him.

He turned in the water to speak to her. 'Hello, Caryl. I swim a lot to keep fit.'

'It's fit you are, all right, although I can't say I haven't cause to be thankful for it.' She gave him a sly look and then kissed him.

'I've offered to help Mr Jones the Bread prepare for the Eisteddfod,' he told her. It's been worrying him, and it's no trouble as far as I'm concerned. It just means I'll be missing for a while.'

'That's a fine thing you're doing,' she said, kissing him again. 'The poor man used to struggle with his back and shoulders something cruel.

His wife comes to me for his herbal treatment, so it's not as bad now, but it can't be easy, doing the kind of work he does.'

'I didn't realise that, about his back and shoulders, I mean.'

'Well, only you knows about it, so don't go telling them down the pub. He wouldn't want any of them to know that his wife does business with the Witch of Llandaron.'

'I wouldn't dream of it.'

'No, I don't suppose you would.' She shivered suddenly and said, 'I'm going to dry myself. You coming?'

'Of course.'

As they dried themselves, Jeff wasn't surprised to learn that Caryl wore nothing beneath her dress, although he commented on it.

'What's the point? Anyway, it's too warm for knickers.'

He could only agree, content for the moment to lie beside her and accept her free-spirited ways. After some time, he asked, 'Do you know if Mr and Mrs Jones the Bread have any family to take over the bakery?'

'They have a son.' Her tone was quite dismissive. 'I've met him a few times.'

'Is he a baker, too?'

'I don't know what he's doing with himself now, but I know Jones the Bread trained him.'

'What else do you know about him?'

'Only that he's not as good in bed as you are.' She smiled cheekily and kissed him to make her point. 'I thought you'd like to know that.'

'Thank you, Caryl, but I've never felt that I had to compete with past lovers. I prefer to think of them as forgotten in the new rush of excitement.'

'You're just full of yourself, Jeff.' She stood up and said, 'Shall we go back to my cottage?'

'Why not?'

'Why not indeed, if it'll stop you looking up my skirt.'

He got to his feet and picked up his towel. 'I like to view you from every angle, Caryl,' he said, 'you're so fascinating.'

'And you're full of *cachu*.' The word needed no translation.

A Baker's Round

The time came when Mr Jones had to call on Jeff, who was ready to oblige. Knowing, now, about Mr Jones's arthritis, he insisted on handling the paper sacks of flour and leaving him the lighter jobs. As Mrs Jones had pointed out, it was hard work, but Jeff had done it many times before, and he was happy to do it, although it was unfortunate that he could do nothing for them in the long term. He'd wondered briefly about making Mr and Mrs Jones an offer for the bakery; it might have given them a comfortable retirement, but then Caryl had told him about their son. He was secretly glad he was hopeless in bed.

The Eisteddfod itself was a new experience for Jeff, and he was impressed not only by the sheer number of competitors, but by their considerable ability.

Most of the primary and intermediate events took place outside, where the weather could not have been more accommodating, and it added to the general enjoyment, but the finals took place in the large village hall, where Jeff experienced something he knew he would never forget. A student from the Welsh College of Music and Drama performed her final guitar recital, playing pieces by Albeniz and Villa-Lobos with such delicacy and heart-rending pathos that she must surely be a strong competitor for the title.

In the end, Jeff heard her name read out by the Chief Judge as the Outright Winner of the 1990 Eisteddfod, and he was delighted. He also resolved never to pick up a guitar again. As Mrs Jones had said, the Eisteddfod was about *proper* music.

No longer required in the bakery except for occasional heavy work, he spent his evenings in the Red Lion and his daylight hours with Caryl, who seemed to have sensed that their days together were drawing to a close.

'That's how it has to be, I'm afraid,' he told her. There was nothing to be gained by evading the subject.

'It's just as well, really. If you'd stayed any longer, I might have fallen for you in a big way, and that would have been a disaster.'

'I did consider, just for a moment, making Mr and Mrs Jones an offer for the bakery. I've grown very attached to Llandaron, and I have to say, I've grown attached to you, too.'

The idea seemed to appeal to Caryl. 'What made you think again?'

'It's for them and, eventually, their son to decide the future of the bakery. It seems to me that in a tightly-knit place such as Llandaron, businesses are best kept in the family.'

She nodded before asking, 'Are you rich or something, talking about making them an offer?'

'Or something, I'd say, although I suppose I am rich compared with many people.' The sale of his London flat was proceeding well, and, with his investments, he could be considered well-healed.

With a tone that somehow lacked conviction, she said, 'If I'd realised I was sleeping with a rich man, I'd have worked harder at keeping you here.'

'No, you wouldn't, Caryl. You're an independent spirit, and you'll make your own way in life. Rich men like to be in control, and you'd hate that.'

'I know.' She reached downward to carry out a physical check, lent a few moments of encouragement, and finally knelt above him as she had the first time.

'Heaven help any man who tries to control you, Caryl.'

'Amen to that.'

He stroked her thighs and hips, torn once more between the bliss of the moment and his need to go on looking for a future.

When Caryl lay beside him again, still and satiated, he kissed her slowly and with much fondness.

'Was that a goodbye kiss?'

'I'm afraid so.'

'In that case, you'd better bugger off now, before I tie you down.' Her eyes were wet.

He kissed her again and reached for his clothes.

A Baker's Round

In the morning, Mr Jones came in to see him just as he was finishing breakfast.

'I hear you're leaving us today, Mr Mortimer.'

'Only because I have to,' he assured him.

'Well, I was grateful for your help with the Eisteddfod. I can't say I didn't need it.'

'It was no trouble, Mr Jones.'

The door opened, and Mrs Jones came in, probably alerted by her husband's voice.

'I hear your son is a baker.' He thought it was safe to mention it.

'Yes,' said Mrs Jones, 'he's in the motor car business, now, but we hope he's going to come back to baking. Like you, he chose a different path.'

'It seems to me that with his father's training he'll be an excellent baker when the time comes, Mrs Jones.'

'Let's hope so,' said his father. 'Meanwhile, good luck in whatever you choose to do.' He held out his hand and, for the first time, shook hands with Jeff.

'Thank you, Mr Jones. Good luck to you, too, and to you, Mrs Jones, and thank you for looking after me so well.'

'It was a pleasure.'

'Yes,' said her husband. '*Ffarwel.*'

'*Ffarwel.*' It was another word of Welsh that needed no translation. Jeff took his leave of them and carried his bags out to the car, mindful that he needed to fill up with petrol for the drive ahead, that he estimated would take him at least two hours.

It was purely on a whim that he'd decided on Derbyshire, and particularly Bakewell, home of the famous tart. He'd never been to Derbyshire, and he liked Bakewell tart, so what other reason did he need? He was less well-acquainted with Bakewell pudding, but that was probably another good reason for making the town his next destination.

He headed back towards Oswestry, because that was the route the AA recommended. There, he would find petrol and, hopefully, the M56, that would take him northward in a wide arc, passing through parts of Cheshire and Lancashire, before making his approach, south-eastward towards Bakewell. Pressing onward, he reminded himself yet again of the need to avoid interfering in the business of others and letting his libido dictate his movements.

The sky was more clouded than it had been for some time, and when he heard the weather forecast, he wasn't surprised. It was almost as if he were leaving the sunshine as well as all the other good things behind him in Wales. He hoped not, and consoled himself with the knowledge that the weather was a fickle entity, unconnected with the good or bad things in life. Derbyshire beckoned, and his natural optimism reappeared.

13

Good Intentions

As he approached the Peak District, he questioned the wisdom of his choice of destination. Under the lowering sky, the countryside seemed dark and forbidding, although that was maybe down to the weather. He'd no way of knowing, but he drove on, ever hopeful.

Whilst the sky remained cloudy for the rest of the journey, he became conscious of a lightening in the countryside outside Bakewell, and he could easily imagine that, in better conditions, it would be much more appealing. With that happy thought, he drove into the town and was immediately captivated by the local limestone architecture that was unlike anything he'd seen on his travels so far.

Remembering that accommodation was high on his immediate list, he consulted the addresses the tourist office had given him, and realised that one of them was in a side turning off Matlock Street, where he was currently, and illegally, parked. To rectify the matter, he located a public carpark and set out for the address on foot.

The guest house turned out to be in an Edwardian, or possibly more recent, building. More importantly, however, a sign in the window informed him that the Lauriston Guest House had vacancies. He rang the bell and waited.

After a very short time, the door opened, and a slender, dark-haired woman stood in the doorway. She asked, 'Can I help you?'

'I hope so. I'm looking for bed and breakfast, a single room, if you have one.'

'For how many nights?'

'I don't know.' The question followed him everywhere. 'A week, to begin with, I should think.'

'Please come in.' She led the way into what was presumably a dining room that doubled as an office, as it contained a cash register as well as a large table, and the scale of charges was displayed on the wall beside it. The rate for a single room was apparently eleven pounds fifty, which was quite acceptable. 'There's a registration form to fill in,' she said, handing him the required document.

'Of course.'

She offered him a ballpoint pen, but he said, 'Thank you. I prefer to use my own.'

Watching him, she said, 'It's unusual to see someone use a fountain pen nowadays.'

'It's just one of my little foibles.' Having written his full name, he said, 'My address is debatable. I've all-but sold my flat in London, and I'll soon be of no fixed abode, however briefly.'

'If you haven't actually sold it, put down your London address. It's the truth, and the form is a formality, anyway.'

'Very good.' He completed the form and handed it to her.

'What brings you to Bakewell, Mr Mortimer?' That was the other question that landladies seemed to regard as mandatory.

'Mainly curiosity, but to some extent, the possibility that it will offer a clue as to where my life is heading.'

'I'm sorry. I shouldn't have asked. It's obviously a very personal thing.'

'Personal, yes, but it's not a sensitive matter. I'll tell you about it sometime, if you like, hopefully without boring you too much.'

For the first time, she managed a half-smile, and said, 'I'm Ms Copley, and this, as you can see, is the dining room, where you'll have breakfast. It's served between seven and nine-thirty. If you like, I'll take you upstairs and show you your room and the bathroom.' She led him up a flight of stairs and showed him the bath-*cum*-shower room and a small but very adequate bedroom.

'Thank you, Ms Copley. I'm impressed.'

'Whereabouts is your flat in London. I forget.'

'Hatch End.'

'Of course. This must seem very ordinary after a flat in Hatch End.'

A Baker's Round

'It was my choice to leave that life behind me.' Realising that he was probably speaking in riddles as far as she was concerned, he said, 'I'm not really a man of mystery, Ms Copley. Honestly, I'll explain it when you have time to listen.'

She shrugged. 'If you'll join me in a cup of tea, I'll be happy to hear your story.'

'A cup of tea would go down well, thank you.' He followed her to a spacious and seemingly well-equipped kitchen.

'Take a seat.'

He took one of the chairs at the deal table while she filled the kettle.

'This isn't one of the services I usually provide, but I must confess, you've aroused my curiosity. Are you sure you don't mind talking about it?'

'Not in the least.' Now that he was able to see her properly, he guessed her age at around early to mid-forties; there were flecks of grey in her dark, bobbed hair, and she had a trim figure. Even so, he felt he would be able to keep his resolution on this occasion. He waited until she'd scalded the tea, before speaking.

'Believe it or not,' he said, 'three months ago, I was lead guitarist with a rock band called Tantum Somnium. My hair was longer, then, and I wore disreputable clothes, just like the others you see.'

Her mouth had fallen open, a fact that she realised and corrected immediately. 'I'm afraid I'm not really *au fait* with pop music, but you're not at all what I would have expected.'

'Good. I made the break because I felt it was no longer for me.' He decided not to go too deeply into the reason for his decision. In truth, he preferred to regard his mini-career in the world of rock 'n' roll as a temporary aberration, and put it firmly behind him.

Ms Copley stirred the tea and poured it out. 'Help yourself to milk and sugar,' she said.

'Thank you, I don't take sugar.'

'So, what's the connection with Bakewell, Mr Mortimer? Do you see it as a step towards finding your true destiny?'

'Broadly speaking, yes. I intend to go on journeying, and experiencing the benefits each place has to offer, until something of real significance occurs to me, and then the odyssey will have run its course.'

'I see, but you told me earlier that you'd come to Bakewell partly out of curiosity.'

'That's right.' He wondered how best to explain his haphazard journey so far, and settled for the truth. 'I've chosen towns that mean something to me, either because of a childhood memory, or because, long ago, I was a baker, and I'm naturally interested in regional specialities.'

'Ah.' Clearly, the Bakewell connection made sense. 'Where else have you been?'

'I started in Banbury, where I taught the proprietress of the B and B where I was staying, to bake Banbury cakes. 'Next, I went to Oswestry, home of the Shrewsbury biscuit, but I left them well alone. Instead, I taught the proprietress to make French *pâtisserie*, and her nieces to bake all kinds of things.'

'Fascinating.'

'It gets better. Next, I found myself in Llandaron, Wales, where I helped the village baker prepare for a local music festival. He's troubled with arthritis, and large quantities of dough present a problem.'

'Good for you, Mr Mortimer, and now, Bakewell.'

'Where, let me tell you, I have no intention of interfering in the preparation of tarts or puddings.' He naturally made no mention of his other good intention.

'It's just as well, Mr Mortimer, because I don't bake.'

'Ah.' He waited for her to refill his cup, and asked, 'Do you mind if I ask why not?'

'Not at all. It's basically because I'm no good at it.'

Memories of Lynn in Banbury came to him, and he asked, 'Has someone told you that?'

'Yes.'

'An expert?'

'He would call himself that, yes.' Uncomfortably, and almost like making a confession, she said, 'It was my husband.'

'That's a shame, Ms Copley. Many people find baking relaxing and even therapeutic.'

'I'll take your word for it, Mr Mortimer. Happily, my husband and I are separated, now, so criticism comes only in instalments, when we have to speak to each other.'

A Baker's Round

Aware that he was about to break his first good intention, Jeff asked, 'Thinking of cakes, biscuits and the like, Ms Copley, what do you most like to eat, given that someone else has prepared it?'

'Oh....' Ambushed as she was, she had to think about her answer. Eventually, she said, 'More than anything, I like a fruit cake. I don't necessarily mean a rich, Christmas-type cake, but one with lots of fruit in it.'

'In that case, with your permission, I'll teach you to make the easiest fruit cake of all, and you'll love it, but more importantly than that, we'll put an end to your belief that you're no good at baking. Anyone can bake if they're taught properly.'

'That would be very kind of you, Mr Mortimer. Do you think my partner might join the class as well?'

'I'm sure he could. Does he help you with the guest house?'

'No, she has her own career as a legal secretary.'

'I beg her pardon.' Now he knew he would be able to keep one of his resolutions.

Jeff had already noticed a gym with a sauna on his way into the town, and he spent a useful time there before shopping for the necessary ingredients. It appeared that Ms Copley also lacked the basic equipment for baking, so he attended to that at the same time.

From time to time, he thought about his broken resolution, and concluded that he just couldn't bear the idea that someone could be made to think badly of herself, presumably because it suited the ill-natured judge in question for that state of affairs to exist.

Satisfied that he was acting out of the best of motives, he took the ingredients and equipment back to the guest house and left them in the kitchen.

'Right,' said Jeff, 'hands washed, pinnies on, and we can start.' He'd actually bought himself a proper baker's apron for the occasion. The

Mses Copley and Fawcett – he thought he'd got the plural of 'Ms' right – had hidden their hair sensibly beneath towels tied up like turbans.

Ms Fawcett, a severe-looking woman of around forty, asked, 'Why have we so many little pots?'

'Because you're going to weigh out the ingredients individually and have them ready when you need them. Are you more confident with metric or imperial?'

'Oh, pounds and ounces, I'm afraid,' said Ms Copley.

'There's nothing wrong with being old-fashioned,' he told her.

'I'm just old.'

'Nonsense. Anyway, you need to weigh and sift eight ounces of self-raising flour.' He watched her weigh the flour and pick up the sieve. 'Gently with the sieve,' he cautioned, 'or the flour will go all over the table. Just tap it gently with your free hand.' He placed the recipe in front of her. 'Now you're in the driving seat,' he said, 'but I'll be behind both of you, so you've no need to worry.'

Ms Fawcett put an egg into a small bowl, measured a quarter of a pint of water, and weighed four ounces of butter. 'What now?' She asked herself the question, and a quick look at the recipe provided the answer. 'Four ounces of caster sugar.' She weighed that into another pot.

'That's my girl.' He winced as he spoke. 'Now, this is the fruit you were talking about, Ms Copley. Twelve ounces of it.' He realised she was smiling, a fairly rare occurrence, and he asked, 'What's the joke?'

'We "girls" are about twenty years older than you.'

'Surely not.'

'How old are you, Mr Mortimer?'

'Twenty-ni… no, thirty.' During the time he'd spent in Wales, a birthday had come and gone almost unnoticed.

'In that case, I'm fifteen years older than you.'

'And I'm ten years your senior,' Ms Fawcett told him.

'It's hardly worth mentioning. Anyway, when you're under my tutelage, you're officially "my girls". It comes under "*Droits du Maître Boulanger*".'

'I'm not so sure about that,' said Ms Copley, 'but we'll let it pass for now. I think it might be better, however, if we dispensed with formality. My name's Hilary, and this is Valerie.'

A Baker's Round

'Excellent. I'm Jeff. What's the next step?'

' "Put the sugar, butter, water and fruit into a saucepan and simmer for twenty minutes on the hob." '

'Okay, go ahead.' When she'd set the pan to simmer, he said, 'Put the lid on and save its embarrassment, and then the next two jobs are to line a cake tin with a greaseproof liner, and load the dishwasher with what we've used so far.' He watched Valerie line the tin. 'Good girl.'

'It wasn't difficult,' she protested.

'I know. I was just winding you up.'

She smiled again. 'I feel like a girl, doing this with you.'

'So do I,' said Hilary.

'There, I told it was therapeutic, and don't forget to keep smiling.'

'Why?'

'Because you're both very attractive women, and smiling intensifies that appeal.'

'Oh, Reg,' said Valerie. It came out as a dismissive sigh. 'If only that were true.'

'It is, at least, as far as I'm aware. Now, your oven is calibrated in Celsius, so now we have to go metric and preheat it to a hundred and fifty.'

When the twenty minutes of simmering were done, he left them to add the beaten egg and stir in the flour. 'Stir it until there's not a speck of dry flour in sight,' he told them. 'Now, pour the mixture into the cake tin. Use a spatula to get every trace of the mixture out of the bowl, and then stick that in the dishwasher.

With that done, Hilary put the cake into the oven and set the timer.

'Make it an hour and twenty to begin with,' he advised. 'We'll have a look at it then, and decide if it needs more. Then we wash the tabletop and have a drink.'

'Oh,' said Hilary, 'I don't think we have much of anything in the house.'

'I brought a bottle of wine in this afternoon. I just need three glasses and a corkscrew, please.'

'You're incorrigible, Jeff,' said Hilary. 'Let's take it into the sitting room,' she said, setting down the glasses and handing him the corkscrew.

'All right, but there's one more important job before we do that.'

'What's that?'

'Stand in front of me, look me straight in the eye, and tell me what was difficult about any of that.'

'Nothing at all. It was… fun.'

'Good. Now smile again.'

Self-consciously, she obliged.

'Well done. Let's all go and have that drink.'

As they sat down in the sitting room, Hilary said, 'I still don't believe it. This afternoon, I unburdened myself to a paying guest who's fifteen years my junior, and now he's taught me how to bake a cake.'

'And me,' said Valerie.

'Exactly, and it wasn't difficult. You see, criticism is one thing if it's well-intentioned, but even then, unless it comes from an expert, it's not worth a great deal. Unfortunately, you seem to have taken your ex-husband's criticism about your baking to heart, Hilary. I take it he's not a baker?'

She laughed mirthlessly. 'No, he's a civil servant. At least, that's what he's called. He stopped being civil towards me some time ago, and he's always expected me to be the servile one.'

It was difficult to know what to say without being openly critical of her husband, so he asked, 'Have you always been in the B and B business?'

'No, I was a secretary until I met my husband. He decided this was the ideal thing to keep the little woman busy and out of mischief.'

Still trying to avoid criticising her husband, Jeff merely looked sympathetic.

'It wasn't just about baking,' she said.

'Oh?'

'No.' She looked nervously towards Valerie, and said, 'He resented my friendship with Valerie.' She added, 'That was before it became a relationship, you understand.'

'Quite.'

'I hope I haven't embarrassed you.'

'Not in the least.' He hoped he sounded sincere. 'I'm enjoying the company of two charming and fascinating people, and that, Hilary and Valerie, is all that matters.'

'I've always been self-conscious about my name,' said Hilary.

A Baker's Round

'They used to ask me at school what the weather was like on Mount Everest.'

'Ignorant people,' said Jeff. 'It's always been a popular name with me, because it was the name of my favourite term.'

'What?' It was Hilary who spoke, but they were both apparently puzzled.

'The Hilary Term,' he explained, 'the one that ended in early July. It was always my favourite because it came before the long holiday.'

'We always called it the "Summer Term".'

'Oh well, my school was lost in another age.' He shrugged the matter aside and asked, 'Ladies, have you anything planned for tomorrow evening?'

They looked at each other, and Hilary said, 'Tomorrow? No, nothing.'

'Will you both join me for dinner? I'll find a good restaurant, unless you know of one.'

'For dinner? Yes, we'd love to, wouldn't we, Valerie?'

It was an unusual dinner date for Jeff, but a very enjoyable one. His two guests were excellent company, and the meal was no less agreeable. It was also a suitable prelude to his departure the following morning.

14

A Boston Tea Party

The journey to Boston, Lincolnshire would have been lengthy, even without the unplanned detours that were a feature of Jeff's navigation. It involved skirting Chesterfield and Newark, and a drive almost to the east coast.

His reason for choosing Boston as his next destination was as whimsical as the rest, as well as being quixotic. He'd learned at school of the Boston Tea Party, and it seemed to him that only a nation of coffee drinkers could treat tea in so disrespectful a fashion. He'd always regarded tea, given the appropriate time of day, as something to be appreciated and relished, and he intended to enjoy it in the original town of Boston. He felt that to do so would go some way towards redressing the wrong perpetrated more than two hundred years earlier.

Eventually, he arrived, and the clock on the car fascia told him it was a little before four. Very appropriately, it was teatime. He parked in the first carpark he saw, and set about finding accommodation.

He had no luck with the first address on his list, but a 'Vacancies' sign hung in the window of the second, which was advertised as a café with bed and breakfast, so he walked into the café and took a seat at one of the tables. After a few minutes, a man of fifty or so in a short-sleeved shirt and chinos came to his table.

'I'm sorry if you've been kept waiting,' he said. 'My wife looks after the café, but she's on the phone. Can I get you anything?'

'Just a pot of tea, please. I'm actually looking for a single room for a few days, maybe a week or so.' He offered the information, as it had been the first question he'd been asked everywhere else. He added, 'It can wait until your wife's off the phone.'

'I think we can accommodate you. I'm Charles Woodhouse, by the way.'

'Jeff Mortimer.' They shook hands.

'What kind of tea would you like?'

'Oh.' He looked at the menu and said, 'English Breakfast, please. Just a small pot.'

'I'll get that for you.'

During his absence, Jeff was able to look around the café, and he was impressed. Everything looked very fresh, and he suspected that the place must have been redecorated fairly recently.

Someone, who was most likely Mrs Woodhouse, appeared with a tray. She looked around the café, and when her eye fell on him, he attracted her attention by raising his hand.

She asked with an open smile, 'Are you Mr Mortimer?'

'That's right. You must be Mrs Woodhouse.'

'I am, and I believe you're looking for bed and breakfast.'

'That's right.'

'We have a single room available, but enjoy your tea and we'll talk about it later.'

'That's a good idea. I've had a long drive.'

'In that case, I'll go and leave you in peace.'

'Thank you. I'll see you later, Mrs Woodhouse.'

She was as pleasant as her husband, and about the same age. Also, on looking at the menu, he gained the impression that someone on the premises was an enterprising cook, and most likely a competent one, all of which led him to the conclusion that his twin resolutions were as good as kept. He relaxed and enjoyed the tea, wondering yet again what had possessed the Americans to behave in such an irresponsible and cavalier fashion. Objecting to taxation was one thing, but sacrilege was quite another.

As he was wondering, albeit half-heartedly, Mrs Woodhouse returned.

'Can I bring you some more tea, Mr Mortimer?'

'No, thank you, but I'd like to make arrangements about the room, if that's convenient.'

'I'll get my husband.'

It seemed a fair division of labour. Jeff waited, and Mr Woodhouse joined him within a couple of minutes. Jeff paid for the tea and followed him into the house.

'As it's the high season,' said Mr Woodhouse with a hint of apology in his tone, the charge for a single room is fourteen pounds.'

'That's absolutely fine.'

'If you follow me, I'll show you the room.' He looked around Jeff's feet and asked, 'Have you any luggage?'

'It's in the car. I left it in a carpark.'

'I'm afraid we can only offer roadside parking.'

'That's all right.' He followed Mr Woodhouse upstairs to the room, which was easily as good as anything he'd experienced so far. 'Thank you,' he said. 'It's a very nice room.'

'I'm glad you like it. We've only been in the bed and breakfast business three years, since I was made redundant, so we're still feeling our way, in a sense.'

'I'm sorry, about the redundancy, I mean. What did you do before that?'

'I was a draughtsman.' He gave a half-hearted laugh. 'It was very different from this business.'

'How's it going, though, generally?'

'Generally, very well. The only villain in this business is the taxman.'

'He's the demon in any business.'

'Well,' said Mr Woodhouse, laughing again, 'we all have our problems. Let me tell you about breakfast.'

'Is that a problem?'

'No, it's a welcome diversion.'

It seemed to Jeff that the tax situation must be particularly trying, for his host to make such a point of it, but he kept the thought to himself and followed him downstairs.

'Breakfast is from seven until ten-thirty, and it's served in the café. After that, we start preparing the lunch menu.'

'Who does the cooking?'

'My wife. At least, I do breakfast, and she does the rest.'

Thinking about the menu, Jeff said, 'I get the impression your wife is a consummate baker.'

A Baker's Round

'I've always thought so, and we've never had any complaints from customers.'

'I should think not.'

'Have you tried her baking?'

'Not yet, but the complexity of some of the items on offer tells its own story.'

'I well,' said Mr Woodhouse confidently, 'you have a treat in store.' A little belatedly, he said, 'I take it you have some knowledge of baking?'

'Before I allowed myself to be side-tracked, I was a baker,' confirmed Jeff. By this time, it had become a habit.

'And after you were side-tracked?'

'I was lead guitarist with a rock band called Tantum Somnium.'

Mr Woodhouse stared. 'Surely not,' he said in genuine disbelief.

'This civilised human form you see before you is a disguise, hopefully a permanent one.'

The man was still nonplussed, so Jeff explained, 'Not all rock stars are churlish, monosyllabic, inarticulate potheads. Many of them are, I'll grant you, but not all of them. In any case, I was tired of the whole business, so I got out.'

Still visibly in disbelief, Mr Woodhouse said, 'Let's go through to the café, and you can try some of my wife's baking.'

'Why not?' Once again, Jeff followed his host.

He ordered another pot of tea and a plain scone, which was as much as he wanted, so close to dinner.

When the scone arrived, complete with cream and the blackcurrant jam he'd requested in preference to strawberry, he forgot the jam for the moment, and examined the scone closely, because it was the fluffiest he'd ever seen. He cut it carefully in half and inspected the texture, which was as light as he'd hoped. Rather than confuse his taste buds at first with jam and cream, he broke off a piece and tried it on its own. It was both light and delicious, and the rest of the scone proved no less enjoyable.

Mrs Woodhouse came to him after a while, and asked he he'd like anything else. 'The café closes at five-thirty,' she explained.

'Nothing else, thank you,' he said. 'The scone was superb. I can't get over the lightness, but I suppose that's a trade secret.'

'No,' she said, 'that kind of thing's too petty for words. Do you make yours with self-raising flour?'

'Yes.'

'So do I, but I add baking powder as well, and another ingredient, which is just a drop of boiling water. Just a teaspoonful per dozen will do the trick.'

Now he thought about it, hot water and baking powder would, but it had taken Mrs Woodhouse to remind him of that. 'Thank you for that,' he said. 'I'm very grateful.'

'Well, now that I've told you that, will you tell me something?'

'What do you want to know?'

'Why did you leave what you were doing to come here?'

Evidently, Mr Woodhouse had told her about Jeff's former life. For possibly the fifth or sixth time since leaving London, he recounted his disillusionment with the music industry and his need to find a more meaningful existence. 'Boston is just one step on the road,' he told her 'Hopefully, I'll find what I'm looking for soon.'

After a comfortable night and, he had to say, an excellent breakfast, Jeff went out to explore the town. He saw the famous Boston Stump and the historic Guildhall, before going on to the Maud Foster Mill, with its seven storeys.

Lunch beckoned, and where better than the café where he was staying? There, he had a magnificent Welsh rarebit, a dish that had passed him by during his stay in Wales, but, as he told himself, he had fitted an awful lot into a short time.

After lunch, he wandered along the River Whitham, and then rounded off the afternoon with an hour at the gym.

He ate at the Roper's Arms, where he spent the rest of the evening.

A Baker's Round

He didn't see the Woodhouses until the next morning, when Mr Woodhouse brought his breakfast, and Mrs Woodhouse called in to make sure everything was satisfactory.

'Mr Woodhouse,' he said, 'you mentioned the fact that the taxman was spoiling the party. I don't like to pry, and I'm not an accountant, but I've had experience of these things. I just wondered if I might be able to give you a tip or two, as you're new to self-employment.' To give them the option, he said, 'Tell me to mind my own business, if you will.'

'We'll come back when you've eaten,' said Mr Woodhouse, looking freshly serious. 'We'll have coffee with you and we'll discuss it then.'

It was a good idea, and Jeff enjoyed his second breakfast cooked by a most hospitable man, who clearly had a problem. If he could help the couple at all, he would do it gladly.

Mr Woodhouse brought fresh coffee, while his wife cleared the table of used cutlery and utensils. Presently, she returned with two extra cups and saucers, and took a seat.

After what seemed a very deep breath, Mr Woodhouse began. 'When we bought this place, we received the usual tax rebate, which was very welcome. Both the house and the café needed a great deal of work and, fair enough, we were able to claim the expenses against earnings, but the big problem that remains, after that first year, is that of cashflow. We paid the first instalment of the current tax bill, but it's the second that's the problem. We could repay it over the next three months, but they want it now. They're even threatening to send the bailiffs to force an entry and take away assets against the debt.' He was quite obviously worried, but there were tears in Mrs Woodhouse's eyes.

Jeff felt desperately sorry for them both. 'Have you made them an offer to pay over three months?'

'Yes, and they just refused to accept it. Someone always phones us, as well, at about four to four-thirty each Friday, badgering us for payment.'

It was a familiar story, and one that Jeff had experienced. 'Have you spoken to your accountant about it?'

'Yes, he's not very helpful. He said our offer was worth a try, but that's all.'

'What a helpful person he turned out to be.'

'There's nothing you can suggest, is there, Mr Mortimer?' Mr Woodhouse shook his head as he spoke.

'Yes, there is. Do you think I might have some more coffee, please?' He needed the lubrication.

'Of course.' Mrs Woodhouse plied the coffee pot.

'You may as well know that their biggest weapon is fear, and they'll not hesitate to use it. Phoning you late each Friday afternoon is a cheap trick. They'll probably give a list of numbers to a school-leaver, and leave him to threaten you and leave you the whole weekend to worry.'

'We do that, all right,' said Mr Woodhouse.

'They know it would take them longer to get the money through the court than if they waited for you to pay by instalments. They're just trying to bully you into finding the lump sum. Now, here's my advice. I think you should write to them, reminding them that they won't get the money any quicker by sending the SAS to burst through your windows and seize your assets. Enclose three post-dated cheques. They won't like it, but they can't touch you, because you're making a genuine effort to pay them.'

'Are you sure?' Mr Woodhouse sounded desperate to know.

'Positive. Now, in accepting your offer, they'll most likely make ugly noises. They'll tell you it's the last time they'll accept such an arrangement, and they'll threaten you again with the bailiff if you default on it, but that's just sabre-rattling. They have to preserve the status quo, that they are there to be feared.'

'Are you absolutely sure, Mr Mortimer?'

'Yes, I've been through that process, but my accountant was infinitely more helpful than yours, and that's something else you may wish to think about.'

'We're very grateful to you, Mr Mortimer,' said Mr Woodhouse, looking immensely relieved, as did his wife.

'Yes,' said Mrs Woodhouse. 'Will you accept tonight's accommodation as a token of our gratitude?'

'That's very kind of you, but I have to be on my way today. If I'm ever down this way again, I'll be sure to look you up.'

'Oh, please do.' They meant it.

15

A Face From the Past

So far, Jeff's odyssey had taken him more or less in a zig-zag route, vaguely towards the north, but now, acting on a whim, as he usually did, he turned south towards Cambridgeshire and, in particular, Stilton, home of the celebrated, blue-veined cheese.

It seemed that Saint Christopher was smiling on him on this occasion, because he found the village without difficulty; at least, he put it down to saintly intervention, because he knew his navigation skills were never going to improve.

It was a relatively short journey, as well, taking only an hour, so he was still feeling quite fresh when he drove into the village and parked.

He'd been so intent on helping the Woodhouses out of their difficulty, that he'd quite forgotten to phone for a list of B and B addresses. Still, there was a perfectly good sub post office and general store close by, so he decided to do the old-fashioned thing and enquire within.

He opened the door and realised at once that he was going to be there for some time. A woman, presumably operating a cottage industry of some kind, was posting parcels of various shapes and sizes, each of which called for a Certificate of Posting and individual receipt. He looked around to see if there was anyone behind the general store counter, but he was disappointed. Still, he was a man of leisure, and he could afford to wait.

As he waited, he heard the doorbell tinkle, and then a woman's voice behind him said, 'I hope you're not in a hurry.'

He turned to face the owner of the voice and saw a tall, slender woman of forty or so, or perhaps a little more than so, in a French navy blouse and fitted jeans. With a nod towards the woman with the parcels, she said, 'She always takes forever.'

'I only came in to make an enquiry,' he told her.

'By the time you get to the counter, you might have forgotten what you came in to enquire about. Is it a Post Office matter, or a general one?'

'Very general. I'm looking for B and B accommodation.'

'In that case, you're in luck, and it's just possible that I am too. I keep a B and B close by.'

'Really? Can you remember, off hand, if you have a single room vacant?'

'Just off the top of my head, yes, I have. If you wait just a minute, while I make a *quick* transaction, I'll tell you more.' The emphasis was for the benefit of the poster of parcels, who was just leaving the counter.

'The Post Office is here for everybody to use,' the woman said sourly.

'I couldn't agree more.' She went to the counter and bought a sheet of postage stamps. 'Now,' she said, 'is that your Volvo outside?'

'Yes. How did you know?'

'I don't know anyone else in this village who has one, so it was odds-on, really. If you don't mind giving me a lift up the lane, I'll show you where to park.'

It seemed a good idea, so he unlocked the car and let her direct him up a short lane and on to a paved area, where there was room for maybe four cars. One, presumably hers, occupied the farthest space.

'Thank you,' she said, climbing out. 'Come inside and I'll tell you what you need to know. I'm Jill Curzon, by the way.'

'Jeff Mortimer.' He shook her hand.

'You'll actually be the only guest tonight. I get the passing trade, you see. No one stays for long, but they find my place useful.'

'As far as I'm concerned, it's more than convenient.'

'Good. I charge fourteen pounds for bed and breakfast, which is served between seven and nine-thirty.'

'Excellent.'

'Come in and I'll show you your choice of rooms. Other than mine, there's a double and two singles.' She led him upstairs and showed him the options.

A Baker's Round

'Honestly,' he said, 'I'm happy with either.'
'I'd take Room Three,' she advised. 'The bed's marginally better.'
'Thanks for your advice. I'll take it.'
'Good. Let's go down and sign the register.'

On the way downstairs, Jeff noticed photographs of two people he recognised from childhood. 'Good grief,' he said, being careful to mind his language.

'Yes, Stan Stennett and Billy Dainty. I worked with them both.'
'In the theatre, presumably?'
'Yes.' She reached into what appeared to be the dining room and picked up the register. 'Would you like to sign in?'
'With pleasure. I have to give my London address. I've sold the flat, but it's not finally settled.'
'That'll do for me.' She watched him write his name and address, and said, 'How nice to find someone who still uses a fountain pen.'
'I wouldn't be parted from it, Ms Curzon.'
'Jill.'
'In that case, I'm Jeff.'
'With a "J",' she observed, glancing at the register. 'Would you like coffee or tea?'
'At this time of the morning, coffee would be perfect, thank you.'
'Let's not stand on ceremony. Come and join me in the kitchen while I make it.'

He followed her through the passageway, between yet more photographs of theatricals, some signed, but others of past colleagues who were presumably friendly enough not to add a signature.

'Stan Stennett and Billy Dainty both did a lot of pantomime, didn't they? I believe Stan Stennett's still around.'
'Still alive,' she confirmed, 'and still very active.' She measured coffee into a cafetiere. 'In case you're wondering, I did a lot of pantomime, too.'
'I wondered.'
'I'm glad you didn't say, "Oh no, you didn't". Most people feel they have to.'
'I wouldn't dream of it.' He had to ask, 'Principal boy?'
'Right in one.'

Her slim figure and long legs rather gave the game away, although he kept that assessment to himself, at least for the time being.

'I did a lot of musical theatre at one time,' she told him, 'but pantomime was special, somehow. Maybe it was because it was part of the Christmas tradition, the innocent fun, and kiddies getting a hundred percent out of it, but it meant a lot to me and a great many others.'

'But it still goes on, doesn't it?' Jeff hadn't seen one for about twenty years, but he was aware of them happening around him.

'Oh, it does,' she said, pouring hot water into the cafetiere, 'but I was talking about *my* past.'

'Not long past, I'm sure.' Her figure had a Sigourney Weaver-like willowiness about it, although her features were somewhat finer, with deeply-expressive, brown eyes. Her dark hair was flecked with grey, but that was no detriment.

'Long enough, Jeff. Anyway,' she said defiantly, 'pantomime's not what it was.'

'In what sense?'

'Oh, it's become a vehicle for loud pop music of the worst kind.' She pushed down the plunger and poured two mugs of coffee. 'Help yourself to milk and sugar.'

'I'll just take it black, without sugar.'

'Fine. So, what's your story, Jeff? What brings you to Stilton, as if I didn't know?'

'Fair enough, I love Stilton cheese, and I want to try some of the plum bread I've heard of from the next-door county, but those things are only a small part of the great escape. You'll be dismayed to hear that, until early this year, I was a perpetrator of "pop music of the worst kind". I was Jeff Mort, lead guitarist with a band called Tantum Somnium.'

'I'm amazed.' She added, 'Not that I've ever heard of them.'

'You haven't missed anything, Jill.'

'So, what happened? What made you decide to sin no more?'

'I was sick of the whole business, but most of all, the pretentiousness that goes with it. I was born in nineteen-sixty, so I've never really known anything else, but it still irritated me.' He tried his coffee and found it too hot for immediate consumption. 'Basically, I'm trying to find a way forward. I was a baker before I was lured away by the music industry, but I can't see myself getting back into that.'

A Baker's Round

She'd been listening to him, nodding occasionally, and clearly interested in his story. 'Now,' she said, 'I can't suggest a way forward, but I can help you with the Stilton cheese and Lincolnshire plum bread. Don't move.'

'I don't intend to.' He waited while she took cheese from the fridge and cake from a tin, finally presenting him with a piece of Stilton cheese and a slice of plum bread on a plate.

'Would you like butter with the plum bread? Most people like to butter it.'

'Thank you,' he said. 'That's very kind of you, but I'll try it without butter. This is a new experience for me.'

'Gosh, a defining moment. Let's treat it with true reverence.'

'Don't mock, Jill. This is important to me.' He broke off a piece of loaf and tasted it. 'Enriched bread,' he remarked. 'Excellent.'

'Thank you. I used dried yeast. It's not traditional, but it works for me.'

He tried some more, almost groaning with ecstasy when he encountered the luscious currants, raisins and sultanas. 'You soaked the dried fruit in tea, I imagine?'

'Black tea, yes.'

'Just the right amounts of cinnamon and allspice.'

'Thank you. I don't think my baking has ever been appreciated in such detail.'

'It's no more than it deserves, I'd say.'

'You're too kind. What are you going to do with the rest of the day?'

'I'll have a look around, commune with nature, and then find somewhere to eat.'

It was a little before nine when he returned to the house, and he was about to go upstairs, when the sitting room door opened, and Jill asked, 'Would you like a drink, Jeff?'

'How kind. Yes, please.' Because he was driving, he'd had only a glass of wine at the restaurant. He joined her in the sitting room.

'What would you like? If it helps, I've just opened a bottle of red wine.'

'That sounds inviting, Jill.'

'Okay, I'll pour you a glass. I'm glad you've come back in good time.' She patted a photo album on the low table. 'I've unearthed some photos for you to look at. That's if you want to see them.'

'Of course I do.' He joined her on the sofa and accepted a glass of wine, prepared at once to be transported back to the pantomime days of his childhood.

She opened the album and announced, '*Goldilocks and the Three Bears*, Tenby, nineteen sixty-four.'

'Of course, they usually make the principal boy Robin Hood, don't they?' He was looking at Jill in her Robin Hood costume, complete with *chapel à bec* cap, doublet, tights and high-heeled shoes. She looked irresistible. 'Magnificent.'

'Thank you. You said you were born in the sixties, didn't you? I'm afraid these must be before your time.'

'I was four, then, and some things are never out of time.'

'If only. I was twenty when this was taken.'

'You were lovely, and you've retained your charms, whatever you say.'

'Flatterer.' She turned the page and announced, '*Dick Whittington*, Rhyl, nineteen sixty-five.' In the photograph, she was challenging King Rat, with her sword drawn and ready for action.

'Glorious,' he said. 'You know, when I was a toddler, it came as an annual disappointment to me that the heroes of pantomimes were always girls.'

'I think you might just have missed one of the essential tenets of pantomime, Jeff.'

'Yes, but as I grew older, it made increasing sense that they should be. I mean, it's never too late to learn, is it?'

She simply smiled and turned another page. '*Jack and the Beanstalk*, Droitwich, nineteen sixty-six,' she announced. 'Oh, I had trouble with that giant.'

'I suppose it's in a pantomime giant's job description to be difficult,' he said.

A Baker's Round

'Not in the way he had in mind,' she assured him, turning the page again. '*Cinderella,* Croydon, nineteen sixty-seven.'

'Croydon? Let me look.' He put down his glass and ran his eye excitedly over the label. 'I was in the audience.'

'Were you really?'

'It was only my… my third pantomime. I wanted to go to the stage door with the other kids and meet the cast – they all seemed very real in those days – but we had to leave.'

'Oh Jeff, and the hurt has stayed with you all these years. Still, you got to meet Prince Charming eventually. You just had to wait twenty-three years for it.' She smiled good-naturedly and said, 'I wonder how many children wanted to meet Jeff Mort and…. What was the band called?'

'Tantum Somnium. Don't, Jill, the memory's painful enough as it is.'

'Why, for goodness' sake?'

'The kids thought we were wonderful, and all the time, we were peddling rubbish. What you had to offer was quality, and there's a world of difference.'

She considered that briefly and asked, 'How do you know it was quality? You were very young at the time.'

'It's there, in the photographs. I don't just mean that you looked stunning and glamorous, although you certainly did. I mean that you and the others created a world of make-believe that was sheer magic for every child in the audience. All we did was to perform cheap tricks of a kind that would earn the censure of a fifth-rate magic turn.'

'Well, you got out of it, didn't you? And you did something tonight that was genuinely good.'

Mystified, he asked, 'Did I?'

'Yes,' she laughed, 'you made me feel glamorous again after all those years.'

'You shouldn't need me to make you feel like that, Jill. You're only forty-six, not eighty-six.'

'Keep telling me that, Jeff.'

'I'll do more than that. Will you join me for dinner tomorrow evening?'

With only a slight hesitation, she said, 'You know, I'll be happy to do that.'

16

The Inevitable Line

Jill wore a plum-red wrap dress that had gained Jeff's immediate approval from the outset.

'Wouldn't you have preferred Lincoln green?'

'Not for one moment. I want to spend the evening with Jill Curzon, not Robin Hood,' he said, smiling as a stray thought occurred to him, 'or even Maid Marian.'

The George Hotel of Stanford was evidently popular, judging by the number of diners, and the staff had been busy throughout the evening, but always on hand when they were needed. Jeff asked, 'Would you like to look at the menu again?'

Jill screwed up her face in thought and made her decision. 'No, thank you.'

'Coffee, another drink?'

'I can offer you those at home.'

'Good thinking.' Turning to the waitress, he said, 'Just the bill, please.'

'Very good, sir.'

Jill looked around her again and said, 'I never expected to be taken to the George.'

'Where else, considering the pleasure you gave me in nineteen sixty-seven?'

Leaning towards him, she said, 'Tell me, do you make a habit of wining and dining women sixteen years older than you?'

'Only when the woman in question is fascinating and alluring. You're obsessed with numbers, Jill. I wish you'd forget them.'

A Baker's Round

'You know, Jeff, you're nothing like my idea of a rock star.'

'Good, I'll take that as a compliment.' He took the bill from the waitress and paid in cash. 'That's fine,' he said. The change would cover the tip. 'Thank you. It was an excellent meal.'

'I'm glad it was to your satisfaction, sir.'

'Oh, it was much better than that. Will someone call a taxi, please?'

'Of course, sir.'

The taxi arrived within minutes, and Jeff climbed in beside Jill. 'Stilton, please,' he told the driver.

'You must have an unusual background for a guitarist in a rock band,' said Jill, intent on pursuing her current fascination.

'Most unusual,' he agreed, 'in fact, almost unique.'

'I mean the whole pop music scene.'

'If you mean that I don't smoke pot, dress like a scarecrow and communicate in, at my most articulate, bi-syllabic expletives, it's probably down to a superior upbringing.'

She digested that information and asked, 'Posh school?'

'Very, although I was invited to leave at sixteen.'

'Oh?'

'*Cherchez les femmes*,' he told her, 'or, more exactly, *les jeunes filles. Les femmes* were beyond my reach at sixteen.' To reassure her, he added, 'I've developed a moral conscience since then.'

'I'm glad to hear it.'

By way of further explanation, he said, 'It helped that my father and grandfather were both men of the cloth. My brother is also of that persuasion, but he wields no influence over me.'

The taxi left the A1 and entered Stilton. The driver asked, 'Whereabouts in Stilton, sir?'

'About a hundred yards past the Post Office, there's a lane to the left,' Jill told him. 'If you drop us at this end of the lane, that'll be fine, thank you.'

The driver dropped them, and Jeff paid him. As Jill took his arm, she said, 'This is something else I wouldn't expect a conventional rock star to do.'

'Oh, they have more pressing urges, believe me.'

'I do.' She opened the door and led the way to the sitting room. 'I'll put the coffee on while you pour yourself a drink.'

Jeff found a bottle of Hine and poured himself a measure. He was inhaling the heady vapour when Jill re-joined him, carrying a cafetiere and two mugs on a tray.

'What would you like?'

'The same as you, I think.'

He poured her a measure and handed it to her.

'It was a lovely meal,' she said, touching his arm. 'Thank you.'

'It was an occasion. I'm glad you could be a part of it.'

He took a seat on the sofa, and was surprised when she opted for an armchair.

'You know,' she said, pushing down the plunger, 'it was good to get those photos out last evening. More than anything, I think, it was what you had to say about them that did me the most good.' She poured two mugs of coffee.

'Rest assured, I meant every word.'

'I believe you.'

'Have you still got the photo album handy?'

'Yes.' She reached beside her chair and picked it up.

'If you've no objection, I'd like to see some more.'

'You're a glutton for punishment, Jeff, but here goes.' She got up and sat beside him. 'Where did we get to, last night?'

'Cinderella, Croydon, Nineteen sixty-seven,' he prompted, remembering it exactly.

'You even remembered the date.' She opened the album, leafing through it until it lay open at '*Babes in the Wood*, Nottingham, nineteen sixty-eight.'

'Robin Hood again,' he remarked, 'and you looked a treat.'

'You say the nicest things. Have you a favourite pantomime?'

'Oh yes, Cinderella wins every time.'

'Twice as many legs in tights?'

'I'm only human, Jill. I've never been able to see the point in Prince Charming and Dandini swapping hats, but I'm happy for them to do anything they like, as long as they're on stage.'

She laughed. 'Fun for young and old alike. Do you want to see nineteen sixty-nine?'

'I can't get enough of it.' He slipped his arm round her shoulders to make his point.

A Baker's Round

'*Aladdin*, Blackpool, nineteen sixty-nine,' she announced.

'There's no doubt about it, Jill. You beat Widow Twanky hands-down for glamour.'

'I should hope so.' Laughing, she turned, and her forehead brushed his cheek.

'I'm new to the B and B way of life,' he said, 'so I'm unsure of the protocol.'

'What protocol is that?' It was clear that she knew what he meant.

'If a paying guest wants, very keenly, to kiss the landlady, does he put in a written request, or does he just ask her very casually if she has any objection?'

'The situation has never arisen, so I think his best plan would be to play it by ear.'

Taking her at her word, Jeff bent his head and let his lips touch hers, like strangers at first, touching gently and then becoming bolder as she responded. At one stage, he heard the photo album make contact with the floor. Thereafter, he was conscious of nothing but her scent, the eager questing of her lips and his own growing need.

After a while, she said, 'I'm not altogether keen on the idea of being a hostage to nature.'

Caught off-guard, he asked, 'In what sense?'

'It used to be called "Vatican roulette".'

'I don't blame you,' he told her. 'Don't worry, I have the means.'

'That's a relief. Will you give me a couple of minutes?'

'Take as many as you like.' He could afford to be generous.

'Three or four, anyway.' She slipped out of the room, and he heard one step creak as she climbed the stairs.

He undressed down to his shorts and, when five minutes had elapsed, carried his clothes up to his room.

He tapped on Jill's door and pushed it open. The room was lit by a bedside lamp, and he could see immediately that five minutes had not been enough, because she was sitting on the bed in her underclothes and hold-up stockings, which she was currently removing. To see those magnificent limbs properly for the first time was sheer self-indulgence, and he had to force himself to speak.

'I'm sorry, Jill,' he said, clearing his throat. 'I should have given you longer.'

'It's all right.' She finished undressing, draped her stockings and underwear over a chair and slid beneath the duvet. He cast his shorts aside and joined her.

'It's been a long time,' she said, taking him into her arms.

He lay still, savouring the silky feel of her body against his. It was a sensation that never lost its novelty.

'I really wanted this to happen,' she said. 'I just didn't want you to feel I was encouraging you.'

'I needed no encouragement,' he assured her, postponing further dialogue by kissing her on the lips and then behind and beneath her ear, aware all the time of her growing arousal. He turned his attention to her neck, kissing it repeatedly and lingering there for some time, and then he moved slowly downward to her shoulder. At this point, he felt her hands, one on each side of his face, lifting him gently, and he responded by kissing her again on the lips, slowly and deliberately.

His onward journey was gradual, via her chin, her throat, and finally, her breasts. He began with the cleft between them, straying after a while to its neighbours and their proud nipples, which he treated with equal consideration.

He continued downward, burying his face in her midriff and kissing it luxuriously, until he felt her hands again, urging him to return to her pillow, which he did, retracing his earlier route.

Again, they kissed urgently while he explored further, his hand stroking its way to her lower abdomen and beyond.

She moaned excitedly until, no longer able to contain her longing, she made room for him.

He followed her bidding, hesitating when she whispered an urgent question, and he answered, reassuring her that he'd taken the necessary precaution.

After a while, he became conscious of her long legs wrapped around him and, all at once, he was a prisoner of Dick Whittington, Jack Trott, Prince Charming, Dandini and Robin Hood among others. It was a pantomime he'd never known, and it was just as magical as those he had.

A Baker's Round

He slept soundly, because the next he knew, he was being shaken gently. 'I'm dreaming,' he said. 'I've just woken up, and I can smell tea. I hope I'm not going to wake up properly just yet. At least, not until I've actually tasted it.'

'It's real enough,' Jill told him, removing her bathrobe and climbing in beside him. 'I thought I was dreaming, too, when I woke up, but there you were, next to me.' She bent and kissed him. 'Just think of it,' she said playfully. 'Last night, I experienced what must have been a hopeless fantasy for many young girls.'

'Steady on, Jill. I appreciate an endorsement as much as the next man, but let's not get carried away. I'm quite human, really.'

'I was talking about sex with Jeff Mort of Tantum Deliciae.'

'Somnium, actually.'

'Let me remember it my way, Jeff. It was *deliciae* from beginning to end.'

It was too much to cope with first thing in the morning. 'Excuse me for a minute,' he said, pulling the duvet back. 'I'm going to look in the mirror, and I bet you anything you like, the image I'll see will be plain, old Jeffrey Mortimer, as ordinary as they come.' He went to the bathroom and, having relieved himself, rinsed his mouth with some of Jill's mouthwash, which he replaced on the shelf, as before.

'I pinched some of your mouthwash,' he told her, climbing in beside her again.

'You fiend,' she said, kissing him. 'Giants, wolves and king rats have been slain for less.' Gesturing towards the tray, she asked, 'More tea?'

'No thanks, it doesn't mix at all well with mouthwash.' He settled down beside her and said, 'Last night, you mentioned gambling with nature. Did you really think I'd put you at risk?'

'No, I was talking about relying on the menopause. I started early, about three years ago, but it's no safer than Vatican roulette.'

He was beginning to see a fuller picture, now. 'This preoccupation of yours with ageing,' he said, 'must have something to do with the menopause.'

'It's an important signpost,' she agreed, 'but if you were to leave tomorrow, which I hope you won't even consider, you'd still have made a huge difference to me.'

'Have I convinced you that you're a very attractive and desirable woman with a tremendous figure as well as legs that go on for ever?'

'More or less,' she laughed.

'And that looking at pictures of yourself at twenty, and comparing them with the way you see yourself now, is unrealistic as well as pointless and unhelpful?'

'Yes.'

'I've done little enough for you, Jill. Anyone could have done that.'

'Oh no, they couldn't.'

'Oh yes, they could.'

Like everything that had taken place since his arrival, their descent into pantomime was inevitable.

17

Celebrity and a Little Coaching

Life with Jill over the next few weeks was blissful, and Jeff was tempted very strongly to extend his stay, but they both knew that their future together was limited, and so the time eventually came for him to move on.

He felt both guilt and loss as he drove away. The loss was real enough, but he realised after a while that he wasn't at fault, and that Jill's tears had been inevitable. In time, he remembered, also, how he'd helped her improve her perception of herself, and that was vitally important.

Those were his thoughts as he set out for his next stop, which was to be Buxton in Derbyshire. For a reason he couldn't identify, stranger that he was to self-examination, he was keen to try Buxton Pudding.

By some happy accident, he found the A1M without difficulty, and even managed to join the northbound carriageway, thus avoiding early annoyance and the need to retrace his course.

Thereafter, the journey became an ordeal by signpost. He negotiated, renegotiated, avoided and re-encountered the B6387, the A616, the A632, he A617 and the A619, and it was at this point he realised he was within a very short distance of Bakewell, a town of recent memory. Had he considered Buxton Pudding when he was in Bakewell, the journey would have been a mere nothing, but that called for planning, and he was a creature of impulse.

Braving the A6020 and the A6, he eventually found himself in Buxton, where, emerging gratefully from his driving seat, he went in search of accommodation.

After such a journey, even a modest stroke of luck was welcome, and it came in the shape of a guest house with vacancies, the first on his list, and on a Friday evening, too. Sighing with relief, he rang the doorbell.

The woman who opened the door was dark-haired, statuesque, severe and instantly forbidding, although Jeff didn't see that necessarily as a disadvantage. For one thing, it would enable him to keep at least one, and possibly both, of his resolutions.

'Can I help you?'

'Yes, please. I'm looking for a single room, just for two or maybe three nights.'

'I'm afraid the single rooms are taken. I have just two doubles left.'

It surprised him that she was afraid of anything. 'Look,' he said, 'if it's all the same to you, I'm quite happy to take a double room. I've had a long and trying journey and, frankly, I could sleep in a dog kennel, although a bedroom would be more inviting.'

'A double room is twenty-eight pounds per night.'

'You're talking to an exhausted man. Twenty-eight pounds is more than acceptable.'

'Very well. Have you any luggage?' She looked around him as she spoke.

'It's in my car.'

'The carpark is to the rear of the house. Anyway, you'd better come inside.'

She opened the register, which lay on the hallstand, and said, 'I have to ask you to enter your name, address and telephone number, if you have one, and sign your name at the end, there.'

'I have a name and a signature,' he told her, taking out his pen, 'but I have no permanent address and therefore no telephone number.' The news of the completed sale had reached him during his stay with Jill.

'Oh?'

'I've sold my London flat and I've yet to find somewhere to live.' Taking in her stony expression, he said, 'Look, I'm quite prepared to pay for two nights in advance. It's unlikely that I'll be around much longer than that, anyway.'

'Oh, that won't be necessary.' Reaching behind her, she took down a key and handed it to him. 'You're in Room Four on the first floor.

A Baker's Round

The smaller key on the ring is for the front door. All I ask is that if you come in late, you do so quietly. Breakfast is served in the dining room between seven and nine-thirty. Dinner is also served there from six-thirty pm, although you arrived too late to reserve a table.'

'Don't worry, I'll find something.'

'Good. I'm Mrs Fuller, by the way.'

'Jeffrey Mortimer.' He shook her hand, surprised that any man could have survived a relationship with her. If he were still around, Mr Fuller was evidently a force to be reckoned with. 'I'll fetch my car and luggage,' he said.

He'd parked the car behind the house, and had only just opened the door to his room when Mrs Fuller called to him from the top of the stairs.

'Mr Mortimer, I'm sorry to disturb you. Can you spare a moment?' Her manner was completely at odds with her earlier attitude, and Jeff could only conclude that she wanted a favour, although he couldn't imagine how he could possibly help her.

'By all means.' He put down his grip and waited to hear what she had to say.

'I'm sure this is very tiresome for you, but we have another late arrival, a couple wanting a double room, but they're particularly keen to have one with a double bed, and the only room available has twin beds.'

Jeff struggled not to laugh. There were occasions when his amorous ambitions had suffered a minor hiccup because a double bed wasn't available, but he'd made the best of things, maintaining that it was a poor workman that blamed his tools.

'I wonder if you would be prepared to take the twin-bedded room and let them have yours. I'd only charge you for a single, of course.'

'In that case, Mrs Fuller, how could I refuse? Where is the twin-bedded room?'

'At the end of this landing,' she told him, pointing in the general direction. 'Thank you, Mr Mortimer. I'm very grateful.'

'Not at all.' He gave her the key and carried his grip to the double room at the end of the landing.

Having deposited his luggage, he locked the door and left the room with the intention of finding a pub where he could get a meal. As he reached the stairs, however, Mrs Fuller reappeared with a middle-aged man and a young woman, whose appearance, had Jeff been more judgemental than he was, he might have described as bimboesque. He naturally stood back to let them reach the top of the stairs, and Mrs Fuller opened her mouth, presumably to introduce them so that they could thank Jeff, when the young woman gave an excited squeal and said, 'You're Jeff Mort! You *are* Jeff Mort, aren't you?' Mrs Fuller remained open-mouthed, and the middle-aged man followed her example.

'Yes, I am.' The ease with which the young woman had penetrated his disguise demonstrated very clearly that his glasses afforded little cover, and that he was overdue for a haircut. 'I am,' he confirmed, 'I admit it and I'm happy to swap rooms with you, as requested.'

'I can't believe it! Excitedly, she swept back her blonde hair, revealing her dark roots. 'When Tantum Somnium split up, I thought I'd never see you again! This is too fantastic!'

'I'm not in the music business now…. I'm sorry. What's your name?'

'Lauren.'

'Right, Lauren, when the band split up, that was me for good. I have nothing to do with the industry now.'

She stared at him rather like a child that's been told the unpalatable truth about Santa Claus. 'No, Jeff,' she said, almost on the point of tears, 'you can't say that.'

'I'm sorry, Lauren, it's the truth.'

'No!' It was evident that Lauren had never been taught to cope with disappointment, because she clung to him, saying, 'No, you can't do that! Everybody says you're going to start up another band. We're all waiting for the news.'

'Well, I'm afraid they're wrong.' He was aware that the middle-aged man was looking more irritated by the minute, so he said, 'Listen, Lauren, your….' He'd no idea what label to give her companion; Lauren wasn't wearing a ring, and he didn't believe in fairies, anyway, so he said, 'You're supposed to be inspecting the lovely room I've just vacated for you.'

Slowly, she released him and, looking at him through a frame of diluted mascara, said, 'I'll never believe in anything, ever again.'

'I'm sorry, Lauren.'

A Baker's Round

She looked at him with such longing, he feared for one embarrassing moment that she was going to kiss him, but she turned away to join the now openly angry man with whom she was going to share the room.

As their door closed, Jeff said, 'That was unfortunate, Mrs Fuller.'

'Never mind. It wasn't your fault.'

Lauren's angry voice came clearly from inside the room. She was saying, 'Stop bossing me around, Robert! We're not at the office now!'

'Oh dear,' said Mrs Fuller, 'I didn't realise that was the situation.'

Jeff couldn't help wondering what she had thought when a man in his fifties arrived with a woman of barely twenty.

'Will you come downstairs and have a drink?'

'In normal circumstances, Mrs Fuller, I'd be pleased to, but I really must find somewhere to eat.'

'The staff haven't eaten yet, and neither have I. There'll be plenty, if you'd like to eat here. You could join me in the dining room.'

He wondered a little at the difference in her manner since his arrival, but he simply said, 'Thank you, Mrs Fuller. That's very accommodating of you.'

As they went downstairs, he said, 'I got your address from the tourist office, but I didn't realise you did half-board.'

'Yes, we don't offer lunch, because guests are usually out and about at lunchtime, and they make their own arrangements.' She led him into the sitting room, where a few guests were being served with drinks by the waitress. 'What would you like, Mr.... That young woman called you "Mort", didn't she?'

'That was my stage name. My agent thought that "Mortimer" was a shade too respectable. I'd like a dry sherry, please.'

'I'll join you with that. Two dry sherries, please, Joanne.'

'Right you are, Mrs Fuller.'

The drinks arrived, and Mrs Fuller said, 'Shall we go to the dining room?'

They found the room empty, so they took the first table they came to.

'At the risk of being impertinent,' said Mrs Fuller, 'I have to say that I would never have expected a pop music star to be quite like you, Mr Mortimer, or to ask for dry sherry.'

'I'm not exactly typical of the species, Mrs Fuller. I entered the business almost by accident, but I left it very deliberately.' He gave her an abbreviated version of the story he'd told so many times, and described his haphazard route through the British countryside.

'And Buxton is the latest stage in your odyssey?'

The waitress who'd previously served them with drinks came to their table and took their order. Mrs Fuller asked Jeff, 'Is a red Bordeaux acceptable?'

'More than acceptable.'

'And a bottle of the house red, Joanne.'

'Certainly, Mrs Fuller.'

Picking up the conversation again, Jeff said, 'That's right. My journey so far has taken me from one regional speciality to the next, so I came to Buxton with a view to trying Buxton Pudding. I should explain that I was a baker before I stumbled into pop music.'

'That makes you even more fascinating, and by the way, will you call me Jane?'

'By all means. I prefer to be called Jeff, anyway.'

'I must confess, we haven't offered Buxton Pudding here for as long as I remember, and it's certainly not going to happen soon, as we're between pastry cooks.'

'That's a shame. I'd rather like to have a shot at making it. I have a recipe, but I've never tried it.'

'My word, you are keen.'

He was. 'Jane,' he said, 'if I buy the ingredients, would you let me use your kitchen, just for as long as it takes to satisfy my curiosity?'

'Of course, and don't worry about the ingredients. If you make enough, we'll put it on the "Specials" board.'

'Thank you, but there's just one thing. It calls for stale white bread, not sourdough or anything fancy, just the stuff you'd toast for breakfast.'

'As breakfast cook, I can probably manage that, but I'll have to go down to the kitchen and look at the bread situation. We only use fresh bread from the bakery.'

'Right, so it'll go stale fairly quickly.'

'Yes. How much bread do you need?'

He thought. 'About eight ounces, two hundred grams.'

'Right,' she said, standing up, 'I'll go down now, before Joanne brings our order.'

A Baker's Round

She was gone only for a few minutes. When she returned, she said, 'I've left a large loaf out overnight.'

Jane turned out to be an excellent breakfast cook, as Jeff was quick to assure her. She was now quite friendly, and he realised that she was basically shy until she was over the initial meeting. It was easy, he reflected, to confuse shyness with aloofness, and he smiled to himself when he compared Jane's reserve with Lauren's impassioned outpouring of the previous evening.

Jane came down to the kitchen as he was laying out the ingredients. She asked, 'Have you everything you need?'

'I don't know. To keep the portions manageable, I need a couple of eight-inch tart tins. Seven-inch would do. I just want to avoid using a large quiche or flan dish.'

Jane opened a large cupboard and took out two eight-inch, loose-bottomed tins. 'Are these all right?'

'Thank you, they're perfect. I think I can find everything else.'

'I'll help you, if you like.'

'All right, will you run half a glass of water and fill up the rest of the glass with ice? Then you can start weighing out the ingredients for the pastry. Put them into separate containers.' He looked at his recipe. 'Three hundred grams of plain flour.'

She busied herself with the scale, weighing out the flour. 'Done.'

'Sixty grams of caster sugar. You can leave the butter in the fridge for now.' He watched her weigh out the sugar, and asked, 'Do you know how to separate an egg yolk?'

'I'm not very good at it,' she admitted.

'In that case, it's time to learn how. Take a clean bowl and crack an egg into your hand.' He watched her. 'Now, let the white run slowly through your fingers.' He picked up another bowl and said, 'Chuck the yolk into there. Easy, wasn't it?'

'I've only seen it done on television, passing the yolk and the white between two halves of the shell.'

'That's just showing off. Right, you can do another one.'

'Just like that?'

'You've proved to yourself you can do it.' He left her to do that while he re-checked his recipe.

'Done.'

'Good girl, well done. Will you get me the chilled water and a hundred-and-fifty grams of butter? If you do that, I'll make the pastry while you weigh the rest of the ingredients.' He pushed the recipe across to her and got on with the pastry, mixing the flour and sugar with a pinch of salt, and then rubbing in the butter until the mixture was at the desired consistency. He added the egg yolks and two tablespoons of iced water, mixing the dough with a knife. Next, he floured the table and tipped the dough on to it, kneading it for about half a minute.

Jane asked, 'Aren't you going to knead it more than that?'

'No, if you overdo the kneading, the gluten in the flour spoils the consistency.' Looking around, he asked, 'Have you any clingfilm?'

'We should have.' She looked around and said, 'Silly me. There it is, on the wall.'

He wrapped the dough and put it in the refrigerator to chill. Then he put a flat baking sheet in the oven and set the gas at Mark 4.

Jane asked, 'What do I do with the bread?'

'Tear it into pieces and blitz it until it turns to crumbs, and then leave it to continue drying. He looked at the rest of the ingredients and said, 'Good girl.' A second later, he winced and said, 'I'm sorry. It's a very bad habit.'

'Not at my age. I take it as a compliment.' Looking at the recipe again, she asked, 'What's next?'

'We have a cup of coffee while the pastry chills and the oven comes up to temperature. Have you anything for blind baking? Beans, or anything like that?'

'I remember buying some ceramic beans, some time ago.' She tried several cupboards before finding them.

'Good girl, thank you.' He rolled the pastry out to the required thickness.

'There's something special about seeing a man use a rolling pin,' said Jane, filling the kettle for coffee.

'You just like to see us do all the hard work.' He lined the tin with pastry and, taking a sheet of parchment, filled the recess with ceramic

A Baker's Round

beans. Finally, he opened the oven and placed the tin on the baking sheet. As a possible hitch occurred to him, he asked, 'Have you anybody staying here who's gluten intolerant?'

'No.' She was definite about that.

'Good, but it's worth noting that you can make this thing with gluten-free flour.'

'You think of everything. I'd have simply offered an alternative,' she said, passing him a cup of coffee.

'Thanks. You know what to do with the rest, don't you?'

She checked. 'Spread the jam over the bottom, beat the butter, beat in the eggs and sugar, fold the breadcrumbs in and spread the topping over everything.'

He nodded approvingly. 'You've got the idea.'

'Only because you gave me the confidence.'

'You had the ability to do these things, Jane. All I did was to put you on the spot, and suddenly you found the confidence.'

'Most professionals don't take the trouble to explain things. They just get on with them because it's quicker that way.'

'That's not my way. I'll tell you what. If I hang around for a few days, I'll be able to show you how to make quite a few things, and then you needn't be in such a hurry to find a pastry cook.'

'If you're happy to do that, I'm more than ready.'

'Okay, let's take out the pastry, and we'll turn the gas down a bit, shall we?'

18

A Coping Strategy

Over the next two weeks, Jeff taught Jane to make a variety of puddings, suggesting that she might even stop looking for a pastry chef, and do the job herself. She was only sorry that he would no longer be available, but he explained to her that he was looking for more than a part-time position, and she understood.

When they parted, she was almost tearful, and they hugged in a way he could never have envisaged on his arrival. Finally, he kissed her on the cheek and took his leave of her, taking with him her good wishes and the satisfaction of knowing that, yet again, he'd been able to keep one of his resolutions.

As he drove away, he thought idly of Lauren and her employer. He hoped for her sake that the double bed had been a success. After the devastation of learning that Jeff Mort would never ride again, she needed some kind of consolation. She also needed to learn that life did have a tendency to bounce up and down, and not just in the carnal sense.

He had to concentrate and stay on the A53 until he reached the A6, signposted to Manchester and other exotic places. He was bound for Eccles in Greater Manchester, to track the celebrated Eccles cake to its town of origin. He remembered comparing it with the Banbury cake, and resolved to avoid disagreement wherever possible, although he was uncomfortably aware that two resolutions had been hard enough to keep. A third would present an added problem, and to keep all three might prove impossible.

According to the AA, the journey would take about an hour,

A Baker's Round

although, allowing for wrong turnings and corrections, he reckoned at least two hours. It was usually better to expect the worst and, when he read the sign for the M60, Ring Road (W)/Liverpool/M62 etc, he battled with rising panic, but he finally found himself on the A57, and the sign told him he was on the way to Eccles. There was calm, as usual, after the storm.

He had a full list of B and Bs, which was as well, because he was down to number five before he found one that had vacancies. It was a three-storey house built probably in the early part of the century.

The landlady was an attractive red-head with a friendly smile, an ample bosom and a wedding ring. The description 'motherly' sprang readily to mind, and it seemed that one resolution wouldn't be too hard to keep.

'Hello,' he said, 'I'm looking for a single room. It'll be for a few days, or maybe a week. I'm afraid I can't be more definite than that.'

'That's all right, chook. Easy come, easy go. Come in, anyway.' She opened the door fully and stood aside in invitation.

He stepped into the hallway that was bright and clean. As ever, brilliant white paintwork was very much in evidence.

'A single room with breakfast is nine-fifty, and I serve breakfast from seven 'til nine-thirty. I'll give you a key for t' front door. All I ask is that you try not to wake the kids up when you come in. It's hard enough getting 'em to go to bed in t' first place.' She smiled broadly and said, 'Still, we've all got our problems, haven't we?'

'We have.' He wasn't sure that he had a problem, other than in finding a solution to his quest, but she was nice, and it felt natural to agree with her.

'Come upstairs and I'll show you the room. Have you got luggage with you?'

'It's outside, in the car.'

'You can park round t' back. Where everybody else has a garden, we use it for parking.'

He followed her upstairs, where she showed him a small, but well-appointed single room. 'There's a couple of chaps here until tomorrow morning, and I'm on the second floor with the kids,' she said, but it should be quite peaceful for you.' Possibly to clarify the situation, she said, 'My husband's in the Army, but he's not likely to be home much before Christmas.'

'That'll make Christmas special for you and the children, I expect.'

'It will,' she agreed. 'Anyway, let's go downstairs, and you can sign t' register. I'm Helen Crawshaw, by the way.'

'Jeff Mortimer.'

She stopped and stared for several seconds. 'I knew I recognised you. You're Jeff Mort, aren't you?'

'I'm afraid so.'

'There's nowt to be ashamed of. Far from it.' She continued down the stairs. 'If you don't mind me askin', why did t' band split up?'

'Two of the members joined a new Heavy Metal band, and the other didn't care what was happening. He probably wonders occasionally why Tantum Somnium haven't had any gigs on Mars recently.'

'I still can't believe it. You know, Jeff— You don't mind me callin' you that, do you? You can call me Helen, by the way.'

'There's no problem there.'

'I was going to say, you're not what I expected, really. If you don't mind me sayin' so, you seem a bit posh for a rock star.'

'Far too posh,' he agreed, 'but I'm not a rock star now.'

'Aren't you? What are you doing now, then?'

'Let me sign the register, and then I'll explain everything.'

'Right,' she said, taking him to an open book in the hallway, 'just print your name, address and phone number, and sign at the end of the line.'

He took out his pen, saying, 'I've no permanent address or phone number. I've just sold my flat in London.'

'That's all right. It's only so that I can send on anything you might leave behind....' She broke off to say, 'That's a posh pen.'

He laughed. 'Well, I'm a posh bloke, as you said.'

'What sort of brew do you fancy? Tea or coffee? I'll make one, an' then we can have a chat.'

He consulted his watch. It was almost two forty-five. He said, 'At this time of the day, tea will be very welcome.'

'Right.' She pointed to the sitting room. 'Sit yourself down and I'll see to it.'

Jeff took a seat in a leather armchair and looked around him.

A Baker's Round

There were two framed crests on the chimney breast. One was of the Lancashire Fusiliers, and the other, the Royal Regiment of Fusiliers, which, presumably, included the original regiment. Mr Crawshaw evidently took his Army service seriously, quite rightly, too. Other pictures were of various Lancashire scenes, which meant little to him as this was his first visit to the county.

He was studying one of them, a print of a place called Pendle Hill, when Helen arrived with the tea.

'I see you're making yourself at home,' she said. 'That's good.' She poured the tea and said, 'I'll leave you to help yourself to sugar.'

'I don't have sugar, thank you.' He took the tea gratefully.

Helen shook her head in lasting disbelief. 'I still can't get over it,' she said. 'You were going to tell me what you're doing now.'

'The short answer to that is that I'm doing nothing, at least, nothing in the way of work.' He told her how he'd put his flat up for sale and taken to the road in search of a new life.

'You're just like Dick Whittington an' all that lot,' she remarked, 'goin' off to seek your fortune.'

'I'm not a bit like Dick Whittington, Helen. You really wouldn't want to see me in tights.' Memories of Jill came to him, bringing with them a pang of guilt, but he dismissed them as Helen spoke again.

'The kids'll be home soon,' she said. 'They give 'em a shorter lunchbreak, now, and send 'em home at half-past three.'

'How old are they?'

'Daniel's nine and five months, and Amanda's seven and five months. It's all to do with the main leave period, you see.'

'It makes sense,' he said, a little surprised by her frankness.

'Well, it's only to be expected, really. They live like monks while they're with the regiment. At least, I hope they do.' She appeared to reflect for a few seconds before saying, 'Steve's very steady, really.'

'I'm sure.' To change the subject as much as for any other reason, he asked, 'Is there a gymnasium near here?'

'There's more than one, but I can recommend Worsley Leisure Centre. Steve uses it when he's on leave.'

'Thank you. I'll give it a try.'

'He has to keep active, you see.'

'Evidently,' said Jeff, thinking of the leave periods.

There was the sound of a door to the rear of the house being opened and then closed noisily, and Helen said, 'That'll be the kids.' Running footsteps in the passageway seemed to confirm that deduction. A moment later, both children appeared at the sitting room door.

'Come in, you two,' said Helen. 'This is Mr Mortimer. Do you remember Jeff Mort who was with Tantum Sonum?'

Jeff let it go. Helen wasn't the only fan who'd struggled with the band's name.

Daniel was staring at Jeff as a naturalist might view a particularly rare species.

'I'm afraid I don't do that now,' said Jeff.

Amanda seemed unmoved by the revelation. It was more than likely, considering her age, that she'd never heard of him.

Helen asked, 'What homework have you got, Daniel?'

He tore his eyes away from Jeff to answer. 'English,' he said, 'p-p-punctuation.'

'Well, you're all right at that, aren't you?'

'A b-bit.'

'I wish I had homework,' said Amanda.

Daniel's look suggested that she would be welcome to his share.

'I expect you're good at punctuation an' that, aren't you, Jeff?' It seemed that being posh carried responsibilities, and Jeff expected to be given the job of helping Daniel with his homework.

'I can't say I've ever struggled with it.' There were times when it was mistake to sound too confident.

'Show Jeff your homework, Daniel.'

Daniel looked unsurely at him, perhaps waiting for confirmation.

'Yes,' said Jeff, 'let's have a look at it.'

Daniel opened a sport bag that was far too big for him, but which carried the logo for street cred., and took out a duplicated sheet.

'Right, so you have to re-write this passage with proper punctuation. Where do you have to write it?'

'In m-my b-b-book.' He delved into the bag again and produced a dog-eared exercise book.

Jeff looked at the passage. It read:

A Baker's Round

marie asked what on earth do you think youre doing im making a boat to sail on the pond that thing will never float it will insisted matthew

It went on, but Jeff decided to tackle a little at a time. 'How do we know when there's a new paragraph?'

Daniel stared at the passage and said, 'Th-there's a s-space.'

'Good lad, we start a paragraph with an indent, and then what should every sentence begin with?'

'A c-c-capital l-letter.'

'Good. Marie is asking a question. What comes after "asked"?'

Daniel thought hard and said, 'A c-c-comma.'

'Good lad, you can make a start, now.' He watched the boy kneel down and write in his book, using the coffee table.

Jeff took him through the rest of the passage and, when he was finished, Helen said, 'Say "thank you" to Jeff for helping you, Daniel.'

'Th-thank you.'

'You're welcome.'

'Right, you can both go upstairs and watch the telly, now,' said Helen.

When they were out of the room, she said, 'They both miss their dad when he goes away. In fact, it's the only time Daniel stammers.'

'Is it?'

'Yes, as soon as he comes home on leave, the stammering stops.'

'Poor lad.'

'Amanda, too, only she doesn't show it as much, but they both get the blues when he's away.'

Jeff was thinking. So much was obvious to Helen, who asked, 'What's on your mind, Jeff?'

'I was thinking about the children.'

'What about the children?'

'About them missing their dad so much.'

Helen shrugged. 'The only cure for that is for him to be here, but that's impossible. If it comes to that, I miss him, too, but we've got to be realistic. Steve's got another three years to do, and that's unless he signs on for more.'

'Agreed. What I'm saying is that the children need to adopt a coping strategy.'

Helen stared at him. 'What's a coping whatsit, when it's at home?'

'A coping strategy? It's a special way of coping with a problem. You see, what the children need is a distraction from missing their dad. He'll be at the back of their minds for much of the time, but when they're missing him most of all, they'll have something to do, something else to think about. Do you see what I mean?'

Clearly, she was unconvinced. 'I get the drift, yes, but where's this special thing going to come from?'

'Before I answer that, is anyone in your family gluten intolerant?'

'No, why?'

'Because the special thing will come from your kitchen. In fact, it's going to happen there. If I buy some ingredients, will you let me use your kitchen when you're not using it?'

''Course I will, but what can you do in a kitchen? You're a fella, when all's said an' done.'

That was true, but Jeff knew something she didn't.

19

If You're Feeling Low, Get Baking!

That Saturday afternoon, Jeff, Helen and the children gathered in the kitchen. Only Jeff knew what they were going to do.

'We're going to make Eccles cakes,' he told them, 'and I'm going to get you all involved.'

A note of dissent came from Daniel, who said, 'G-g-girls d-do c-c-c-cooking.'

'This is baking, not cooking, and it's not restricted to girls, Daniel. I made my living as a baker before I went into the music industry, so pay attention.' Indicating the ingredients on the table, he said, 'The only thing that's missing, here, is pastry, and that's because it's in the fridge, chilling. Now, I really enjoy making pastry, but you two are just starting out as bakers, so we're using ready-made pastry from the supermarket, and in this case, it's flaky pastry. At a pinch, you could use puff pastry, but if you use short pastry, you'll get a surprise, because you'll pull your baking out of the oven and find you've got Chorley cakes instead of Eccles cakes. Got that? Right, let's get started. What's the first job?'

They looked at him blankly.

'I'll tell you. The first job is always for Mum and Amanda to tie up their hair. Use a cruncher, if you have one.'

'A *scrunchie*,' Amanda told him.

'You can use one of them. I don't care what you use, as long as your hair's out of the way.' With the necessary adjustment made, he went on. 'The second thing is for everybody to wash their hands. Hygiene is everything. On your marks, get set, scrub!'

When their hands were clean, he took them through the rolling out of the pastry, which he then divided into eight squares. Next, he supervised the mixing of the filling and had them share it between the squares of pastry, now on a baking tray.

He turned the oven on at 200 Celsius. 'Now for the clever bit. Wet your fingers with water and take two opposite corners of the pastry, like this.' He demonstrated how to join them in the middle. Daniel's first attempt went awry, so he helped him repair it.

'If the filling spills out,' he told them, shove it back inside, and then dry your hands, flour them, and press all the edges together.' He watched them, helping whenever necessary. 'You as well, Mum,' he said. 'I shan't always be here.' Satisfied that all was well, he said, 'Turn them over, so that the bits you've stuck together are underneath. Now, with floury hands again, make a proper circle. What do you notice about the top, Daniel?'

'It's bulging out.'

'That's right, so we press very gently, because we don't want the filling to come squirting out, do we?'

'No.'

He broke an egg into a bowl and handed it to Amanda with a fork. 'Whisk that, Amanda,' he said. When she'd finished, he asked, 'What shall we use to coat them with egg, Daniel?'

'I don't know.'

'Come on, it's easy. We're going to paint the tops with egg, so what do we use?'

'A brush.'

'Good lad.' He risked a quick look at Helen, who was clearly taken aback, not so much by Daniel's reply, but by the absence of a stammer.

When each cake was coated with egg, he showed them how to sprinkle sugar over them. 'Good,' he said. 'How's the oven?' It was up to temperature, so he put the tray in the middle of the oven and set the timer for twelve minutes. 'We'll have a look at them then, and see if they need longer. How was that, Amanda?'

'Great.'

'How was it for you, Daniel?'

'Great.'

'Mum?'

A Baker's Round

'Fantastic. Thank you, Jeff.'

'You're welcome. Now, I also bought some Lancashire Tasty cheese, which we can have with the Eccles cakes when they've cooled.

As if on cue, Daniel said with genuine enthusiasm, 'Brilliant.' It rather summed up the exercise for Jeff.

Later, when the children had gone to bed, Helen said, 'I couldn't believe it when Daniel spoke without stammering.'

'He'll stammer again, but not when he's baking. It'll take so much of his concentration, he'll forget about missing his dad until later, when he's not concentrating on anything in particular. Even so, baking could still be a life-changer for them both. I'm going to leave the recipes that we use with you, so that you'll be able to give the children and yourself some baking therapy whenever you need it.'

'But how did you think of it?'

'It's the only thing I know, apart from writing naff songs, of course, and taking people for a ride. Seriously, though, you must have been into a proper bakery at some time, rather than a supermarket.'

'Yes, I have.' She thought for a moment. 'It were a while ago,' she admitted.

'Can you remember the mood of the other shoppers?'

'You're joking. It must have been... two years ago.'

'Were they miserable and complaining?'

'No.' She thought again. 'They were happy enough. I do remember that.'

'Well, there's your answer. Baking makes people happy. Buying meat and groceries makes them concentrate on how much it's all costing, and that's a recipe for misery, but just the smell of freshly-baked bread puts heart into people, and suddenly, the world's a happier place.'

'So is this house, Jeff, thanks to you. Have you thought what you're going to teach us next?'

'Oh yes, but you'll have to let it be a surprise.'

With October half-term poised to begin, Jeff had to think about recipes. To fill the children with sugar and carbohydrates would do them no good at all. The emphasis had to be on fun without fats or, at least, with minimal fat, so the first recipe he chose was for low-fat biscuits. The ingredients were plain flour, baking powder, baking soda, salt, and the all-important non-fat yoghurt.

With hair tied up and hands washed and dried, Helen and the children assembled round the kitchen table.

'With this recipe,' he said, 'we use both baking powder and baking soda. I'd gladly tell you why, but I don't think you'd be very interested. Amanda, will you switch the oven on at two hundred and twenty, please?' He watched out of the corner of his eye and, satisfied that she'd done it properly, went on to the mixing stage. 'Daniel, will you weigh out four hundred milligrams of plain flour, and Amanda, get ready with the baking powder?' He checked Daniel's flour, which was on the heavy side, so he spooned some back until the scale stood at four hundred. 'Now, Amanda, a tablespoonful of baking powder.' He gave her the measure. 'And then half a teaspoonful of bicarb and half a teaspoonful of salt.' Now, one of you can stir it all up until everything is mixed. 'Mum, I haven't forgotten you. Will you measure three hundred millilitres of yoghurt and add it gently to the mixture?'

When the mixture was ready, he floured the surface of the table and spread the dough until it was about twenty millimetres thick. 'I bought two two-inch cutters, and I'm going to show Amanda and Daniel how to cut these things, starting carefully at the edge.'

'I must pay you for the equipment and ingredients, Jeff,' said Helen.

'Fiddlesticks, as my old grandmother used to say. The cost is nothing beside the satisfaction of doing the job.' He picked up a can of cooking spray and coated a flat baking tray. 'I use this stuff,' he said, 'because it's very low in fat and because it's not as messy as butter.' He showed the children how to pick up the circles of dough with a palette knife and place them on the baking sheet. 'Whatever you make,' he told

A Baker's Round

them, 'get your mum to put it in the oven and take it out again when it's done. That's very important.'

'Why?' Daniel had an enquiring mind.

'Have you ever burned yourself, Daniel?'

'Yes, on the iron.' Again, it was noticeable that there was no trace of a stammer.

'It wasn't nice, was it?'

'No.'

'Well, ovens can be spiteful as well. I can tell you that from experience.' He showed them a scar above his wrist. 'This was worse than an iron burn,' he told them, placing the tray in the oven and setting the timer for twelve minutes. 'We'll have a look then and see if they need any longer.'

Amanda asked, 'Does everything take twelve minutes?'

'I'm afraid not. Christmas cakes take at least four hours.'

'That's a long time.'

'They're worth waiting for,' he assured her.

By the end of half-term, the children had an impressive collection of recipes, which Helen kept in a folder.

'They're going to be heartbroken when you go,' she said. They were in the sitting room. The children had gone to bed.

'And the whole idea was to make them happier. I'll tell you what, I'll stay a while longer, just until they can start looking forward to their dad coming home.' It wouldn't help him in his quest, but he reasoned that the happiness of two children was worth a break of a few weeks. In any case, he hadn't had much luck with his quest so far.

'I don't want you to go out of your way, Jeff.'

'Don't worry, I can hang on for a while longer. They'll be happy enough when their dad's due to arrive, they'll be blissful when he comes, and then I'll be forgotten.'

'Not forgotten, Jeff, no. That will never happen.' She was quite emphatic.

'Well, let's say, not as important. When their dad goes back to his regiment, you'll be able to bake with them. You could even do some cooking. That would keep them occupied.'

'Except that I'm not brilliant at cooking.'

'All the more reason why I should stay a bit longer, wouldn't you say?'

Reluctant to leave Daniel and Amanda unsupported, and disheartened by his lack of success in finding a new livelihood, Jeff stayed for the next six weeks, concerning himself with the children's welfare and taking no interest in outside matters. When he came into the house on the evening of the 22nd of November, and Helen told him that Margaret Thatcher was standing down as Leader of the Conservative Party, and therefore as Prime Minister, he was only mildly surprised.

Helen asked, 'What's to do, Jeff? Something's on your mind. Everybody else in this country's either rejoicin' or goin' into mournin', an' you act as though you couldn't care less either way.'

'I'm sorry, Helen, and you're right. I have something on my mind. I'm very conscious that I've been on the road since April this year, and I've been tempted just twice to stay and make some kind of future. Otherwise, I've found nothing.'

'Tell me about those two places.' As she settled comfortably to listen, it occurred to Jeff that she must have been a rewarding child at story-time, last thing at night.

'The first was in Wales, where I stayed at a bakery.'

'Just right for you, then.'

'Yes, the baker was an elderly chap with back problems, so I helped him with the bread-baking at a busy time. It was a lovely, friendly place, and I was tempted to make the baker and his wife an offer for the bakery.'

'You can't be short of a bob or two, then.'

He smiled at her turn of phrase. 'You could put it that way. What I got for my flat in London would have bought that bakery and the house four times over.'

'So why didn't you?'

A Baker's Round

'I found out that they had a son. He'd gone into the motor trade, but he was likely to be their sole beneficiary, and his father had trained him in bakery, so I thought again. In that kind of community, businesses are best passed down from father to son. Continuation is very important to such people.'

'If he was in the car trade, he might not have been interested in baking.'

'You're right, Helen.' Smiling at her concern for his welfare, he said, 'Even so, it was for him to decide.'

'Oh.' Then, remembering that there'd been two occasions, she asked, 'What about the other place?'

'That was in Stilton, in Cambridgeshire. I thought of looking for work thereabouts, but I'd have been on a hiding to nothing. It's an agricultural area, and there'd be very few openings. I looked out for businesses for sale, but there was nothing in the bakery line.'

'In that case, what was it about Stilton that attracted you?'

'The landlady.'

'You're jokin'.'

'No, I'm not. She was lovely, an ex-theatrical. She'd been principal boy in lots of pantomimes.'

'Oh, aye. Nice-lookin' an' with spectacular legs, I imagine.'

'Yes, but she was a lovely person as well.'

'Did you get off with her?'

He smiled again at the colloquial expression. 'Yes, I got off with her.' To avoid misunderstanding, he said, 'She was a single woman, so it was perfectly above board.'

She adopted a wistful look and said, 'I do like to hear about people finding romance. It's just a shame when it ends in disappointment, as it did for you.'

'I can't argue with that, Helen.'

'As you've got a bit of brass behind you, you could go on looking for a business,' she suggested.

'Oh, I shall.'

Word came, three days before Christmas, that Steve Crawshaw would be home the next day, and the news provided Jeff with the camouflage he needed. He said goodbye to the children, who were sad that he was leaving, but happily distracted by the imminent arrival of their dad, and then to Helen, who was understandably tearful.

'Things will be better now,' he assured her.

'I'm sure they will, but you won't be here. You've done so much for Daniel and Amanda,' she said, 'and me, too. We're all going to miss you badly.'

'And I'll miss you.' He held out his arms and gathered her into a hug, kissing her on her wet cheek. 'Always remember,' he said, 'if you're feeling low, get baking.'

20

Washing-Up

The AA route told him that his destination would take fifty-five minutes. With his unflinching lack of faith in his own navigating ability, he reckoned at least two hours.

As far as he knew, Blackpool wasn't associated with any regional delicacy beyond the usual seafront offerings. His only reason for choosing it as his next staging post was simply that it was famous and that he'd never been there.

The word 'famous' and the context set him in mind of 'Albert and the Lion' by J Marriott Edgar.

There's a famous seaside place called Blackpool,
That's noted for fresh air and fun,
And Mr and Mrs Ramsbottom
Went there with young Albert, their son.

'E were a grand little lad, were young Albert,
All dressed in his best, quite a swell;
With a stick with an ''orse's 'ead 'andle,
The finest that Woolworths could sell.

He couldn't remember any more.

Of course, the Ramsbottoms had every right to take little Albert to Blackpool, and Jeff had just as much right to go there, even though Helen had tried to warn him against it. He'd put her reservation down to professional jealousy; B & B proprietors in Blackpool had the advantage of a famous location, whereas Helen did not, so it was with an open mind that he set out on his journey.

The road to Worsley was easy enough; he'd taken it regularly to the sports centre. However, once off the roundabout, he was faced with a sign for: *Ring Road (North)/Salford/M602/Mcr City Centre/Liverpool/ M62/Bolton/M61/Leeds.*

It was time to panic. After much dithering and hyperventilating, he merged on to the M60, taking the M61 exit towards Preston, Wigan and Bolton.

It was time to merge again, and that always worried him, but he managed to join the M6, taking the M55 (Blackpool) exit to the A6, which threatened to lead him to Preston and/or Garstang. He continued along the M55 with white knuckles and a dry mouth, finally taking the A583 to Blackpool, and the ordeal was over. He could breathe again.

It was time to start looking for accommodation. Helen had warned him that the B & Bs would all be closed, and that his best chance would be a hotel. Chances were, she said, that the smarter hotels on the North Shore would be booked up by people escaping for Christmas, possibly with the intention of doing some serious dancing in the Tower Ballroom. He should therefore try the South Shore, where hotels were less luxurious, and good luck to him.

He actually tried two of the rather grand-looking hotels on the North Shore, only to receive the news, imparted quite condescendingly, that they had no vacancies until after the New Year.

The South Shore beckoned, and three private hotels later, he was rewarded.

'We've had somebody give backword,' said the proprietor, sounding particularly camp. 'Death in the family, apparently. You don't want that, do you? Not at Christmas.'

Jeff refrained from telling him that it hadn't been an occasion for unbridled merriment when he lost his parents on the first Sunday in Lent.

'So, it's a single room you want, then? The whole bag of tricks? Full board and the Christmas meal?'

'Yes, please.'

'Where are you from, then?'

'I've just driven over from Eccles, but London, originally.'

'London, eh?' It was as if Jeff had given his place of origin as the capital of Mars. 'What are you doin' up here, then?'

A Baker's Round

'Just looking around.'

'Right, well, if you'll sign the register, I'll give you the key.' With an elaborate gesture, he reached for the register, no doubt still marvelling that someone from London had heard of the Jolly Fisherman Hotel in Blackpool. Jeff explained that he had no permanent address, prompting the proprietor to ask if his journey to Blackpool was for the purpose of finding somewhere to live. If so, he had a friend whose house was about to go on the market.

'I'm looking for somewhere,' he said, but not necessarily in Blackpool.'

'Oh, do you not fancy it, then?'

'I've only just arrived, so I've really no idea.'

'Oh well, you never know. You might take a liking to it.'

Jeff agreed that most things were possible, although he omitted to say that Blackpool had so far to win his vote.

He took his luggage up to his room, which was adequate and what he might have expected for the rate he was paying. He took off his coat, jacket and shoes and lay on the bed. It was quiet and peaceful in his room and, best of all, he could escape, just for a while, from the garrulous proprietor.

That afternoon, he donned his raincoat, turned up the collar, pulled his hat firmly down against the wind and rain, and set out for a walk along the Promenade. The hat, a trilby with a wide brim, was a souvenir of Buxton, and he hoped it would prove its worth in the Blackpool climate.

Incredibly, he found he wasn't the only eccentric in Blackpool that day, because people of all ages were braving the elements, and apparently enjoying the experience. Another remarkable thing was that they all wanted to exchange greetings. 'Gradely, isn't it?' 'You can't beat it, can you?' 'There's nowt like a bit o' Blackpool air.' These were just a few of the pleasantries that passed between them, and it wasn't long before Jeff shook off his London reserve and joined them, equally raucous and enthusiastic. The fact was that they were actually very friendly and welcoming.

He stopped when he came to South Pier, surprised again by the number of people who'd turned out in the wind and rain, and who were now walking along the pier.

A voice beside him said, 'Just wait 'til tonight at high tide. You won't be able to see t' pier for rods an' lines.' He gave Jeff a friendly grin and asked, 'Do you go fishin'?'

'I'm afraid not. I like to eat them, but I've never tried catching any.'

'Aye well, it's not for everybody. Are you just up for Christmas, then?'

'Yes.'

'I live here,' he said cheerfully. 'I wouldn't live anywhere else, even though it's goin' downhill as a resort.'

'Is it really?' Jeff had no idea.

'Oh, aye. Folk don't come here for holidays, these days. They're all off to Benidorm an' them places. I'll tell you what we get, now. We get stag an' hen weekends. Mind you, their brass is a good as anybody's.'

'I suppose it is.' The possibility had never occurred to Jeff. 'Are you in the tourism business?'

'Me? No.' He laughed, as if it were a joke. 'I'm an electrician. They still need me, even now the holidaymakers have gone to t' Costa del Sol.'

'Good for you.'

'Anyroad, I'm supposed to be meetin' the missis, so I'll say tarra.'

'Tarra, then. Nice meeting you.'

'Aye.'

Jeff realised he just uttered his first word of the local vernacular. He wondered if he might be turning cosmopolitan.

On Christmas morning, he went down for breakfast and sat at his single table. Breakfast was surprisingly good, with a choice that included scrambled eggs with smoked salmon, and Jeff opted for that. In fact, he'd just been served by a man he understood to be the partner of the one who'd welcomed him, when another of the guests approached him. He was middle-aged and comfortable-looking, as most of them seemed to be.

A Baker's Round

'You don't mind me askin', do you? Are you on your own? I mean, you're not waitin' for somebody, are you?'

'No, I'm alone.'

'That's no good. Not at Christmas-time. Come and join us at our table. There's only me and my wife, so there's plenty room. What do you say?'

He looked at the man beside him and then at his wife, who was waiting at the next table, two vessels filled with goodwill. 'I'd say that's very kind of you both. I'd like to do that. Thank you very much.'

'I'm Arthur Rossendale, and this is my wife Sybil.'

'Jeff Mortimer. I'm glad to meet you both.'

He learned that Arthur was employed as a fitter and turner in a machine shop, that the couple had no children, and that they were very keen on ballroom dancing, hence their regular pilgrimage to Blackpool. Jeff had to admit that he was a stranger to the art.

'We'll be going dancing, this afternoon,' Arthur told him. They get up to all kinds of silliness, here. Malcolm and Lee, who own this place have their own ideas, in more than one sense, really—'

'Arthur,' said Sybil, 'there's no need for that.'

'I'm only sayin' that if Jeff wants to get out, he's welcome to come with us, if only to watch. Mind you, it might suddenly appeal. You never know.'

'That's very kind of you,' said Jeff, 'but, after a substantial meal, I'll probably go out for a run along the Promenade.'

'Rather you nor me, Jeff. T' weather's not brilliant. No,' he concluded, 'we'll work it off by dancing.'

'Each to our own thing, Arthur.'

After a well-cooked and ample Christmas meal, Jeff left the others, as planned, and changed into his running clothes.

One part of his plan, however, had to change. The Promenade was so crowded with post-prandial walkers that he found it impossible to maintain a steady pace. He therefore set off along the nearest side street and left his route to chance.

After half-an-hour or so, he was lost, although that was no surprise. As he made his way through the drizzle between houses that had been in better repair, a feature that reminded him of his conversation with the cheerful electrician who enjoyed fishing from the pier, it seemed to him that he must be able to find someone who could direct him back to the Promenade. In the distance, quite faintly, he could hear the sound of 'O Little Town of Bethlehem' being sung to organ accompaniment, and he followed the sound, more for the pleasure it gave him than with the immediate intention of eliciting directions.

His musical homing sense brought him to a large, stone-built church. Judging by the style of its fussy detail, it was probably built in the Victorian era. Certainly, it dated from a time when greater numbers of worshippers were expected than in the present day. From within came the sounds that had caught his attention and guided him to the spot, and a large sign told him that food was being served in the crypt. Purely for the sake of curiosity, he followed the signs that brought him eventually to an extensive, stone-flagged basement furnished with long tables of the folding kind used for public functions. Each table was host to men and women, many of them of shabby appearance that told of straitened circumstances, some in footwear ill-suited to the northern winter, but all of them enjoying the Christmas meal served to them. As he watched, he was conscious of the mixed aromas of turkey, gravy, vegetables, potatoes, Christmas pudding and mince pies. It was an experience he'd never shared, and it was all the more touching for that.

A woman's voice close-by said, 'Happy Christmas, love. Have you come for your Christmas dinner?'

Turning, he realised she was addressing him. 'No,' he said. 'Thank you, that is. I ate earlier at the hotel where I'm staying.' Looking down, he understood her mistake. He was soaked and looked as bedraggled as some of the people at the tables. 'Look,' he said, 'can I... I mean, is there something I can do?'

The woman chuckled good-naturedly and said, 'There's a pile of washing-up you can get started on, if you've a mind, chook.' She pointed to a much-overloaded sink. 'I fancy we'll be needing some of them plates an' that cutlery before very long.' She looked at him oddly. 'Are you all right, love? You're soaked to t' skin.'

'I'll be all right, thank you. I've been out for a run.'

A Baker's Round

The woman shook her head, no doubt in mystification that anyone would do that in such hostile weather. Jeff simply smiled at her and walked over to the sink.

It occurred to him that, apart from during his various baking episodes, he'd last washed dishes in April, before he left the flat. Even then, it had been a matter of loading the dishwasher and washing the occasional saucepan by hand. Still, it held no mystery for him as he ran hot water and squirted a drop of washing-up liquid into the sink.

He found the rising warmth from the hot water strangely comforting, and the row of pristine dinner plates satisfied him as he washed and stacked them.

Soon, he was conscious of a companion wielding a tea towel. He turned to greet him and saw a man in a clerical collar. 'Hello, Reverend,' he said.

'Hello. I'm Mark, the curate. A happy Christmas to you. The vicar's upstairs, leading the singing.' He laughed self-consciously. 'It's just as well, seeing as I'm tone-deaf.'

'Happy Christmas, Mark. I'm Jeff. How do you do.' Jeff offered his wet hand, and Mark took it awkwardly.

'Are you local?'

'No, just visiting. I was out for a run, and I heard the singing.' Unable to explain adequately, he said, 'I thought I'd get involved.'

'God bless you, Jeff.' Almost immediately, Mark froze. 'You're Jeff Mort, aren't you? I knew I recognised you.'

'I was. Now that I've come to my senses, I'm Jeff Mortimer again.'

'Of course. The band is no more, I believe.'

'It's no loss, Mark. We were pretty dreadful.'

'Well, Jeff Mort or Jeff Mortimer, you're just as welcome here.'

Jeff turned to view the full tables and said, 'I didn't know this kind of thing happened.' In his father's well-heeled parish, there was no need of such a thing.

'It does, Jeff, but not often enough. A great many people have to dig deep into their pockets to make this happen just once a year. Otherwise, the kitchen provides a more modest meal at other times. We call it the Agape Kitchen.' He pronounced it 'aggapay'.

'I'm sorry,' said Jeff, breaking off from the dishes for a second, 'I'm afraid that's lost on me.'

'*Agape* is the Ancient Greek word that describes love for our fellow man and woman, as mentioned in St Paul's First Letter to the Corinthians.'

'I should have known that. My father and grandfather were both men of the cloth.'

'Were they really? You would hear a great deal, I imagine,' said Mark, 'but you couldn't be expected to remember it all.'

When he'd dried himself and changed, Jeff wrote a cheque in favour of St Ethelred's Church. It would possibly pay for a few *agape* lunchtimes.

When he arrived downstairs, he found Arthur and Sybil in the bar, so he bought them a drink. He asked, 'Did you enjoy yourselves this afternoon?'

'We'd a gradely time,' said Arthur. 'You don't know what you're missing.'

'I didn't know what I'd been missing until this afternoon,' said Jeff.

Sybil asked, 'Did you go out running in this weather?'

'Yes, but I didn't spend the whole afternoon running.'

'I should think not.' Sybil was clearly concerned for his wellbeing. 'So what else did you do, then?'

'I did some washing-up.'

21

A Recipe Means What it Says

Knowing he would never find St Ethelred's again, Jeff posted the cheque the next morning. Blackpool had been quite a revelation for him. Gaudy and flashy in part, otherwise shabby, forgotten and depressed, it was nevertheless a town of warm, open-hearted, welcoming people, and he would never forget his experience in the crypt at St Ethelred's.

They say that maturity involves coming to terms with one's limitations, and in a mature moment, Jeff decided to abandon cold-calling on B & Bs and spend some time on the phone beforehand. His next stop was to be Grasmere in Cumbria, home of Grasmere gingerbread, and his third phone call was successful. He took his leave of Arthur, Sybil and the two hotel proprietors, took a deep breath and headed for the A5230.

He surprised himself by finding the A5230 and followed the signs for Preston, the M6 and the M61. Incredulous at finding himself on the M55, where he was supposed to be, he continued to junction 32. After three circuits of the roundabout, he took the M6 towards Lancaster and breathed a little less apprehensively. At junction 36, he took the exit, hoping that fate would point him towards the A590 and the A591, which, if not fate, some agency did, much to his relief. The rest fell into place, and by the time he joined the B5287 to Grasmere, his heartbeat was down to a mere twice its normal rate.

An hour and forty-five minutes after leaving Blackpool, he rang the doorbell of the address on his notepad.

After another ring, the door opened, and Jeff came face to face with a grey-haired woman of possibly sixty or so. She had a pleasant smile.

'Mrs Schofield?'

'Yes.'

'I'm Jeff Mortimer. I phoned you yesterday about a single room.'

'Of course. Come in, Mr Mortimer.'

He followed her inside, where she said, 'I decided to stay open through the winter, to catch what business I could.'

'Have things been difficult?'

'Not in terms of trade. No, it's been quite brisk. The reason I said that was because this is my first year on my own, you see, since my husband died.'

'I'm sorry to hear that.'

'That's kind of you.' Changing the subject, she asked, 'Did I tell you about the room rate?'

'I believe you said it was fourteen pounds for a single room.'

'Yes, that's right. The dining room is through here.' She showed him round the house, which was clean, light and generally appealing. His bedroom window even gave him an unimpeded view of Helm Crag.

'This is excellent,' he said.

'Would you like to sign the register?'

'Yes. By the way, I can't give a permanent address, because I haven't got one.'

'Oh?'

'That's right, no fixed abode. I sold my flat in London a short while ago, and I haven't found anything I like yet.'

'That's all right.' She watched him take out his pen and write his name and signature in the register. 'What do you do for a living, Mr Mortimer?'

'Since April, nothing. I made myself redundant, and I'm trying to decide what to do next.'

'I see. Redundancy's not always a bad thing, is it? It was my husband's redundancy that led us to buy this place, and then life became so much pleasanter. How long will you be staying, Mr Mortimer?'

'I'm afraid I don't know yet. A few days, maybe. I'll know more when I've had a look at the local newspaper.'

A Baker's Round

'I have a copy of the *Westmorland Gazette*. I'll get it for you.' She disappeared for a minute and returned with the paper.

'Thank you. That's very kind of you.'

'What are you going to do while you're here?'

'I don't know. I suppose I'll have a look at the beautiful countryside.' Glancing through the window, he said, 'That's when the rain stops. Then, I suppose, I'll find out where Wordsworth lived and maybe try some Grasmere gingerbread.... That kind of thing.'

'I can point you in the direction of Dove Cottage, where Wordsworth lived. It's at the top of this street.'

'Is it really?'

'And the Grasmere Gingerbread Shop's in the middle of the village.'

'Mrs Schofield, you amaze me. If you don't mind, I'll have a quick look at your paper, and then I'll be out of your way.'

'I was about to make coffee when you arrived. Will you join me?'

'That's very kind of you. Yes, please.'

He sat down with the paper while she went into the kitchen. There was one business for sale, and that was something connected with farming, a closed book as far as he was concerned. Even so, he thought, maybe this was the way to do it. Instead of touring the country and finding places that appealed to him, maybe he should search the papers for opportunities, and then concern himself with where they were. It was Friday, and the national dailies would be on sale. For the time being, though, and for no better reason than idle curiosity, he flicked through the newspaper until Mrs Schofield arrived with the coffee things.

'Would you like to come into the sitting room and sit comfortably?'

'Let's do that,' he agreed. 'I'll bring the tray.' He followed her across the hallway into a fairly large, well-furnished room, setting the tray down on a low table.

'Please take a seat.'

He sat in an armchair while she perched on the sofa and poured the coffee. 'You're my only guest,' she told him. 'I don't get many at this time of the year, as you can imagine. Just the occasional one, like you.'

'There can't be all that many like me, Mrs Schofield.'

That seemed to jog her memory, because she said, 'Yes, you told me you'd made yourself redundant. How on earth did you do that?'

Before he could answer, she put a hand to her mouth and said, 'Oh, I forgot. Would you like some gingerbread? It's gingerbread cake, not the Grasmere kind.'

'If it's not a lot of trouble.'

'Not at all. I won't be a minute.' She went to the kitchen, returning after a minute or so, with a piece of gingerbread on a plate, which she handed to him. 'I'm trying not to eat too much of this kind of thing,' she said. Then, with a look of apology, she said, 'Actually, it didn't come out quite right. Things often don't when I make them.'

He tried a piece and said, 'It tastes good. Did you mean the way it sank in the middle?'

'Yes, it keeps happening. They say banging the oven door can cause cakes to sag, don't they? I try not to, but… well, if it tastes all right, that's something, isn't it?'

It was a unique approach to baking, and one that Jeff wasn't inclined to encourage. 'How many eggs did you put into this, Mrs Schofield?'

'Oh well, the recipe says two, but I thought an extra one would make it richer.'

'I see. In this case, it seems to have caused it to rise beyond its own expectations and then… experience a crisis of confidence.'

'Is that what made it sink the way it did?'

'It's more than likely.' Feeling guilty, now, that he'd criticised his hostess's baking, he said, 'Still, as you said, it tastes good.'

'Do you do a lot of baking, Mr Mortimer?'

'Not nowadays, but I used to be a baker by trade.'

'Oh,' she said, looking as if she'd been caught out, 'and I gave you some of my awful gingerbread.'

'It's not awful at all, it tastes very good, but it just sank in the middle. You see, baking is very different from cooking. If you make a stew, for example, you can experiment, adding things that take your fancy, and there's usually no harm done; in fact, you can often improve on the recipe. Baking, though, is about a chemical reaction between ingredients. If you change those ingredients, you change the formula, and it often reacts by biting you on the bum.' He pointed to the sunken gingerbread as an example.

'Well, I never knew that. No wonder I can never get anything to rise.'

A Baker's Round

Now feeling very guilty, he said, 'Don't feel bad about it, Mrs Schofield. What's your favourite thing that you like to bake?'

'I'd say a fruit cake, supposing I could ever get one to rise.'

'All right, I'll get some ingredients, and then I'll show you how easy it is to make a fruit cake that'll rise.' Before he spoke, he realised that he'd fallen into his usual trap, but at least, he was confident that he would be able to keep his other resolution.

With his recipe book open on the table, he watched his pupil weigh and measure the ingredients, occasionally reminding her that the recipe meant what it said. 'No extra sugar, Mrs Schofield. Be a good girl and put the bag away now.'

'I'm nearly sixty years old,' she protested.

'That's no excuse for rewriting the recipe. Behave yourself.'

He waited until she'd put the fruit, margarine, sugar and water into a pan, and caught her putting it on to a high setting. 'Let it come up to simmer,' he prompted, 'not a rolling boil, and then cover the pan and leave it for twenty minutes.' It was the recipe he'd used with Ms Copley and Ms Fawcett in Bakewell, except that he was now dealing with a capricious child of fifty-nine. 'While we're waiting for it,' he told her, 'you can beat an egg and weigh out the flour.'

'Just one egg?'

'Just one,' he confirmed. 'Don't be naughty.'

'I haven't enjoyed myself so much for... a long time.'

'Good. That's what baking's about.'

'Do you really think so?'

'Yes, I forgot that for a while, but then it came back, like a faithful dog, to remind me.'

'Did you make yourself redundant from baking?' Her tone was one of disbelief.

'No, worse than that.' He told her about serving his apprenticeship as a baker, about the sudden death of his parents and his illogical decision to enter the music industry. Finally, he told her how he'd turned his back on it to search for a way forward.

'You're a bit like me, Mr Mortimer,' she said. 'I've been wondering what to do with myself since I lost my husband. I suppose I could sell up and retire, but then what would I do? I love this village, and I enjoy taking in guests.'

'I think that answers your question, Mrs Schofield.'

'You know, I think it does, although I've never thought about it so simply.'

'When we're involved in tragedy, we don't always think clearly and simply.'

She seemed to be nerving herself to say something, and then she spoke. 'There are two things I'd like to ask you,' she said.

'Ask away.'

'One is, I feel that we know each other quite well, now, so will you call me Patricia?'

'With pleasure. My name's Jeff.'

She hesitated before asking, 'Now that you've bared your soul to me and told me about losing your parents, is it all right for me to give you a hug?'

'I think that's just about in order.'

She wrapped her arms round him and held him close. 'Mm.'

'That's a lovely, comforting sound, Patricia.'

'Now,' she said, releasing him and addressing her task once more, 'Eight ounces of flour.'

'And no more,' he warned.

'I'm a reformed character.'

'I'm glad to hear it.'

When the mixture had cooled, and with the oven set to a hundred-and-fifty, she poured the egg into it and added the flour. 'Oh,' she said in one of her characteristic dilemmas, 'I haven't greased a tin.'

'There's no need.' He handed her a tin containing a paper liner. 'These are much better,' he told her, 'and they make washing-up a lot easier. Now, fill the tin, making sure the mixture goes right to the edges.' With the oven door closed, he set the timer. 'We'll look at it after an hour and twenty minutes,' he said, and take it from there. Meanwhile, let's adjourn for a drink.'

'I'm afraid I've nothing in the house.'

'I have,' he said, taking a bottle of Burgundy from the carrier bag.

A Baker's Round

They went to the sitting room, where Jeff opened the bottle and poured two glasses. 'Here's to your baking future,' he said.

'And to your future, wherever that may be. What's your next port of call?'

'I don't know yet. I'll have a look at the daily papers tomorrow and make a decision.'

'Are you looking for anything specific?'

'Only a business opportunity. It's so long since I've worked for anyone, I really think I'd be a poor employee.'

'In that case, let's hope you find the right opportunity.'

Whatever Patricia's shortcomings were as a baker, her breakfast was one to remember for the best reasons, and it enabled Jeff to begin the day on a note of confidence.

He was right to feel confident, because a notice in *The Daily Telegraph* (Scottish Edition), procured in Penrith, listed a bakery for sale in Dumfries. It had not been a functioning bakery for some time, and was therefore offered under the Scottish system as an asset purchase. Jeff made arrangements with the agents to visit the property on the next viable working day, which was Thursday, the 3rd of January. He hoped that those involved would not be suffering in the aftermath of the New Year celebrations.

22

A Desirable Residence

Even after such a short time, parting with Patricia was like saying goodbye to an old friend. Incredibly, however, Jeff had once again been able to perform a service for his landlady, and without troubling his conscience unduly.

Feeling virtuous as a result, whilst apprehensive by habit, he negotiated the B5287, the A591, the B5322 and the A66. The latter was something of a miracle, and he was still feeling bewildered when he had to join the M6 (North) to Carlisle. Thereafter, the familiar nightmare began, and with something akin to panic, he joined, albeit at the last minute, the A74M. The A75 exit presented itself all too soon, confusing him with its list of possible destinations. It offered him SW Scotland, Dumfries, Stranraer, Gretna and, in case he fancied a lucky dip, the B7076. Eventually, he encountered the A75, which led him to the A780, at which point the cold sweat began to dry, because he was now within a sensible distance of Dumfries.

On this occasion, he'd booked a room at a local hostelry, the Fox and Ferret. When he arrived, the landlord and several patrons wished him a 'guid new year', and he responded as well as he could whilst admitting to himself that he really did need a good one.

Whilst daylight remained, he set out to have a look at the bakery from the outside, but when he arrived, he found that the windows were so dirty, it was impossible to see very much. The main doors were dilapidated, with old and peeling paint, and the whole impression was one of neglect. If there was one thing, he reflected, of which a bakery had no need, it was dirt. He returned to the Fox and Ferret to think and to eat. He found the food that evening particularly good.

A Baker's Round

The hotel offered a 'Full Breakfast', which suggested to Jeff that the word 'English' was considered superfluous. He made no mention of it, however, but asked simply for the advertised Full Breakfast. When it arrived, it consisted of eggs, bacon, sausages, mushrooms, tomatoes, baked beans and a slice each of black pudding and haggis, the whole offering accompanied by a slice of fried bread, which oozed oil or fat, he wasn't sure which. He could only conclude that the breakfast cook was in a different league from the regular chef, who had prepared dinner the previous evening.

The greater part of the meal was actually very good, and it was only when he tried the black pudding and haggis that his appreciation sagged. They, like the fried bread, appeared to have soaked up the oil in which the rest had been fried. It was a shame that, in such an appealing town as Dumfries, he'd found the breakfast he would have paid to avoid.

At the appointed time, he arrived at the bakery, where he was to meet a representative of the agent and, five minutes or so later, he was rewarded.

'Mr Mortimer, I believe?' The representative was tall, elegant and slim, evidently not a devotee of the Full Breakfast. 'I'm Rory Walters.'

'I'm glad to meet you, Mr Walters.' He shook the outstretched hand.

'Are you familiar with the Scottish system of buying and selling businesses?'

'Not in any great detail, but let's have a look at the premises, first, shall we?'

'Of course. I take it you are conversant with the baking industry?'

'I'm a baker, yes.'

'Excellent.' Mr Walters took out a bunch of keys and unlocked the main door. 'The premises have not been in use for almost a year, now, so things are a little dusty, I'm afraid.'

It was a triumph of understatement, because the place was filthy. Cobwebs abounded, although the spiders seemed to have been selective, because dead flies, unfettered by any web, littered the window sills and work surfaces. Maybe the spiders had taken an extended New Year holiday. At all events, a massive clean-up would be required by whoever bought the place. The equipment, too, was in poor condition.

'Mr Walters,' said Jeff, 'I don't want to take up more of your time. I'm afraid this bakery is of no interest to me. It was clearly a large bakery at one time, and one that employed staff, so the investment in personnel alone would be considerable. Also, the equipment is obsolete, and the place is lost in dirt.'

'It does present a challenge,' said the euphemistic agent. 'That I'll allow, but an advantageously low minimum price has been set.' He showed Jeff the document on his clipboard, and Jeff shook his head. 'Not even at that price,' he said.

It was time to consult the newspapers again, and Jeff returned to the Fox and Ferret with a collection, the only missing items being the obvious ones that provided titillation and gossip at the expense of hard news and the kind of advertisement he was seeking.

After some time, his eye fell on an estate agent's advertisement for a grocery with living quarters, and it seemed to him that, depending on the size and extent of the living quarters, there might be the possibility of starting a bakery on the premises. The shop was in Morpeth in Northumberland, which he'd never visited, but that made it no different from the other places he'd visited since his quest began. He picked up the phone and dialled the agent's number.

'Hello, Wicken's, the Estate Agents.' It was the voice of a young woman, and she sounded pleasant. 'This is Julie speaking. How can I help you?'

'Hello. I've just read your advertisement for the shop in Morpeth, and I'd like to find out more about it.'

'Would you like me to send you the information in the post?'

'No, thank you. I'm staying in a hotel in Dumfries, so I shan't be here for very long.'

'Lovely.'

'Yes, I'd really need to know more about the living quarters. In

A Baker's Round

particular, I'm wondering if there would be room to set up a bakery on the premises.'

There was silence, as the young woman presumably re-examined the details and plan of the premises. Eventually, she said, 'I don't see why not. There's a fairly spacious kitchen above the shop. Of course, I'm not an expert on bakeries; in fact, I don't know the first thing about them, but I can't see any reason why that wouldn't be possible.'

'Okay, I'd like to come over and have a look at it, if that can be arranged.'

The young woman took his name and gave him the address of the property, finally arranging to meet him there at eleven-thirty in two days' time. The process was very pleasant and, just before he rang off, she said, 'It's funny, Mr Mortimer, but when you gave me your name, I thought you were going to say "Jeff Mort". That would be a turn up for the book, wouldn't it?'

'I imagine it would.' He decided not to let her into the secret immediately. It was always possible she wouldn't recognise him when they met, and he would be spared the distraction.

The taciturn young man serving breakfast came to him for his order.

'Could I have the Full Breakfast, please, but without the black pudding and haggis, and could I have toast instead of fried bread?'

The young man greeted his request with a shrug. 'You'll be wanting the Full English, then?'

'I'm afraid so.'

'There's not many English folk can take the haggis and the pudding, and the fried slice doesn't get many takers either.'

'We're an effete lot,' admitted Jeff, feeling somewhat noble.

With the necessary adjustment made, breakfast was an enjoyable and satisfying start to the day.

With only a day to spare, he was naturally unable to obtain either a list of places offering accommodation or a route from the AA, so he elected to take pot luck on the B & Bs and work out a route the hard and complicated way, using the map.

With only moderate difficulty, he found the A780, and then, negotiating the roundabout twice, he managed to stay on the A780 until it was time to change to the A75, where he was distracted by references to Gretna Green. It occurred to him, whilst looking anxiously for a sign to the M6, that a great many eloping couples must have been very determined in following their hearts' dictate, to have braved the traffic system in that region.

At junction 44, he took the exit towards Carlisle, and that was when his handwritten set of instructions deserted the fascia panel for the seclusion of the passenger footwell.

Eventually, he was able to pull in and restore the list to its former place, at which point, he realised that he was about to approach the A69.

Having survived that crisis, he continued along the A69, scarcely able to believe the respite, which lasted a welcome half-hour.

His temporary relief was shattered when he read the sign for the A1. 'Morpeth' spoke for itself, but 'Airport', 'Jedburgh' and 'A696' were three distractions too many, and it was with jangling nerves that he merged on to the A1.

Thereafter, life slowed down, and he was able to follow a series of roundabout signs to Morpeth, arriving rather more than two hours after leaving Dumfries. Drained but relieved, he decided against trawling the B & Bs, and checked in at the Cock Robin Hotel.

Surprisingly, after the previous day's adventures, he found the shop easy to locate, and he was there, chatting with the seller, when Julie from the estate agency arrived. She was dark-haired, with an engaging smile and what looked like fun in her eyes, and she was slender, at least, as far as he could see, because she was wearing a long, grey, winter coat. Jeff was about to introduce himself, when she gasped and said, 'You *are* Jeff Mort! You *bugger!*'

Laughing, the owner of the shop said, 'Mr Mortimer's from London, Julie. I don't suppose he's all that used to being called a bugger.'

'I'm sorry, Mr Mortimer. It was the shock. One minute you disappear

A Baker's Round

without trace, and then you turn up in Morpeth, of all places.' Turning to the owner, she said, 'Didn't you recognise him, Angie?'

Angie shook her head. 'No, you'll have to let me in on the secret, Julie.'

'He's Jeff Mort. He used to be lead guitar with Tantum Somnium, except they split up a while ago.' Still eyeing him with something close to veneration and shaking her head in disbelief, she repeated her earlier greeting with a little less excitement. 'You *bugger*.'

'In the north-east,' explained Angie for Jeff's benefit, ' "bugger" can be a friendly greeting as well as an insult.' Then, turning to Julie, she said, 'I think you'd better show Mr Mortimer round the place.' With a wink, she said, 'Try not to offend him, won't you?' It was a timely suggestion, because a customer was about to enter the shop.

'Right,' said Julie, 'you can see the extent of the store room from here, so let's go upstairs.' Then, almost to herself, she added, 'I cannot believe I just said that to Jeff Mort.'

'Never mind, Julie. Lead the way.'

She took him up a wooden staircase and showed him two bedrooms, a double and a single, a small sitting room, a tiny bathroom, and the kitchen. At that point, his spirits sank. 'I don't think you're going to sell this place to me, Julie,' he said as gently as he could.

'Don't you think so?' Maybe her feelings were still buoyed up by her unexpected meeting with Jeff Mort, but she didn't seem excessively disappointed. 'Go on, tell us why not.'

'It's the kitchen, basically. It's not big enough for a bakery, and there's nowhere else to put one.'

'I'm surprised to hear you say that. Me mam manages to bake in a kitchen like this one.'

'Ah, but does she bake two dozen loaves at a time?'

'No, there's only her and me brother.'

'I'd say that explains it.'

'I suppose so. I told you I knew nothin' about bakin'.' As an afterthought, she said, 'Don't say anythin' to Angie, will you? I'll tell her later that it's not quite what you were lookin' for.'

'You know, Julie, you don't sound at all like you did when you answered the phone yesterday.'

'Well, you see,' she said distinctly, 'that was my business voice.'

Lapsing again into the broad vernacular, she said, 'I have to sound a bit posh, workin' in Morpeth.' Changing the subject abruptly, she said, 'If it's not too much trouble, do you think I could have your autograph before you go?'

He was reminded fondly of Donna, the hair stylist. 'Julie,' he said, looking at her ringless left hand, 'a girl like you must have a bloke.'

'No, that hit the ground a month ago. Why do you want to know?' Her expression betrayed nothing but curiosity.

'Meet me tonight for a drink.... No, as you're such a loyal fan, join me for dinner. Will you do that?'

She beamed. 'I won't object to that, Jeff.' Suddenly remembering herself, she asked, 'Is it all right to call you that?'

'Just about. Where do you live?'

'I've got a flat not far from here. I couldn't afford anything in the posh part of town.'

'Give me your address and I'll pick you up. Is seven o' clock okay?'

Like a child that's been offered a treat, she said, 'Why aye. I'll see you then.' Writing her address hurriedly on one of the firm's leaflets, she asked, 'By the way, where will we be goin'?'

'The Cock Robin. It's where I'm staying.'

'That's posh.'

'As I said, you're a staunch fan.'

They went downstairs to take their leave of Angie and then walked into the street, stopping beside Julie's car, a Ford Fiesta. A teddy bear in a Newcastle jersey occupied the passenger seat. It seemed fitting.

'I'll see you tonight, then, Jeff.'

'Seven o' clock at your place,' he confirmed, leaning forward and kissing her on the cheek.

With a look of wonder, she said, 'It just keeps on gettin' better.'

Julie's flat was in the same street as Angie's shop, so it was easy to find. There had to be some exceptions in life.

The block of flats had two storeys, access to the ground floor flat

A Baker's Round

being via the front door, whereas an exterior staircase led to the upper flat, of which Julie's was one. Jeff pushed the bell and heard it chime reassuringly inside the flat.

When Julie opened the door, she was wearing the same grey coat she'd had on earlier, but it was unbuttoned to reveal a dark-green dress with, as far as Jeff could see, a spiral motif in a lighter green. She'd gone to a great deal of care with her make-up and hair, which hung in loose waves.

'Julie, you look better than ever.'

'Thank you.' The words came with a deep sigh of pleasure. Then, in a more down-to-earth tone, she said, 'This staircase is a pain in the.... Everybody can see who's coming and going.' She added hastily, 'Not that fellas come and go all that often, you understand.'

They reached the bottom of the steps and, simply out of habit, he offered her his arm.

'Oh, now I really don't believe it.' Nevertheless, she took it and they walked to the car. Jeff opened the door and held it for her, waiting for her to gather her skirts before closing it.

When he got into the driving seat, she said, 'You're not at all what I expected, Jeff. You're a lot posher, and this is a lovely car, but not what I associated with you.'

'Does it help that I went to a posh school and, until eight months ago, I had a Porsche?'

'Why did you get rid of it, then?'

'It was all part of breaking with the past. That's why I bought the Volvo and stopped wearing jeans with holes in them. I had my hair cut, as well.' He pointed to it in case she hadn't noticed. 'Have I spoiled your treat?'

'Don't be daft. I just thought I'd mention it.' Pointing to a street sign, she said, 'If you don't mind me mentionin' somethin' else, you've just missed a turnin'.'

'I do that all the time. You wouldn't believe the trouble I had driving from Dumfries yesterday.'

'I would, now I think about it. Just turn left at the next junction an' I'll direct you from there.'

'Welcome to my life, Julie,' he said, patting her hand. 'You're just what I need.'

'You want to be careful, sayin' things like that.' She peered through the darkness and said, 'Left again at this crossroads.'

'This must be what it's like to have a guardian angel.'

'Even a one that calls you a bugger?'

'I'm sure they come in various forms. It's quite a novelty to get the Geordie kind.'

'I've heard a few lines in me life, but now I've heard 'em all. Next left, an' it's on your right.'

He swung into the Cock Robin carpark, marvelling at the expertise with which she'd brought him from confusion to certainty, so it was with a sense of gratitude that he opened the passenger door and offered her his hand.

'I'm not helpless, Jeff,' she said, smiling, 'but it's nice of you, all the same.'

They went to the bar, where Jeff said to the girl there, 'Mortimer, Room Four. I booked a table for two in the restaurant.'

'Right, Mr Mortimer. Would you like to have a drink first, or go straight to your table?'

Jeff asked Julie, 'Would you like a drink, or shall we go straight in?'

'Yes, let's do that.'

The girl asked, 'Would you like to follow me?' She guided them to their table and took their coats. 'I'll bring you the menu and the wine list.'

As they took their seats, Julie said, 'I'm not used to bein' treated like this. They usually turn up at the flat, they say, "Get your coat on, pet, you've pulled," an we go to the pub for a drink. Then, I usually sit an' watch 'em play darts.'

'You deserve much better treatment than that.'

'You're full of it, Jeff, but you're nice.'

He took the menu and the wine list from the waitress. 'Thank you. There, Julie, you can decide on your starter and main course.' While she did that, he studied the wine list.

Eventually, all decisions were made, and Jeff gave the waitress their order.

When she was gone, Julie said, 'Go on, then. Tell us why Tantum Somnium split up and why you haven't formed another band.' Shaking her head in wonder, she said, 'I still can't believe I'm sittin' here with Jeff Mort.'

A Baker's Round

He'd explained it so many times, such was the price of even bubble fame, but he told the story again because she was eager to know, and she was entitled to a proper answer. 'Two of them joined a new Heavy Metal band, one that was more in-keeping with their intellect and ability. I wanted a change, to do something different.' He made no mention of the real reason for his disenchantment. Julie had followed the band in good faith, and she didn't deserve to be disillusioned as well as disappointed.

'So, in that case, what are you going to do?'

'I don't know. Before I went into the music business, I was a baker.'

'Ah, that was going to be my next question.' She crossed it off her pretend list with a stroke of one finger.

'Good, because I think that whatever I do will be connected with baking. I just have to find the right business.'

Not surprisingly, she seemed disappointed. 'I've got all your singles and albums,' she said.

'Julie, I don't deserve a fan like you, and neither did Tantum-bloody-Somnium.' He squeezed her hand reassuringly.

'It's just as well *we* thought you were good,' she protested. 'Somebody had to appreciate you, even if you didn't appreciate yourselves.'

'The other three were happy enough with themselves, although Sam, the drummer, was happy with anything as long as he was away on coke, smack or whatever. For what it's worth, my ex-girlfriend called me a loser.'

'Some women don't appreciate what they've got.'

'True, but I appreciate you. You're the best kind of fan, and I'm sorry it had to end for you.'

She squeezed the hand that was holding hers and said, 'I've got you tonight, and that makes up for a lot.'

'I won't be around for long, Julie.'

'I realise that. I'm just goin' to enjoy havin' you around while you still are.'

The waitress brought the wine for Jeff to taste, and he gave it his approval.

'You mentioned your ex-girlfriend, Jeff. You're not married, are you?'

'No.'

'Have you got another girlfriend?'

He shook his head. 'I've been on the road since last April, Julie, and you know that a rolling stone – and I'm not talking about Mick Jagger – gathers no moss.' Crossing his fingers under the table, he said, 'It doesn't usually get to do anything else, either.' Uncomfortably aware that all the focus had been on him and his activities, he asked, 'Have you always worked in estate agency?'

'No, I haven't. Me mam and dad used to have a café. That was after me dad was made redundant, and I worked in that with 'em. I enjoyed it, but even that didn't last. When me dad died, me mam just folded. She didn't want to do anythin', an' that was when she sold the café, and I went to work for Wicken's, who'd sold it for her.'

'I'm sorry, Julie. That was a chapter of horror for you.'

'Aye well, we get through these things.'

When the food arrived, it came as an opportune distraction, and the conversation lightened, so that by the end of the meal, they'd covered a variety of topics.

'I honestly couldn't eat anythin' more, Jeff.'

'Neither could I. Shall we order coffee?'

'I could make coffee at my place.' Seeing him hesitate, she said, 'Ground coffee. I've experience in caterin', remember.'

'I'll take you up on that.' He motioned to the waitress, who brought the bill. He signed it and left a tip.

On the way back, he was careful to follow Julie's directions, and he was surprised at how straightforward the journey was.

'Just run it into this little bit of drive,' she told him. 'It'll be safer here than on the road.'

'What would I do without you?'

'You'll find out soon enough, pet.'

She let him into the flat and took his coat. 'Now, how do you like your coffee?'

'Just white, no sugar, thanks.'

'Right,' she said, switching on the gas fire. Make yourself at home, and I'll be with you in a few minutes.'

The flat seemed very ordinary for a girl who was far from ordinary, but it occurred to him that maybe she spent very little time at home.

A Baker's Round

She probably visited her mother quite frequently, as well. It wasn't surprising, after all, that she hadn't put her personal stamp on the decoration and furnishing.

In what seemed a very short time, Julie came in bearing a tray that contained a cafetiere of coffee, two mugs and a jug of milk. 'There,' she said, pouring both, 'there's no point in paying for it when we can have it at home.'

'Spoken with true northern thrift.'

'Well, you know how I learned that.'

'I do.' He joined her on the little sofa and took a mug of coffee from her.

'That was a lovely meal, Jeff. Thank you.'

'I enjoyed your company.'

'Well, I little thought when I set out this mornin' that I'd be on a date with Jeff Mort. Whose idea was it to shorten your name, anyway?'

'My agent's. He's full of ideas.'

'Ah.' With old-fashioned tact, she said, 'Maybe I ought to stop goin' on about Jeff Mort an' Tantum Somnium, seein' as you've put all that to bed. Just one thing, though, before I do.' What she had in mind was obviously important to her. 'Why did you call it that? I mean, the way I translate it, it means "Only a Dream".'

'That's right. In this case, though, I was thinking of "Only make-believe." It was because I didn't really believe in what we were doing.' He'd said it, now, but she was grown-up enough to live with it. 'Well done, by the way. Most people haven't a clue what it means.'

'I'm not daft. I did Latin at school.'

'Obviously.'

'There was a film on the telly at Christmas. *Showboat*. Do you know it?'

'That's where "Only Make Believe" came from,' he confirmed.

'I thought so. It's a lovely song.' She gave a little sigh and said, 'I get sentimental about songs like that.'

'It's a great song. You've every right to.'

She gave him a straight look and, with no warning at all, said, 'I know I mentioned an autograph earlier, but will you kiss me instead? It'll be better than an autograph.'

Her candid approach reminded him again of Donna. Taking her in his arms, he kissed her, feeling her react readily. After a while, she said, 'It wouldn't bother me if you weren't Jeff Mort after all. You're a lovely fella, an' that's all that matters.' She joined him in a lingering, sensuous kiss, breaking off after a while, to say, 'There's somethin' else that's better than an autograph, an' all. That's if you've got somethin' with you.'

'I have, but are you sure? You know I shan't be around for long.'

'Why aye. Howay.'

He followed her into the bedroom, where she closed the curtains and they undressed.

'It's a pity I've only got a single bed,' she said.

'We'll just have to take turns in it.'

'Don't be daft.' She removed the last of her clothes and got into bed. 'Hurry up,' she said, 'it's cold in here.'

'I know.' He kicked away his shorts and joined her, taking her in his arms again, delighting in her softness as he kissed her repeatedly. 'You've got goose bumps,' he told her.

'I've got more than that,' she said, looking down at her impressive bosom.

'I mean these things.' He ran his hand over her shoulder, which was visibly affected by the coldness of the room. 'Snuggle up and get warm.'

Taking his advice, she said, 'You're patient, Ah'll grant you that.'

He kissed her again, running his hand down her back until he stopped suddenly.

'What's the matter?'

'Your bum's like ice.'

'I know, but it's not half as cold as me feet.'

'Let me have them. I'll warm them for you.'

'Are you sure?' She sounded incredulous.

'It's all part of the service,' he assured her, avoiding her knees as she brought them up to chin height. 'Careful,' he warned her. 'One foot out of place, and I could be helpless for at least ten minutes.'

'I wouldn't do that to you. I've got a vested interest in keepin' you active.'

'I know.' Taking her feet in his hands, he rubbed them to encourage circulation.

A Baker's Round

'You're one on your own, Jeff,' she said, obviously enjoying the process. 'I never expected to have me feet warmed up.'

'Is that better?'

'A lot better, thanks.'

'Good. Roll over.'

'What?'

'Turn over and snuggle up. I'm going to warm your bum.'

'How?'

'Just snuggle up next to me, and it'll be warm in no time.'

'Okay, but this is a new experience for me.' She made the necessary adjustment and backed up against him. 'Oh,' she said, 'you're as warm as toast.'

'That's the idea.' He kissed her shoulder, working his way round to her neck.

'That's lovely. Don't stop.'

Moving her hair aside, he kissed her neck again softly.

'You're full of new ideas, Jeff. Keep 'em comin'.'

He kissed her neck again, and she wriggled over to face him. Then, reaching downward to check on progress, she said, 'He's ready.'

Between kisses, he said, 'He's been ready for a while.'

'Aren't you goin' to put his coat on?'

'No, you can do that.' He took one from the packet and handed it to her.

'Just in case you'd forgotten,' she said.

'I hadn't forgotten.' He kissed her neck and moved downward.

'Gan canny, pet. I'm tryin' to do a job down here.'

'Sorry.' He waited for her to re-emerge, and then kissed her at length.

When she could speak, she said. 'You're not in a hurry, are you?'

'No. Are you?'

'Not if you're not. I keep wonderin' what you're goin' to surprise me with next.'

He kissed her again, feeling her arms tighten around him. Gradually, he reached downwards, running his fingertips through her forest until he uncovered her secret.

'Aah.'

'Nice?'

' "Nice" doesn't begin to describe it, you... aah....' She moaned freely until his mouth covered hers again, and then, after a while, she made room for him with a little cry of greeting.

After some time, when her excitement had ebbed, she said, 'I always knew it would be different, doin' it with Jeff Mort.' Suddenly wary, she asked, 'Is he all right in there?'

'More than all right. As you people are fond of saying, it's a highly desirable residence.'

'I mean, is it safe? If he loses interest while he's still in there....'

'Very safe. He's not lost interest yet.' He lowered his head to kiss her before moving again.

'You bugger, you're goin' to make me come again, aren't you?'

'Not if you don't want to.'

'Don't be daft.'

23

A Word in Time

With absolutely nothing of interest in the newspaper advertisements, Jeff stayed longer in Morpeth than he'd intended, and it gave him a convenient excuse to spend more time with Julie, although he was reluctant to leave it too long, as that would make the inevitable parting harder for both of them.

Eventually, an opportunity arose, this time in the Midlands, another area about which he knew very little, beyond the fact that it had once been well-known for its motor car industry, Cadbury's chocolate and Shakespeare's birthplace. It nevertheless called for investigation.

Parting with Julie was even more difficult than he'd expected. They'd always known their relationship was to be short-lived, but some take root quicker and more surely than others.

She clung to him for the last time, with tears coursing down her cheeks. 'I told meself I wasn't goin' to be daft an' cry,' she said. 'It just shows how little you know yourself.'

'Cry if you have to, Julie. There's no law against it.' His face was wet with her tears. Parting was, as Julie had said earlier, a bugger. There was no getting away from it. 'If Angie's kitchen had been bigger, or if I'd found somewhere that had possibilities, things might easily have been different. It just wasn't to be.'

'Remember us, won't you, Jeff?'

He'd long since become used to the dialect use of 'us', rather than 'me'. It was one of the many natural charms that made her so special. 'I'll never forget you, Julie.' He meant it.

Rather than prolong the suffering, he kissed her for the last time and picked up his bag. 'Goodbye.'

He drove away from the flat, feeling guilty on Julie's account and miserable for himself, and it was some time before he was able concentrate on the familiar process of losing his way.

One day, he imagined, someone would invent a device, rather like one of those funny, miniature computers that children begged their parents to buy for them because they were too young to play Space Invaders at the pub. The device he had in mind, however, would have a voice inside it, that would give clear and concise directions to any destination its owner cared to choose. He thought about that until he realised he'd missed the turning for the A1. On second thoughts, he decided, whilst trying to relocate the elusive trunk road, that his idea was too space-age to be given serious consideration. He would continue to pin his faith in AA routes and try, at the same time, to develop a sense of direction. He went on his way, encouraged by the fact that he would be on the A1 for some time.

After a journey of well over four hours, the fault being down to him rather than the AA, he drove into Wolverhampton and secured a room in the first hotel he could find.

The receptionist asked him, 'Are yeow plannin' to stay long, sir?'

'I beg your pardon?'

The receptionist repeated the question, and Jeff took 'plannin' to stay long' as a clue to translation. 'Just a few nights, I think.'

'Good. Do yeow know where everythin' is?'

'I think so.' It was getting easier.

'Here's your key, sir.'

That was much easier. 'Thank you.'

'Pardon me for askin', but are yeow Jeff Mort, by any chance?'

'No, but I'm often mistaken for him.' It was easier than having a conversation in a strange language. He picked up his key and went to the lift. 'Thank you.'

The room was quite adequate, and it would only be for a short time.

His appointment with the estate agent was for ten-thirty the following morning. That was how he intended to work in future, through estate agents. It would make the job easier and take much of the pot luck out of it. Like the hotel receptionist, his contact at the

A Baker's Round

agency had been difficult to understand, but he would probably get the hang of the Midlands accent, as he had with Geordie, although, of the two, he preferred the latter. It was certainly the friendlier. He made himself think about something else, anything, rather than dwell on Julie and make himself miserable again.

'Are yeow Mr Mortimer?'

Jeff was surprised, because the question came from a casually-dressed woman, who looked nothing like a representative of the agency.

'Yes. Good morning.'

''Morning.' The woman delved into her coat pocket and pulled out a selection of keys. Then, having identified the right one, she unlocked and opened the door.

'By the way,' asked Jeff. 'what's your name?'

She looked at him as if his question were somehow strange, and said, 'Janet. I'm not one of the partners, I just show people round the properties, like I'm doin' now.'

'I just thought we should be properly introduced.'

She gave him the strange look again, but instead of commenting on that observation, she asked, 'Where are yeow based?'

'Nowhere, yet. I'm from London, originally, but I've been travelling since April, looking for a business opportunity. I've just come down from Northumberland.'

She greeted the information with a grin not far removed from a smirk. 'Do they do business up there? They're not civilised, are they?'

He thought of Julie's quick translation of Tantum Somnium. 'I wasn't aware of it,' he said, the words 'kettle' and 'pot' springing to mind. He dismissed the thought as he made his way round the room, examining utensils and equipment of a different kind, which had been left in rather better condition than the contents of the Dumfries bakery. The oven had also been cleaned prior to putting the business up for sale.

'I imagine the seller's solicitor will have access to the firm's books,' he said.

'Yeow'd have to speak to one of the partners about that.'

'Do you know anything about the bakery, what made the owner put it up for sale, and what kind of market there is locally?'

'No, yeow'd have to speak to one of the partners.' It seemed to be her stock response. On this occasion, however, she appeared to be studying him, and it was no surprise when she asked, 'Aren't yeow Jeff Mort?'

'Yes.'

'I thought so. My sister told me Tantum Whatsit had split up. It was never my kind o' thing. If it comes to that, I don't think yeow ever really caught on in the Midlands.'

'I don't suppose we did. I'm told our appeal was more of an intellectual kind.'

'Oh, yeah? I suppose it would bey with a name loike that.'

Having made his point, he asked, 'When did this business come on the market?' He was half-expecting her to advise him to speak to one of the partners, when she said, 'Last week. The owner's retirin',' she told him, adding, 'It's all roight for some. According to Mr Beardall, he's only fifty-foive, an' he should know. They're members of the same Buffaleow lodge.'

'I see. Which of the partners is handling this sale?'

She shrugged. 'Take your pick. There's Mr Beardall and Young Mr Beardall. Either of 'em should be able to tell yeow what yeow want to know.'

'Well, thanks for your help. I'll be in touch with the agency.' They left the building, and Janet got into her car and drove off, leaving Jeff to wonder just how keen the agents were to sell their properties.

He spoke to Young Mr Beardall that afternoon, who told him that the firm's books were not yet available for scrutiny, but he would let Jeff know when they were. All in all, it had not been an informative day.

A Baker's Round

Dinner in the hotel restaurant was quite good and, rather than go straight to his room, Jeff thought he would try the bar, which seemed to be fairly busy.

He tried some of the local brew that was on offer, and changed to Guinness. In doing so, he asked the barman, 'Are you often as busy as this?'

'Through the week, yes. We get businessmen who use it as their local.' He nodded at the unfinished pint of bitter and said, 'It's a pity yeow don't like the local beer.'

'I'm a Londoner,' explained Jeff. 'Tastes vary up and down the country, don't they?'

Later, he got into conversation with one of the local businessmen the barman had mentioned. He owned three hairdressing salons, and he introduced himself as Trevor Alpin.

'So what brings you to Wolverhampton, Jeff?' It was immediately and pleasingly noticeable that the otherwise ubiquitous 'yeow' was missing from his vocabulary.

'I've come looking for a business opportunity,' he said.

'Oh? What line of business are you in?'

'The bakery trade.' It was a relief not to be asked to explain his exit from the music business. Trevor was clearly not a devotee of that kind of music, which made him potentially a welcome companion.

'Right, so have you got your eye on something in particular?'

'Possibly. I came to look at the Edwards bakery.'

'Did you now? I believe Beardall's are handling that one.'

Jeff looked at Trevor's glass and asked, 'Can I get you another?'

'Very civil of you, Jeff. A pint of bitter, please.'

Jeff asked the barman for a pint of bitter and a pint of Guinness, thankful that he, too, wasn't a devotee of Tantum Somnium.

'I heard something about the Ernie Edwards and his bakery,' said Trevor. 'Now, what was it?'

'Here's a pint to refresh your memory.'

'Thanks, Jeff.'

'I believe you said you were in the hairdressing business.'

'That's right, and it's a good business to be in. Hair never stops growing, unless it falls out, that is, and people want it looked after while they've still got it.'

'That's true.'

'If it comes to that, I suppose they'll always want bread, although there's keen competition from the supermarkets.' He stopped suddenly. 'That's what I was trying to remember.'

'About the Edwards bakery?'

'Yes, I remember Ernie Edwards saying he wanted to sell up and retire while he could.'

'Yes?'

'That's right. Business hadn't been too good for a while. He'd lost most of the restaurant trade to the big boys, and the supermarkets were laying the boot in at the same time.'

It made a great deal of sense. 'The big bakeries will always get the restaurant trade, and the supermarkets are too convenient. Shoppers can call at one of those places at any time and pick up sliced bread packed with preservatives. Many of them don't know any better, because they've never tasted quality.'

'There's that and the difference in price,' said Trevor.

'They need to learn that quality is worth paying for.'

'I'll say they do,' said Trevor, finishing his beer. 'Same again?'

'Yes, please.' He was grateful to Trevor for his helpful warning. In time, the books would have told their own story, but time was valuable, because Jeff needed to find something quite soon. The money from the sale of the flat was still there, waiting to be invested, and there was still money in the bank, although he'd spent rather a lot during his odyssey, but it wouldn't last forever.

'Cheers.' He took a pint of Guinness from Trevor.

'I'm sorry to give you bad news, Jeff.'

'Not at all. By telling me that, you've saved me a lot of time and work, finding it out for myself.'

'I hope you find what you're looking for.'

'I will eventually.'

Jeff spent three more days, looking through advertisements, speaking on the phone to agents, and concluding that Wolverhampton was not where he wanted to spend the rest of his life. Part of his feeling of dejection, he knew, was the result of leaving Julie behind. He'd grown more attached to her than he'd realised at first, and it was difficult to be up-beat about anything, so his best course was to keep moving on until he found something that really excited him.

Eventually, an advertisement appeared for a grocery with a hundred square metres of 'useful upper-storey floor space' in Beckworth, West Yorkshire. The premises had once belonged to the Co-operative Society, hence the floor area, he discovered, and it sounded promising. A phone call to the agent resulted in a viewing appointment in three days' time.

24

Fame and Frailty

Jeff was surprised to find himself becoming less intimidated by motorway lanes and road signs. It had taken a long time, but his tour of Britain had done him some good, after all. The journey to Beckworth had taken exactly two hours and forty-five minutes, even with a heavy snowfall, with no wrong turnings or last-minute adjustments. Maybe it was a sign that his luck was changing. He really hoped so, because nine months was a long time to spend in pursuing a nebulous goal. The shop in Beckworth might just be the answer. Maybe it would have a yard and a hoist, which would be very useful in unloading sacks of flour. He was cautiously excited.

When he arrived at the premises, he found Anna Jessop, his contact at the agency, waiting for him.

'I'm sorry to keep you waiting,' he said. 'I'm Jeff Mortimer.'

'Jeff Mort, I know.' Her eyes twinkled. 'I'm Anna, and don't worry. I was here in good time. I've just been having a chat with Esme, the seller. Come and meet her.'

The entrance had been recently cleared of snow, but Jeff stamped his feet as they entered the shop.

Anna introduced them. Esme was a cheerful woman, probably in her sixties, which was a good reason for selling her business. He would find out more about that later. Meanwhile, he looked round the shop,

A Baker's Round

which appealed to him, as old-fashioned grocery shops always had. His main interest, however, was the upper storey, and he followed Anna upstairs with the sense of anticipation he remembered from childhood Christmases.

Anna switched on the lights to reveal a hundred square metres of empty, floorboarded workspace. Jeff had already noticed a load-bearing wall downstairs, that would facilitate the installation of a baker's oven. Otherwise, steel joists would support flour, sugar and all the heavy ingredients that would be needed.

A pair of doors on the far wall took his attention, and Anna happily slid back the bolts to open them so that he could see both the hoist and the yard beneath it, just as he'd imagined them.

Here and there, wet spots were evident on the floorboards, and Anna explained, 'It's a Victorian building, and the roof does need some attention, but that's reflected in the asking price.'

'Has much interest been shown so far?'

'Quite a lot, yes, but no offers as yet.'

'I'm very taken with it.'

'I can tell.'

'I'll be in touch when I've done a few sums.'

Later that afternoon, Jeff drove to Otterburn Estate Agents, and was pleased to find Anna behind her desk. She greeted him warmly.

'I'd like to make an offer on the grocery shop,' he said.

'I thought you might. What's your offer?'

'The asking price.'

'Excellent. How will you finance the purchase?'

'I'll have no difficulty at all.'

She laughed. 'I'm sorry, I meant, where will your finance come from? From the sale of a property, or a mortgage?'

'Neither. The cash is waiting in the bank.'

'That's even better. Now, we have some more people who want to view it, so I'll be in touch when they've seen it and come back to me. I'd better make a note of your hotel phone number.'

The next morning, he made arrangements at the Post Office for his correspondence to be sent there, and returned to the hotel to phone his bank manager. After a couple of minutes' wait, he got to speak to him.

'Mr Lawford?'

'Mr Mortimer, hello.' They exchanged greetings, and Mr Lawford said, 'I'm glad you've phoned me. I've been wanting to speak to you about a large sum of money that has appeared in your current account.'

'And you'd like to help me invest it, I imagine.'

'Well, I think that the first step should be to put it where it's going to work for you, rather than leave it in your current account.'

'Okay, Mr Lawford. There's a branch in this town, so I'll open a deposit account for now. However, I am going to invest the money.'

'Oh, good.'

'I'm going to buy a business.'

It would have been pleasant to go out and explore the countryside around Beckworth, but snow continued to fall, making such journeys treacherous and, in some cases, impossible. All Jeff could do was stay in the hotel and wait for a call from Otterburn's.

The call came three days later.

'Mr Mortimer, it's Anna at Otterburn Estate Agents.' She sounded less than buoyant.

'Hello, Anna. It's "Jeff", by the way.'

'Right, Jeff. There's been one more offer, and I'm afraid you've been outbid, because the offer is for five thousand more than yours.'

It was quite a shock. 'Okay, Anna, I'll see their five thousand and raise them five thousand.' He'd wanted to say something like that for some time, after watching old episodes of *Maverick*.

'Are you sure, Jeff? That's ten thousand above the asking price.'

'I don't know who these people are, Anna, but I want the place more than they do.'

'I wouldn't put money on that, but you seem to be ready enough.'

'Yes, I am.'

'Look, Jeff, I'm not hopeful, but I'll put your increased offer in and see what happens.'

'Thanks, Anna. Goodbye.'

'Goodbye, Jeff.'

It was very odd. Naturally, Anna couldn't tell him who his rivals were, not that he was likely to know them, in any case, but they were obviously keen and they had money behind them. He just hoped they'd reached their limit. After nine months of searching, it would be too bad if he lost out.

When matters are on a knife-edge, a distraction can be a good or a bad thing, and Jeff was in no doubt about the nature of the events that were about to occur. They began with a phone call the next morning.

A pleasant-sounding female voice asked, 'Am I speaking to Jeff Mort?'

Jeff took a deep breath and said, 'Yes. Who's calling?'

'It's the Northern Focus Studio, Mr Mort. Is it all right if I call you Jeff? My name's Louise Stanford, by the way.'

'Yes, that's fine. How can I help you?'

'We've just heard that you're in Beckworth, and I wonder if you'd be kind enough to give us an interview.'

It was inevitable. 'Yes, all right. How did you find out I was here?'

'I'm sorry, Jeff. I can't disclose my sources. Is later this morning convenient, at eleven-thirty?'

'Yes, but where?'

'We'll come over to your hotel. Don't worry, we won't put you to any trouble.'

It was a teaser. As far as he knew, no one on the hotel staff had recognised him, and releasing information about hotel residents must surely be a sackable offence, anyway. The only other people who knew he was there were at the Otterburn office. He phoned their number and asked for Anna, who was apparently out with a client.

He left a request for her to phone him as soon as she returned to the office.

In the event, she called at the hotel in person, about an hour later, looking particularly troubled. She asked, 'Have the media contacted you, yet?'

'Yes, they have. Presumably, you know something about it.'

'I'm afraid so. I'm really sorry, Jeff. My youngest son spoke to the Northern Focus Studio. It was my fault for telling him you were here.'

'Hardly your fault, Anna. Let me buy you a drink.'

'I'd better not when I'm working, but thanks, anyway.' She was still in the throes of remorse. 'I just thought he'd be excited. I didn't realise the little mercenary was going to sell the information to the media.'

'How old is he?' Jeff was genuinely curious.

'Twelve, thirteen next month, if he's allowed to live that long.' Her expression cast doubt on that event taking place.

'He sounds like an enterprising lad. Who else has he told?'

'I don't know. He's only owned up to Northern Focus, so far.'

The only person who was really upset about it was Anna. 'Don't worry about it,' he told her. 'It was always going to happen, and the media got a run for their... whatever they paid him.'

'You're very understanding, Jeff. I've told him he has to give his ill-gotten gains to a deserving cause. He's certainly not going to profit from this business.'

'Ouch. That's going to hit him where it hurts.'

'He was only going to spend it on silly games.' She closed her eyes at the thought. 'He's got all your singles. You'd think he'd show a bit of loyalty, wouldn't you?'

'Maybe he thought he was doing me a favour, getting me some publicity.'

'I don't know how you can joke about it, Jeff.' She looked at her watch. 'When are the television people coming?'

'Eleven-thirty.'

'It's nearly that now. I'd better get out of your way.'

'Okay, but change out of the sackcloth and ashes, Anna. It wasn't your fault, and there's no harm done, anyway.'

'Right, I'm going. Thanks for being so nice about it.' She inclined her face for him to kiss her cheek.

A Baker's Round

'No word from the competition, I take it?'

'None as yet.'

Anna had been gone less than five minutes, when the TV crew arrived, spearheaded by a determined-looking brunette in what looked to be several layers of winter clothing.

'Hello, Jeff,' she said, 'I'm Louise. Thank you for agreeing to this interview.'

'Not at all, Louise. Would you like a drink?'

'Better not, thanks. It doesn't look good on camera.' Glowing in the warmth of the hotel bar, she went on to say, 'The hotel people are happy for us to do this here. I'll just take my coat off before we start.' She doffed her overcoat to reveal yet more woollen layers. 'I hate winter,' she said.

'It shows.' He was quite amused.

'Just while the boys are setting up the camera and sound, is there any particular subject you'd rather avoid?'

'No, I'm not guilty of anything.' It seemed an odd question. 'I thought you people spent your time looking for embarrassing stories,' he said.

His remark earned him an admonishing look. 'This is Northern Focus, love, not the tabloids. We go after lying politicians and crooked businessmen, but we've no axe to grind where you're concerned.'

'I'm sorry, Louise. My mistake.'

'It's all right.'

The sound engineer did a test with the microphone before handing it to her.

'Thanks, Lee.' Turning to the cameraman, she asked, 'Okay, Kev?'

'Okay, Louise.'

'Right, Jeff,' she said, 'we're recording.' Then, in a more practised, professional way, she looked him in the eye and said, 'Well, Jeff, we last heard from you in April of last year, and now, nine months later, you turn up in Beckworth. What have you been doing with yourself in the meantime?'

'Nothing too dramatic, Louise. I just felt like a change.' It was the truth, after all.

'We can see that from the haircut and the smart clothes. Your fans will barely recognise you.'

'Yes, I'm sorry to disappoint so many of them,' he said, suddenly thinking of Julie because it was difficult not to, 'but I really have turned my back on the music industry.'

'We got that impression from the comment you gave *Music Review* and the radio stations, so what now?'

'Believe it or not, before I went into the music business, I was a baker, and I think that's going to be the way forward. At all events, it's what I want to do.'

'That's fascinating, Jeff, and you've certainly kept us all guessing. What have you really been up to, these past nine months?'

There was no harm in telling the public. He'd nothing to hide. 'I've been on a tour of Britain, Louise. I've stayed at bed and breakfasts in Banbury, Wales, Bakewell, Eccles, Cumbria and Blackpool, as well as places in Scotland and Northumberland. You see, in getting out of the high-profile, high-speed world of the music industry, I had to take a step back and spend some time organising my feelings. It's been a marvellous time, and I wouldn't have missed it for anything. As I said earlier, I'm sorry to disappoint my fans, and I'm deeply grateful to them all for their support, but I had to do this.'

'It's a lot to turn your back on, Jeff. You're a talented man.'

He was glad she mentioned that. 'Last summer,' he told her, 'I spent some time in Wales. I met some wonderful people, and I was there when they held their annual music festival. It was a defining moment for me, Louise, because I heard a girl, the winning entrant, play the guitar as I'd never heard it played. I'd never heard classical guitar music at all until then and, having been taken to a different planet by this girl's wonderful playing, I knew I wasn't in the same league. I'm sorry, fans – I should say, ex-fans – but it's the truth.'

Visibly affected by his disclosure, Louise collected herself to say, 'Well, you heard it first on Northern Focus. This is Louise Stanford saying, a very heartfelt "thank you" to Jeff Mort and wishing him every success in his chosen career. Thank you, Jeff.'

'It's a pleasure, Louise.'

The cameraman said, 'Cut,' and Louise relaxed. 'That was powerful stuff, Jeff,' she said. 'When I thanked you, I really meant it.' Looking out of the window, she said, 'And now, I think I've done you no favours at all.'

A Baker's Round

Following her gaze, he saw cars delivering photographers and reporters, all jostling outside and being held there by the obliging hotel manager. 'Don't worry,' he said, 'it's not your fault. I suspect that the little sod who gave you the tip-off tried his luck with the tabloids as well.'

'Oh, I gather you're on to him.'

'I know his mum,' he told her, helping her on with her coat, 'and I can tell you that the money's going to a deserving cause. He might learn something from that.'

'It was only ten quid. Thanks again, Jeff.'

'You're welcome.' He gave her a kiss on the cheek and shook hands with the sound engineer and cameraman, walking with them to the door, to be assailed by a barrage of flashes and clicking shutters.

'I'm sorry about all this,' he told the hotel manager.

'It's no hassle,' the manager assured him. 'It breaks the monotony, if nothing else.'

Raising his voice above the excited shouts of the reporters, he said, 'I'll try and get rid of them.'

'Is it true you're starting a new band, Jeff?'

'What was the problem with Tantum Somnium, Jeff?'

'Is it true about you going Progressive, Jeff?'

Questions continued to come until he held up his hands to them. 'Listen,' he said when the shouting had died down, 'the best thing you can do is to watch Northern Focus tonight. Then, you'll hear the whole story.'

Someone asked, 'What have they got that we haven't, Jeff?'

'Their reporter's better-looking than you are,' he told him, watching the others make a rapid note. It was hardly wit, but it was all they were going to get.

'Have you got a message for the *Daily*...?' The rest of its name was lost in the clamour.

'Yes, I have.' He was conscious of a quietening as reporters waited.

'Go on, Jeff, what's your message?'

'Bugger off. You're making the place untidy.' With a final wave, he retreated inside the hotel just as the police arrived at the manager's request, to move them on.

'Hell's bells,' said the manager, 'I hope I'm never as popular as you are.'

'You can make yourself popular with me, if you like.'

'What can I get you, Mr Mortimer?'

'A pint of Landlord, if you will.' He'd developed the taste for it in the short time he'd been in Beckworth. He hoped it would be a lasting relationship.

Anna phoned the next day, still remorseful after the incident, but with more news. 'I've just heard from the people who are after the grocery, Jeff.' She sounded less than cheerful.

'Go on.' He had an awful feeling about it.

'They've raised their offer again, and they say they'll go on doing it until you lose interest. They're a large organisation with almost unlimited resources, and they really want it.'

'Bugger.'

'Obviously, I can't tell you who they are,' she said, sounding defeated, even though the competition meant a better deal for the Otterburn agency. 'All I can tell you is that they're a chain of convenience shops, and they want to demolish the grocery and build a new store on the site. They'll be as welcome here as measles, but that's for them to find out. I'm really sorry, Jeff.'

It was the worst kind of news, although it would be good for Esme, who was selling the place. 'Once again, Anna, it's not your fault. Thanks for your help.'

It was becoming a bad habit or, more appropriately, a recurring nightmare. Jeff picked up the *Times* and the *Telegraph* yet again, hoping the next possibility wouldn't be too far away. To hope for more than that seemed to be tempting Providence.

In fact, almost a week passed before something occurred. When it did, it sounded too good to be true. The property, consisting of a bakery with a tearoom attached, was in a village called Akengarth, in

A Baker's Round

Netherdale. Jeff had heard about the Yorkshire Dales, and such were the accounts he'd been given, he'd promised himself a visit at some time. Here, though, was the perfect opportunity, and a look at the map told him he didn't even need a route. He could see the road unfolding as he looked: Bradford, Keighley, Skipton and on to Netherdale. Maybe it was a sign that his future lay in the north of England. Hope springing ever eternal, he spent some time on the phone and made arrangements for a visit.

25

Like a Local

Bradford was tricky, and Keighley and Skipton were hair-raising, but the road out of Skipton was a tonic, and beyond that lay the route to Akengarth in Netherdale, his destination. He pressed on, now, with what Sir Winston Churchill had called 'growing confidence.' Was there something about this part of the country, he wondered, that inspired that confidence, a feeling of destiny, perhaps. On reflection, it was better not to conjecture about such things at that stage. He drove on and, almost before he knew it, he was reading signs for Akengarth.

February possibly wasn't the best time to see the Yorkshire Dales for the first time, but he was no less mesmerised by the towering, snow-covered hills and limestone walls. The river also had a kind of freshness that reminded him briefly of swimming with Caryl in Wales. That, however had been in midsummer, whereas the water in Wharfedale, Netherdale, or wherever he was, couldn't be much above freezing. It was better not to dwell on it, and certainly not to swim in it.

Soon, he entered Akengarth and parked in what was clearly the market place, at the top end of the High Street, where, quite incredibly, parking was free except on Market Day.

The White Swan Hotel was just across the road, as was the Pack Horse, albeit two buildings away, but the White Swan looked more like the kind of place he was looking for, so he made it his first call.

He rang the bell on the reception desk, and a receptionist appeared almost immediately.

'Can I help you, sir?' She was young, with red hair, freckles and a serious expression.

A Baker's Round

'I hope so. Have you a single room with a bathroom?'

'We have, sir. How long will you be staying?'

'Certainly for a few days. Maybe longer.' Much depended on the room rate.

As if reading his thoughts, she said, 'The room rate is twenty-seven pounds for bed and breakfast, and forty for bed, breakfast and evening meal.'

'Fine. Let's start with bed and breakfast.' If things turned out well, he would find somewhere less expensive later.

'If you do want dinner, we ask you to give us your order by seven o' clock. Would you like to sign the register, sir?' She offered him a ballpoint pen.

'Thanks, but I'll use my own.'

She watched him take out his pen and print his name. Under *Home Address*, he wrote, *No fixed abode, but where there's life, there's hope*, and then signed his name. Still apparently mesmerised by the fountain pen, she said, 'I haven't see one of them since I left school.'

'I'm just an overgrown schoolboy,' he told her.

Her eyes narrowed a fraction, and she asked, 'Are you, by any chance, Jeff Mort?'

'Yes, but don't tell anyone.' He placed one finger along the side of his nose to emphasise the point.

'Right.' Recovering herself, she said, 'We need your car registration number.' She pointed to the section in the register. 'Parking's in the yard at the back, and it's reserved for residents.'

He entered his registration and asked, 'Do you know Mitchell's Bakery?'

'Yes, the hotel used to get its bread from there, but old Mr Mitchell died. It's up for sale, now.'

'That's what I've come to see,' he said.

'Oh well, good luck with it. Do you need any help taking your luggage upstairs?'

'No, thanks, I'm stronger than I look.'

She gave him his key. 'Number six,' she said, 'on the first floor.'

He carried his luggage upstairs and located his room, which was well appointed, if a little dark. Dark furniture, he decided, had no place in a hotel room, which was supposed to be a home from home, a place of pleasure and comfort. Light oak or beech were much more appropriate. He unpacked and went out to reconnoitre the town.

He didn't fully believe that people lived in such places. The buildings looked so inviting as to exist solely for the use of visitors, but people must live there. They probably carried on their quiet lives in places visitors never saw.

As he walked on, he read a street sign that looked familiar, and he remembered that the bakery and teashop were in Stringer Lane, so he took the turning to investigate. He found the place about a third of the way along the lane and examined it as well as he could from the outside. As far as he could see through the windows, the bakery had been left tidy. There would naturally be dust and so on, the products of disuse, but there was no evidence of neglect, as there had been in Dumfries. A concrete apron in front of a garage, suggested parking for more than one vehicle, which was good, because a van was essential in the bakery trade.

As for the house, which was more of a cottage, there was a small garden to the front and what appeared to be a courtyard to the rear, possibly where teashop customers sat in the summer months. Beyond that, it was impossible to see anything, as the cottage was a private residence. He would see more the next day. Meanwhile, he continued with his walk around the town, seeing a great deal and disliking nothing.

After dinner, which was unremarkable but expensive, he decided to give the bar at the hotel a miss and try the Pack Horse, further along the High Street.

He found that it kept Theakston's Ales, and an exploratory mouthful followed by another to confirm his initial impression made him an instant convert. He was conscious that the landlord was watching him. He lowered the pint by a half and put it down on the bar with an approving nod.

'You sound like a southerner, but you sup like a local,' said the landlord, whose tone was gruff but welcoming. 'Like a local,' he repeated, as if confirming his observation to himself. 'Most off-comed 'uns sip it an' take t' head off, an' then they decide they don't like it. At least, that's what we generally find.'

'If it's good, it's worth drinking, and this is a lovely pint.'

A Baker's Round

'I'm glad you like it.' Possibly unable to believe that a foreigner was capable of such appreciation, he asked, 'Where are you from?'

'London.'

'Oh, aye? What's your line of business?'

'I'm a baker.'

'A proper baker?'

Jeff nodded. 'Artisan-trained. I served my apprenticeship with a master baker who'd have nothing to do with factory methods, and neither will I.'

'I'm glad to hear it.' Inclining his head in the direction Jeff had come from, he said, 'We lost our baker a few months since. His widow's tried to carry on wi' t' teashop, but she's havin' to draw t' stumps, poor lass.'

'That's why I'm here,' Jeff told him. 'It was the advertisement that brought me. I'm looking for a bakery to buy.' He finished his pint. 'The same again, please, and have one yourself.'

'Much obliged. I'll just have a half.' The landlord pulled his pint and went to serve someone else. As he did so, he exchanged a few words with the customer and nodded in Jeff's direction.

When he'd been served, the man walked over to Jeff and said, 'Na then, I'm Dick Foster. I keep t' garage an' petrol station just up at t' top o' t' High Street.'

'Glad to meet you. Jeff Mortimer.'

'Aye, Albert tells me you've come to look at Herbert Mitchell's bakery.'

'That's right.'

'I've only lived here twelve years. I came up from t' West Riding, but I allus think businesses like that should stay in t' family.'

'So do I.' For a moment, he wondered if he was going to be run out of town, but then Dick spoke again.

'It were t' biggest shame about their lad.'

'What happened to him?'

'He used to work in t' business with Herbert, an' then, poor lad, he were on his motorbike when he had a collision with a car. He were dead on arrival at t' hospital. Herbert died just three years after him.'

'That's terrible. I can't imagine what it's been like for Mrs Mitchell.'

'Poor old Anthea, yes, she's had an awful time of it, an' now she's decided to call time. The teashop isn't enough on its own, you see.' He let that information sink in and asked, 'Where are you stayin'?'

'Just for now, at the White Swan.'

Dick closed his eyes and pursed his lips as if he were in pain. 'They'll fleece you at that place. Tell yer what, Jeff. Anthea Mitchell does bed and breakfast. If you're stayin' any longer, you could do a lot worse nor talk to her.'

'Thanks. I'll bear that in mind when I see her tomorrow.' He looked at Dick's pint and asked, 'Can I get you another one?'

'That's very civil of you, Jeff. A pint of Theakston's Bitter, if you will.'

Jeff signalled the landlord and asked him for two pints of Theakston's Bitter.

'Two pints of Theakston's,' he repeated, pulling two more. 'I've just been sayin' to that lot over there, how we'll have to get used to bread bein' baked by a Londoner.' There was the merest suggestion of a smile on his face as he said it.

'I haven't bought it yet. You never know, I could have competition.'

'I don't think anybody's bitten yet, but I could be wrong. T' estate agents'll tell you.' He laughed. 'They're a funny lot.'

'The estate agents?'

'Aye, they write them clever descriptions, an' when you go to look, it's nowt like they say.'

'Oh well, I'll see for myself tomorrow.'

'That's right.' He took the money for the beer and gave Jeff his change. 'Anthea Mitchell's a nice lass. We just hope she gets a good deal.' His sentiments were echoed by Dick, who accepted a pint from Jeff. 'Much obliged, Jeff.' Despite the welcome, their words sounded ominously like a warning.

'You're welcome.' A question had occurred to Jeff, and he asked them both, 'Where have people been getting their bread since Herbert Mitchell died?'

'There's a bakery in Thanestalls,' said Dick. 'Mind you, I don't think it's a patch on Herbert's baking. Do you, Albert?'

'It's all right,' said Albert, 'but not like Herbert's.'

It seemed to Jeff that if he were successful in buying the bakery, he would have to work hard to match Herbert's reputation, at least, in

A Baker's Round

the eyes of Albert and Dick, and the interview, because that was how it seemed, wasn't yet over. Albert asked, 'Do you, by any chance, play the hallowed game?'

Jeff knew immediately which game Albert had in mind. 'Yes,' he said, 'I haven't played for a year, now, but I bowl right-arm medium-fast, and I usually bat at number six or seven.'

'Good.' For the first time, Albert's face creased into a proper smile. 'We have a strong village side, but we won't turn talent away.'

'If I buy the bakery, you can count me in,' promised Jeff.

At closing time, he walked back to the White Swan with rather a lot to think about.

As he retraced his footsteps, the next morning, a black BMW passed him and drew in beside the bakery. Its driver got out and looked around him.

'I think you're looking for me,' said Jeff. 'That's if you're from the estate agency.'

'Bernard Sheldon, yes.' He offered his hand.

'Jeff Mortimer.'

Mr Sheldon looked at his watch and said, 'I think Mrs Mitchell will be ready for us.' He walked up to the door and rang the bell.

The lady who opened it was possibly in her sixties. She wore a spotless apron and gave the impression immediately of being scrupulous in her habits.

'Hello, Mr Sheldon.'

'Mrs Mitchell, this is Mr Mortimer, who's come to look at the property.'

'Oh, good. Come inside, both of you. You know your way round, don't you, Mr Sheldon?'

Jeff shook hands with her and noted her look of surprise.

'Are you a baker, Mr Mortimer?'

'Yes.'

'You seem very young.'

'I'm thirty, but I can still bake, I assure you.'

'Of course. I'm sorry.'

'It's quite understandable.' In her world, a master baker was an old man who'd learned the trade in the distant past. She was quite right to wonder.

'Now, you do understand,' said Mr Sheldon, 'that the complete premises are for sale, the bakery, the cottage and the tearoom?'

'That's how I understand it.'

'Good, I'll take you upstairs first, Mr Mortimer. Is that all right, Mrs Mitchell?'

'Perfectly.'

Jeff followed the agent upstairs, where he found two bedrooms, a bathroom and a small boxroom.

'This has been a tragic business,' confided Mr Sheldon.

'I gather so.'

'Oh? How did you hear of it?'

'I was in the Pack Horse last night, and some of the locals brought me up to date.'

'You're lucky they spoke to you. They're not usually so quick to accept outsiders.'

'Apparently, I "sup like a local".'

'I'm sure that helped.' Addressing the immediate business again, he said, 'If you've seen everything you want to see up here, we'll go downstairs.'

Jeff inspected the kitchen, which was well-equipped, with a pristine oil-fired range that looked new. He asked, 'Does this do hot water and central heating as well?'

'Yes.' Mrs Mitchell sounded nervous, but definite. 'The hob and oven are quite enough for the tearoom.'

'I'm sure they are.'

They looked at the tearoom itself, and then the bakery. Jeff wasn't surprised to see that the equipment had been properly cleaned since it was used; in fact, he was most impressed by the late Mr Mitchell's standards, and it was always good to be impressed. 'This is quite remarkable,' he said.

'Really?' Mr Sheldon seemed surprised.

'Yes, the bakery is up to date and beautifully kept. Of course, it'll

A Baker's Round

need to pass inspection by the Food Standards Agency, but that won't be a problem.'

'Have you seen everything you want to see?'

'I think so. I want to ask Mrs Mitchell about accommodation. I'm staying at the White Swan, and it could work out expensive if I have to stay there for any length of time.'

'Oh.' Mr Sheldon looked serious. 'We don't encourage buyers and sellers to communicate directly.'

'I'm not asking you to encourage anything, Mr Sheldon. I just want bed and breakfast accommodation. Before I do that, though, I want to make an offer for this property and the bakery fixtures and fittings. The figure I have in mind is the asking price.'

'Excellent. I have to ask you, though, how you're going to finance the purchase.'

'Of course. The cash is in the bank, as I'm sure they'll confirm.'

'Well, I'll certainly put your offer to Mrs Mitchell. I imagine she'll be delighted. I'll tell you what. You speak to her about accommodation, and then I'll have a private word with her, if you don't mind.'

'Of course not.'

They returned to the cottage, where Mrs Mitchell was waiting.

'Mrs Mitchell,' said Jeff, 'I believe you do bed and breakfast here.'

'Yes.' She seemed a little taken aback. 'There's just the single room.'

'That's all I need. I'm at the White Swan, but I can move out anytime.'

'Oh well, let me see. I charge twelve pounds a night. Is that all right?'

'Absolutely. Thank you for letting me look at the premises, Mrs Mitchell. I'll go and get my things from the hotel. In the meantime, I believe Mr Sheldon wants to speak to you.'

Sheldon had gone by the time Jeff returned with his luggage, but he'd left behind a delighted seller.

'I suppose I'd better decide what I want to take with me and what I'm going to leave,' she said, clearly ready to make a start.

Ray Hobbs

'Your solicitor will send you a form to fill in, listing all your fixtures and fittings,' he told her, vaguely remembering the process from moving to the flat. 'You can decide then.'

'It's been such a long time since I did this.'

'You'll be all right, Mrs Mitchell. You'll have the estate agent and the solicitor to advise you, and I'm not going make difficulties.' If he did, he knew that the locals at the Pack Horse would have plenty to say on the subject.

26

Assault and Bakery

The first job for Jeff was to make a new *poste restante* arrangement with the Post Office in Akengarth, so that the solicitor wasn't sending his documentation to him care of Mrs Mitchell. He knew that solicitors could be nervous about that kind of thing. His second task was to notify the bank, his solicitor and the firm storing his furniture from the flat. They would need to know when he was likely to move. After nine months of waiting, he felt a boyish kind of excitement about everything.

Mrs Mitchell was equally excited. 'This is a great relief for me,' she said. 'The tearoom can't keep the place going on its own, and it's quite a struggle.'

'Where will you go when you move?'

'I'll move in with my younger sister. She's a widow, as well.' Her need to move out was evidently at the forefront of her mind, because she said, 'Simon, our son, was our hope for the future. He'd learned the trade from his dad, and he was a good baker. He was about your age, but he should have had more sense.' Realising she might have made an unintentional *faux pas*, she hesitated and said, 'I mean, more sense than he had, not more sense than you have.'

'I know what you meant, Mrs Mitchell.'

'Oh good, I'd hate to give offence.'

'There's no question of that,' he assured her.

'It were that motorbike of his that were his undoing, although the accident wasn't really his fault. The driver of the car were to blame, but it came out at the inquest that Simon's bike wasn't roadworthy. Dick at the garage kept offering to service it for him, but Simon would do things his way.'

'I'm sorry, Mrs Mitchell.' It was all he could say, because he had no intention of pursuing the tragedy.

Her financial situation was also causing her some anxiety. He knew that from her expression when she picked up the post each morning, and he could understand her readiness to sell the house and the business.

He behaved as if he knew nothing, but the events that occurred later in the week made it impossible for him to remain in isolation.

He'd barely finished breakfast, when a white van drew up outside, and three men got out. One, a man of fifty or so, wearing a suit, carried a clipboard, whilst the other two, who were much younger and dressed in jeans and T-shirts, hung back, presumably waiting for instructions.

Mrs Mitchell's face had turned white, and her mouth hung open.

'Who are they, Mrs Mitchell?'

Her voice shook as she said, 'It's the bailiff and his men.' The doorbell rang, and she went to let them in.

The bailiff showed his identity and said, 'Mrs Mitchell, I have a County Court Order to collect the remaining balance due on the Rayburn range and installation plus court costs, or to carry away goods to the same value.'

Tearfully, she said, 'I can't... pay that now.'

'In that case, I'm afraid we'll have to carry away goods to the value of one thousand, six hundred and forty-one pounds fifty-six.'

As he spoke, one of the louts in attendance moved forward, knocking Mrs Mitchell out of the way, so that she fell heavily against the newel post on the staircase. His progress was arrested, however, in the most unexpected way, by a punch to the solar plexus and another to the face that left him writhing on the floor, bent double, fighting for breath, and bleeding from his nose and lip.

The other, who had been as surprised as his workmate, faced up to Jeff, who said equably, 'You're welcome to have a go, but you'll get the same treatment.'

'Just a minute,' said the bailiff sternly. 'You've just struck a court officer.'

'Rubbish. These two are yobs, nothing more than hired muscle. You're the only court officer here, and if you want to make a case of

A Baker's Round

it, I'll tell the police how one of your monkeys assaulted a helpless woman.' Mrs Mitchell was now sitting on the bottom stair, sobbing helplessly. 'I gather you're the bailiff. Is that right?'

'Yes, I am.'

'I thought so.'

'Look,' said the bailiff more calmly, 'This is unfortunate. I've warned this man before about his strong-arm tactics—'

'Never mind that. Have you got a card machine with you?'

The crumpled heap on the floor stirred, and Jeff said, 'Make one daft move, and I'll hurt you so that you'll remember it. This lady's a friend of mine, and I don't take kindly to low-life like you knocking her about.' He extended a finger of warning, also, to the other yob. 'Bear in mind what I've said,' he told him. 'There's easily enough floor space for you as well as him.'

The yob merely stared at Jeff, open-mouthed. The bailiff, however, opened his briefcase and took out a card imprint machine.

'Right,' said Jeff, handing him his credit card, 'take it out of this card and then get these thugs out of this house.' Looking at the injured one on the floor, he said, 'You may need a wheelbarrow for this one, but that's your problem.'

Clearly shamefaced, the bailiff took an imprint of the card and gave it to Jeff for his signature. 'I've only been doing this job two weeks,' he said soberly, 'and I'm sick of it already. When I retired from the police force, it seemed the ideal job, but it's anything but ideal, and particularly when they give me numbskulls to work with, like these two.' He looked at the name on the credit card before handing it back. 'I'm not kidding, Mr Mortimer, villains are one thing. They deserve to be caught, but to hell with hounding honest, law-abiding people who are down on their luck.'

'I'm glad you see it that way.' He looked at his credit card receipt and said, 'I'd like a written receipt from you, as well. One that'll stand up in a court of law, in case Rip Van Winkle here decides to prefer charges.'

'I'll write you a receipt, Mr Mortimer, and don't worry about the other matter.' He gestured towards the casualty. 'You'll hear nothing more about this.' Turning to Mrs Mitchell, who was still in a state of emotional shock, he said, 'I must apologise for my assistant, Mrs Mitchell. Are you all right?'

Still tearful, she nodded.

'Are you sure?'

'Yes.'

Using his briefcase as a temporary desk, he wrote a receipt for the full amount and gave it to Jeff.

'Thank you.'

'Right, you two, get back in the van, and don't pick a fight with any garden gnomes on the way. He opened the door for them and said, 'I'm sorry again, Mrs Mitchell. Thank you, Mr Mortimer.'

Jeff joined his distraught landlady on the bottom step and put his arm round her shoulders. 'It's all right now,' he told her, giving her a reassuring squeeze.

'Thank you… Mr Mortimer. I owe you… the money now.'

'That's true, but I won't arrive on your doorstep with two retarded gorillas, issuing threats and offering violence. We can sort out the money when we get completion.'

'You're very… kind.'

'I know, but we both need a cup of coffee. Then we can sit down comfortably, and you can tell me if that's the extent of it or if you need help with anything else.'

Peering with some alarm, she said, 'Your hand's all swollen.'

'He had a hard head, but I think it hurt him more than it hurt me and, to be honest, it was true, what I told him about him knocking you about. You know, I rather enjoy being your minder.'

The story was also enjoyed by the regulars at the Pack Horse.

'Hey, Jeff,' said Dick, the garage man, 'what's this I hear about you brayin' t' debt collector's ear'ole for him when he got tough with Anthea Mitchell?'

The term 'braying' was new to Jeff, but the sense was clear enough. 'Not the man in charge,' he said. 'I could have been arrested for that, not that he'd have stepped out of line, anyway. No, it was one of his thick-ear merchants. He pushed Mrs Mitchell into the stair post, so I taught him a lesson in manners.' It troubled him a little, that Mrs

A Baker's Round

Mitchell's problem was public property, but it seemed to be the way in that community.

'The bugger,' said someone else, who evidently agreed, 'treating poor old Anthea like that.'

'Aye,' said Albert, the landlord, 'an' we've heard how you're treating Anthea fair and square over t' sale.'

Jeff wondered if anything could happen in Akengarth without coming to the attention of the Pack Horse faithful.

'Take your hand out of your pocket,' said Dick. 'You're not buyin' a drink tonight.'

'Aren't I?'

'No, it's on us. You're lookin' after Anthea, so we've decided you're all right.'

'Thank you.'

'Na then, but don't expect it every night.'

The laws of the Pack Horse patrons were like those of the Medes and the Persians, but Jeff was happy to live by them.

———•———

His presence at the cottage turned out, yet again, to be of benefit to Mrs Mitchell, when the wife of the baker in Thanestalls phoned to tell her that her husband was down with 'flu, and therefore incapable of supplying the bread order. Business at the tearoom was slower in the winter months, but still very important. It was the season for hot lunchtime meals, advertised on the menu as 'Winter Warmers'.

'I don't know where I'm going to get bread rolls before tomorrow,' she said. 'People who come here won't be fobbed off with supermarket rolls.'

'What's your bread order, Mrs Mitchell?'

'White and wholemeal rolls, a dozen of each, and four large white loaves and three wholemeal for sandwiches. I've got everything else.'

'Fine, I'll drive over to Ellison's and get the flour and yeast. I'll have to bake it in your kitchen range tonight, I'm afraid. I can't use the bakery equipment until the inspector's seen it.'

'Of course.'

'Don't worry, Mrs Mitchell, you'll have your bread for tomorrow.'

It was a laborious business; there was limited space in the range oven, so the actual baking had to be done in stages, but Jeff was plying his trade again, and that made him very happy. Eventually, the bread order was complete, and he went to his room tired but satisfied.

Feedback was positive and quick to arrive. 'Everybody's saying how much better the bread is today,' said Mrs Mitchell. 'Harold Ghyll's ears must be burning, poor chap. It's bad enough having 'flu without that an' all.'

Kay, Mrs Mitchell's part-time help, came from the tearoom with the same story. 'Your name's up in lights,' she told Jeff. 'They're all talkin' about your bread. It can only serve you in good stead when you take over the bakery.'

'He's a good man to have around, all right,' said Mrs Mitchell.

'I'm surprised you're not married,' said Kay, 'a man of your talents. There's many a woman who'd wed you for your baking alone.' Eyeing his muscular physique discreetly, she said, 'The rest would be a bonus.'

'You're too kind.'

'Seriously,' said Mrs Mitchell, 'isn't there a lass in your life?'

'No, I've been travelling for the best part of a year,' he reminded her, 'and when I've met anyone promising, we've been like ships that passed in the night.' Recent experience had left him reluctant to dwell on the subject.

'Oh well, maybe when you've had time to settle down, things'll change for you.'

It occurred to Jeff that matchmaking was built into a woman's DNA. For the moment, though, he had to concentrate on supplying the tearoom with bread for as long as Mr Ghyll was indisposed, as well as dealing with the paperwork that buying and selling property inevitably generated.

27

April

A Permanent Arrangement

With the exchange of contracts imminent, or so he was told, Jeff had much to organise. The bakery and kitchen would have to be inspected before the takeover was complete, and therefore, with Mrs Mitchell's permission, he stole a little time by giving the bakery a thorough cleaning.

'It's been a while since it looked like that,' she said when he'd finished.

'I just hope I can match up to all your late husband's standards,' he said seriously.

'Get away. You know folk round here can't wait for you to start this place up again.'

'They're very kind, Mrs Mitchell.'

'No, they're just looking forward to being able to buy some proper bread.'

'If you think I'm popular, they'll hold a wake at the Pack Horse when you move out. They only accepted me when they were satisfied I was treating you fairly and squarely.'

'Don't be silly.' Nevertheless, she seemed to like the idea. Then, as she remembered something, she said, 'I've spoken to Kay, and she's agreed to work full-time, just until you get organised.'

'Thank you for that. She'll be a great help.' He surveyed the pile of junk that Mrs Mitchell had accumulated. It was destined for the council rubbish depot. He said, 'I should be able to get that into my car and do it all in one visit.'

'I'll give you a hand.'

'Don't you dare, Mrs Mitchell. I won't have you injuring yourself when I'm around to do these things.'

'You spoil me.'

'Quite right, too. Are you coming for the ride?' It was Wednesday, and early closing.

'All right. I can help you unload everything.'

'No, you can't. Behave yourself.'

She locked the cottage and joined him in the car. 'It's good of you to give up your time on a nice day like this, helping me get rid of my rubbish.'

'It'll make it easier for me to move in,' he reminded her.

After a few miles, she asked, 'Have you given any thought, yet, to what you're going to do with the tearoom?'

'Quite a lot of thought.'

'Just remind me of your options.'

He thought about his answer and said, 'One option is to close it down altogether. That would be the easiest course.'

'Go on.'

'Another would be to let it to a third party. That would involve yet more legal goings-on, but it would probably be worth it. I'd just have no say in how it was organised.'

'What else?'

'The only other option, it seems to me, is to take on staff and keep it going.'

'You've got Kay,' she reminded him. It was immediately evident that the possibility appealed to her.

'And she's worth her weight in gold, but she doesn't want to work full-time.'

'She can't, not with kids at home. Which is your most likely option, the one you prefer?'

'Number three, principally because if I were to go for either of the other two, my life at the Pack Horse wouldn't be worth living.' There was another reason, as well, that he'd had in mind for some time and, now that completion was about to take place, he was keen to set things in motion. However, their conversation had to stop there, because Jeff had just pulled into the council yard.

He opened the rear hatch and started to unload. He'd just dropped

A Baker's Round

two full suitcases of rubbish into the crusher and started back, when he saw one of the staff. He was carrying a heavy, oak bedside table. 'I thought I'd better bring this,' he said. 'A little old lady was trying to pick it up.'

'Thank you. I'll speak to her.'

'Is she your mum?' The man tossed the heavy table into the crusher with impressive ease.

'No, but she's as good as. She's my landlady.'

'You're lucky. You ought to meet mine.' He looked into the car and asked, 'What else have you got?'

'Just these old rugs and a few bits and pieces.'

'You bring the bits and pieces, mate. I'll take the rugs.'

'That's very kind of you.'

'It's only what I'm paid for.'

Jeff got back into the empty car.

'Thank you,' said Mrs Mitchell.

'It was no trouble.'

She seemed intent on pursuing the original topic. Maybe she was concerned about his future, because she asked, 'Do you know anyone who could manage the tearoom?'

He waited until he'd turned into the main road, and said, 'Yes, I do, but it depends on the circumstances.'

'Do you mean how she's fixed, kind of thing?'

'Yes.'

Having dropped Mrs Mitchell at the cottage, he walked across to the public call box and asked Directory Enquiries for the number he wanted.

The operator asked, 'Would you like me to put you through?'

'No, thank you. I'll do it myself.' He was rather looking forward to it. He dialled the number and waited. A man's voice answered. 'Wicken's, the Estate Agents. Jason speaking. How can I help you?'

'I'd like to speak to Julie, please, if that's possible.' There was a short silence. For a moment, he thought he was going to be told that

Julie was out or, worse still, that she no longer worked there, but then the man said, 'Will you hold the line, please?'

The next voice he heard was Julie's. 'Hello? Julie speaking.'

'Julie, it's Jeff, Jeff Mortimer.'

Excitedly, but in a whisper, presumably because she was in the office, she said, 'I know who Jeff is, you bugger. Where are you?'

'I'm in a town in Netherdale, North Yorkshire.'

'That's not far from here.'

He'd forgotten about her remarkable navigation skills. 'Not far at all, Julie. How are things with you?'

'Not bad. What about you?'

'Pretty good.' He had to ask her. 'Have you got a fella?' He thought that was the right word.

'I thought I had, but he buggered off somewhere, lookin' for a bakery.' Almost immediately, she checked herself. 'No, that's not fair. I knew you were leavin'. Anyway, what are you doin' now?'

'I found that bakery.'

'Fantastic.' For a moment, her volume became almost normal, and then she controlled herself again. 'Where is it?'

'Here, in Netherdale. Listen, Julie, if I come up to Morpeth, can you put me up for a night?'

'Of course I can. When?'

'Tonight.'

'Yes!' It was like a hiss. 'I've no food in the flat, mind.'

'I'll take you out to dinner.'

'You're truly wonderful.'

'If I set off now....' He looked at his watch.

'You'll be here by about half-past six.'

'Or a little later, if I get lost.'

'You cannot get lost, man. It's uphill all the way, an' turn left when you get to Newcastle.'

'I'll see you later.'

'Yes. 'Bye.'

''Bye.'

He walked back to the cottage to find Mrs Mitchell. She was in the kitchen. 'I shan't be in tonight,' he told her. 'I'm visiting a friend in Northumberland, but charge me for tonight. I insist.'

A Baker's Round

'If you really insist.'
'I do. I'll just pack some overnight things and I'll be off.'

Once again, he surprised himself by navigating the journey to Morpeth without difficulty, rush-hour traffic notwithstanding, and he arrived within the two-and-a-half hours Julie had predicted.

When she opened the door to him, she beckoned him inside hurriedly, and then clung to him, kissing him ecstatically.

'You're going to put lipstick all over my face,' he told her.

'I'm not wearin' any yet. Oh, Jeff, it's lovely to see you again.' She checked herself quickly and asked, 'You haven't got a girlfriend, have you? Tell me you haven't found a gorgeous, irresistible woman who answers all the criteria.'

'Do you ever stop being an estate agent? I did know a lovely girl who was all those things, but I buggered off somewhere, looking for a bakery. I hope she'll have me back.'

'Of course I will.' Her relief was tangible. 'What time have you booked the table for?'

'Half-past-seven. We can have a leisurely drink before we eat.'

'Right, I'll put some lippy on. What flavour do you like best?'

'Surprise me.'

'I might, yet, but you're usually the one with the surprises.'

Their table was ready when they arrived at the Cock Robin, so they went through to the restaurant and took their places.

Julie shook her head for maybe the fourth time and said, 'I never expected you to come back, an' when you did, it was like a dream come true.'

'I had to.' If he'd needed to convince himself of it, just the sight of her at the table in a pale-green dress against her clear complexion, and with her hair down in loose curls would have convinced him.

'Did you miss me as much as that?' There was an element of surprise in her tone.

'No, much more than that.'

'No kiddin'?'

'I'd have come back to see you, wherever I found myself. It was just pot luck that I found a bakery in the north of England. When I left you, it was to go to Wolverhampton, believe it or not, and then it began to improve when I went up to West Yorkshire.'

'I saw you on Northern Focus.'

'I hope it wasn't too disappointing.'

'No, I felt sorry for you, havin' to admit that you'd lost interest in the music scene. Hearin' you apologise to your fans brought tears to my eyes.'

'That's a generous thing to say,' He reached for her hand and held it.

'You can say generous things an' mean them when you're in…. I mean, when you think a lot about somebody.'

The waitress brought the wine, showed him the label and poured a little for him to taste.

'Thank you,' he told her, leaving her to pour two glasses, that's good.'

'I saw your picture on the front of one of the papers an' all, when I was in the supermarket.'

'Which one?'

'I say "papers", but it was one of the comics.' She thought briefly. 'I cannot remember which one. They're all the same to me. The only paper I have any time for is the *Independent*, 'cause I cannot abide bein' told what to think, as if I haven't got a mind of me own.'

'Well said.'

'I'm glad you agree with me, but how did the reporters know where to find you?'

'Needless to say, money changed hands. You could say that the enterprise economy was behind it.'

'It sounds despicable enough to be somethin' like that.'

He told her about Anna's youngest son and the deal he'd made with Northern Focus.

'The little bugger.'

A Baker's Round

'I think his mother had plenty to say to him.'

'Good.' Impatiently, she said, 'Tell me all about the bakery you've bought.'

Smiling at her excitement, he said, 'I haven't got completion yet, but it's only a week away. It's quite a small bakery that I can manage on my own, but there's also a cottage and a tearoom attached to it.'

'It sounds expensive,' she said, sounding very much like her business *alter ego*, 'especially in the Yorkshire Dales.'

'It is, so it's just as well I'm moving from one of the fashionable parts of London.'

'I see.' Even with her experience at the agency, it was a lot to take in. 'As far as the tearoom is concerned, will you be keeping the existing staff?'

'One person. She's currently part-time, but she's agreed to work full-time until I find a manager. She's very good.'

'Well, a manager could be hard to find.'

'In normal circumstances, yes, I suppose that might be the case. As a matter of fact,' he said, 'I've been wondering if you'd be interested in taking the job.'

She raised herself on her pillow to say, 'We do work well as a team, as I think we've just demonstrated. She laughed in the way that comes so easily after climactic love-making. 'Of course, I'll have to find somewhere to live.'

'Accommodation comes with the job. In fact, you'd be living over the shop. I remember your telling me how you'd helped your parents in their tearoom and how you'd enjoyed it.'

'It was more of a café than a tearoom, but aye, I did enjoy it.'

'So you'll consider it, then?'

She said seriously, 'Jeff, tell me I'm not makin' a complete fool of meself an' fallin' for a man who's not as keen as I am. I mean, I know you want me to work for you, but am I readin' too much into it?'

He leaned over her to kiss her. 'You're not making a fool of yourself, and I'm as keen as you are. I've missed you like hell, and I can't tell you how it feels to be with you again. In fact....' He kissed her once more and whispered the words she needed to hear.

'Why, yer bugger.' It was the softest, gentlest of endearments. 'I love you too, if you haven't already realised it. I take it this accommodation you're talkin' about comes with you as one of the fixtures.'

'That's right, it's a permanent arrangement.'

The End

Lightning Source UK Ltd.
Milton Keynes UK
UKHW010714270223
417728UK00001B/68

9 781636 830469